Digging for Home

Digging for Home

Windy City Publishers
2118 Plum Grove Rd., #349
Rolling Meadows, IL 60008
www.windycitypublishers.com

Published in the United States of America

First Edition: 2013

ISBN:
978-1-935766-64-3

Library of Congress Control Number:

Cover Illustration by Barbara Ball

Digging for Home

By Jimmy Ball

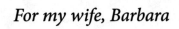

For my wife, Barbara

"You never soar so high as when
you stoop down to help a child or an animal."

Jewish Proverb

chapter 1
WINTER FOLLIES

The most exciting time of year for me is the Christmas season. Especially when I was twelve years old and school was out for two whole weeks. The only major worry for me was arranging my busy schedule around sledding, playing hockey at the lagoon, and getting into snowball fights with Larry and Howard Jenkins, who lived down the block from us.

My name is Benjamin Davies. My seven-year-old brother, Frank, and I were dragging our inflated saucer sleds to nearby Gilberts Forest Preserve, where there were several awesome sledding trails. The one we were headed for was known as Dead Man's Hill. Dead Man's sloped sharply down for almost a hundred yards before leveling off. It was narrow and left little room for error. Anyone sliding off the main path was rewarded with painful scrapes and numerous bruises from the surrounding pine trees and underbrush.

"When are you going to tell Mom and Dad about the other night, Benny?" asked Frank as we approached the top of slope.

The "other night" that Frank was referring to was the Christmas caroling our Wednesday-night religious education class partook in. Our teacher, Mrs. Rupert, decided that a great way to end our first session would be for the class to go serenading in the neighborhood of St. Catherine's. Normally I would have faked some sort of illness to escape such torture, but Mrs. Rupert mentioned that following the caroling we would return to the classroom for hot chocolate, cookies, and a gift exchange. That got my attention.

The night started out innocently enough with bright stars and a nearly full moon. The first few houses we visited were delighted to see our smiling faces. The fact that our singing voices left a lot to be desired didn't seem to dampen their spirits, either. One elderly gentleman seemed worried that we were soliciting donations for our performance and was quick to close the door before our last note could be heard. But all in all, things were going quite well. About twenty minutes or so into our excursion, my friend Denny Picket and I decided it was time for a little mischief. We slunk to the back row of the choir and began rolling up snowballs. My first toss hit Cheryl McAdams square in the middle of the back. She spun around but by then we had our program sheets up and were concentrating on belting out "O Little Town of Bethlehem." Denny's first throw caught Ella Turner in the right shoulder. Her glare was focused right on the two of us, but we pretended to be interested only in our vocals. This continued for several more stops and we got bolder and bolder. The most annoying girl in our class, Rachel Whittenburgh, was right behind Mrs. Rupert. I had total confidence that I could lob one right onto the back of her neck, which would surely get a big-time reaction out of her. Unfortunately, my aim was a little off and the snowball carried a little farther than I anticipated. It landed right on top of Mrs. Rupert's noggin. At first I had to stifle a laugh. Denny was shaking with mirth behind his program. That all stopped when we saw the look on her face. The words "fury," "outrage," and "humiliation" came to mind. As she stormed toward us it was like the parting of the Red Sea—and she was Moses. The grins on our faces betrayed any hope of innocence.

"Why do you two have to ruin everything?" she started. "It's a beautiful evening to extol the joy of Jesus' birth. And all you two can think about is disrupting our performance. The two of you march home this instant and pray for God's forgiveness. Furthermore, you will not be allowed back to class without a note of apology signed by your parents."

When Denny asked if that meant we weren't going to get hot chocolate and cookies, I thought she was going to come unglued. I dragged Denny out of her reach before she could strangle him. As we walked away from the group, I resisted the urge to ask Mrs. Rupert if she could please mail our gift exchange presents to us.

Before we headed down Dead Man's, I tried to convince Frank that I still had a few weeks to worry about the signed note Mrs. Rupert was requesting.

"Maybe she'll forget," I offered. But deep down, I knew that wasn't going to happen. After a half a dozen trips down and back up the hill we trudged back home for a mid-afternoon snack. Home was 207 Monroe Ave., or as some of our neighbors referred to it, that dreadful house where those unruly Davies boys launch their operations of misdeeds from. While Frank gorged himself I decided to head into downtown Glidden for a little surveillance.

Glidden was your typical Midwest city with about 20,000 residents. It was about an hour west of Chicago and surrounded by endless corn and soybean fields. Glidden enjoyed a rich tradition of agriculture and industry. Winding through town was the mighty Blackhawk River and five miles down the road was our very own community college. Truly a Land of Lincoln heartland center if there ever was one.

Christmas Eve was on Friday. Since my mother, Suzanne, who worked at the Piggly Wiggly grocery store in Glidden as a cashier, got paid on Fridays, I thought I'd be able to catch her doing some last-minute shopping. I'd already scoured the house searching for our presents, but there were none to be found. She was probably waiting until the last minute to shop for Frank and me so she wouldn't have to hide them from us.

Knowing that she got off at 3:30, I hung around the downtown area near Helton's Sporting Goods. Sure enough, about 3:35 I spotted our blue Chrysler station wagon rolling past Helton's. She found a parking spot just down the street. I was pretending to be interested in some holiday greeting cards in the Hallmark store directly across the street. Mom entered Helton's and went directly toward the baseball glove display. My heart was racing until I heard "Ahem" from directly behind me. There stood a somewhat elderly lady with pointy glasses and a hideous Christmas sweater adorned with holiday buttons. The buttons all contained various clichés proclaiming seasonal joy and peace.

"May I help you with something, young man?" she inquired as her beady eyes swept over me rather skeptically.

"I'm just looking," I replied, hoping she'd go away and leave me to my spying. Unfortunately, her curiosity got the best of her and she wasn't about to let go.

"How much did you have in mind to spend?" she asked in a suspicious tone.

How can I rid myself of this uninvited shadow hovering over me like a hawk, I thought to myself.

A quick peek across the street found my mother moving over to the bat rack. I knew Frank was wanting a bat for tee-ball next summer, so I missed out on what transpired in the ball glove department.

"Well," she said a bit louder than need be.

"Do you have any Christmas cards for great uncles?" I asked.

"Not that I'm aware of," she cackled.

"Could you please check with the manager?" I asked in my most pleasant voice.

"Very well," and off to the back of the store she stomped. Maybe one of her buttons was sticking through that unsightly sweater of hers and poking her skin. That would go a long way in explaining her unpleasant mood. At any rate, this brief delay gave me more time for surveillance on Helton's. A couple of minutes later my mom strode out of Helton's with two purchases, one obviously a bat and the other, I hoped, my Ron Santo autographed baseball glove. As I spun to ditch out of the Hallmark store, Old Ironsides proudly came clomping up with a card for (you guessed it) "the best great uncle in the world."

"I've found just the card for you, young man," she proclaimed.

Since I didn't have any money on me or a great uncle, I had no other choice but to ad lib.

"I'm sorry, ma'am, but I just remembered that he passed away last summer. But thank you anyway for your help. Have a merry Christmas."

With that I was out the door in a flash. The last thing I heard from her wasn't exactly in the true Christmas spirit. I don't believe there are any buttons with those sentiments on them.

I had to see for myself if Mom had picked out the right glove. I entered Helton's and headed for the baseball glove display. My prayers were answered when I saw an open space where the glove used to be. Yes, there really is a Santa Claus.

With Frank bouncing off the walls and me trying to work on my surprised look on Christmas Eve, Dad announced that it was bedtime. My father, Paul, must have been a lot like me in his younger years because he seemed to "get" me, not an easy task by any stretch of the imagination. Normally I would throw a mild fit at a ten o'clock curfew, but Christmas Eve was no time to rile the parents for fear of reprisals, including the possible withholding of certain presents. Plus, I could always retire with my *Sports Illustrated* and if I turned down the volume on the TV in my room, I could catch some of the Gator Bowl football game, too. With a stiff warning from my dad to Frank that he was not allowed out of his room to spy on Santa like he did last year, Mom marched him up to his room and tucked him in. He was even too excited to beg for a bedtime story tonight.

Dad walked me up to my room and whispered to me, "Make sure you put a towel under your door. That'll block the light from your TV, which gives away the fact that you're watching the football game."

"What makes you think I'm planning on watching the game?"

"Because you didn't complain about the early bedtime and I know you better than you think. You're not as clever as you imagine yourself to be, and don't forget that I was once your age, too. Now brush your teeth and try to act like you don't know what's in your packages before you open them tomorrow morning. And don't forget the towel or your mother will raise Cain with you."

"Good night, Dad."

"Good night, and merry Christmas, Benny."

It was always good when they called me Benny. It's when I heard "Benjamin" that I got nervous.

"Merry Christmas, Dad, and sleep tight, because Frank will be up at the crack of dawn."

"If we're lucky," he said.

It was actually a little before dawn when Frank went racing through the house banging on bedroom doors and shouting at the top of his lungs, "Wake up, sleepyheads."

Mom poked her head out of their bedroom and warned Frank that if he didn't go back to bed she was going to phone Santa to come pick up his presents and return them to the North Pole. That bought us another half hour of shut-eye before he came bounding out like he had been shot out of a cannon. It was hopeless to fight the inevitable, so up we got and trudged down the stairs to the Christmas tree in the living room. Frank was already building piles for everyone by the time we were all assembled. He was delighted that his was the biggest pile of the four.

We let Frank go first in opening presents because he would torture us for being too slow if we didn't. He tore asunder his entire pile in less than ten minutes. It most certainly could have been a world record if they kept track of such things.

I was next and was careful not to open the package that I knew contained the glove first so as not to draw any undue suspicion. I faked genuine happiness at the sweaters, pants, and even the underwear until finally I couldn't stand it anymore. I opened the one with the glove in it and feigned shock.

"I don't believe it," I lied. "Thanks, Mom and Dad. I can't wait to break it in."

Dad and I agreed that no matter what the weather was like, we would break in the new glove with a game of catch before the new year.

"It's a date, Benny," my dad said. "Tomorrow night Merv and I have tickets to the Blackhawks game, so the day after that you'd better have that arm warmed up."

Merv was Dad's best friend and his partner in their carpeting and tile business, Piles and Tiles.

"See if you can pick me up an official Blackhawks puck because I lost the one I had last year at the pond," I said.

"If I had a dollar for every ball or puck you lost, I'd be a millionaire," Mom said.

A loud crash suddenly changed the subject. We whirled around to see Frank holding his new bat and Mom's treasured multicolored ceramic figurine, a wedding present from her parents, shattered all about the dining room.

"Francis," Mom shouted, "I'm already sorry I bought that bat for you."

"You didn't," Frank squealed. "Santa did!"

Mom looked over to where Dad sat shaking his head and asked, "Does Santa accept returns?"

chapter 2

NO DEAL

My dream was interrupted by a ringing sound. In my dream, I was playing third base for the Chicago Cubs, but as dreams often go, not much else made sense. For one thing it was snowing and for another, instead of at Wrigley Field, we were playing under a huge circus tent. Well, maybe the way the Cubs usually play, it made perfect sense after all. The ringing continued and I realized it was our phone. As I glanced at my alarm clock, it read 12:25. Now who would be calling at this hour of the night? Whoever it was would probably get an earful from Dad. That's if Dad was back from the hockey game, which by this time of night he almost certainly would be. My interest was piqued by now, so I rolled out of bed only to turn my ankle on one of Frank's army tanks that he had been playing with earlier while I was applying the final coat of oil to my new baseball glove. As I limped out into the hall, I was alarmed to hear Mom shouting hysterically into the phone in their bedroom. Whoever was on the other end of the line was obviously not handing out any good news.

"Where did this happen? Why can't I talk to him?"

I opened the bedroom door, looked around and didn't spot Dad anywhere. Now it was me who was shouting hysterically. "What's going on? Where's Dad? Who is that on the phone?"

The look on Mom's face reminded me of the look on her face last winter when Frank was sledding down the slope of our front yard and sledded right out into the street and between the front and rear wheels of an oncoming garbage truck. The truck stopped and the few seconds that elapsed before we dashed to the truck and pulled Frank out seemed like an eternity. Miraculously, he was unscathed but panic-stricken. That same look was back now without the look of relief that accompanied Frank's rescue. I immediately wished I hadn't asked where Dad was, because I wasn't sure I wanted to hear the answer. Mom jotted something down on a piece of paper and hung up the phone. At least she tried to hang up the phone, but her hand was shaking so badly that the phone plopped off the nightstand and into the waste can by the bed. Mom stared off toward the opposite wall, refusing to make eye contact with me.

"There's been an accident," she whispered, barely audibly. She was shaking like a leaf.

I couldn't bring myself to ask the question that was too horrifying to hear. She retrieved the phone and quickly called her sister, my Aunt Julie. After hanging up, she walked into the bathroom and shut the door. I could hear her crying uncontrollably from the hallway.

Back in my room, I just sat on my bed and tried to stop my mind from racing. Was Dad going to be OK? If not, what would become of our family? He just had to pull through. Right? My thoughts were interrupted as Mom peeked her head in the door and announced she was on her way to St. Ambrose Hospital, which she thought was about a half hour away. She came over and gave me a big bear hug, said she loved me, and turned, heading for the door.

She looked back once more and said, "Watch over Frankie until Aunt Julie gets here. I'll call when I know more."

"Mom, your sweatshirt's on backwards," I told her, but I don't think she heard me because she just kept on going.

I began to make a "pact" with God. If my father lived and was all right, I was willing to offer some concessions.

1. No more cursing when the Bears blow a lead in the fourth quarter.
2. I'll volunteer to be altar boy once a week for the whole year instead of once a month.
3. I promise to donate ten percent of my lawn mowing proceeds to the Salvation Army.
4. I'll volunteer to work twice a month helping out at the church food pantry.
5. No laughing or teasing Frank about his slight lisp for an entire year.
6. No snatching money out of Dad's change jar to buy a chocolate humdinger shake down at Hank's Dairy Deluxe.
7. No mean tricks on Frank, like the garter snake I put in his bed last summer.
8. I'll even clean my room once a month instead of just shoving everything under the bed.

Now, if I'm not too late, that should be enough, I thought. I prayed more in the next hour than I had in the previous year. Around 1:30, Julie rolled in and did her best to cheer me up while we waited in the living room for the call.

At about two o'clock the phone rang. I was too terrified to pick it up. Julie grabbed it and took it into the kitchen. I tried listening in through the door but my aunt was barely speaking above a whisper. Finally I did manage to catch back-to-back "No, no" and a clear "Oh God no."

I returned to the couch and curled up in the fetal position. As much as I tried willing myself to believe that this was simply a cruel nightmare, deep down it was becoming more and more obvious that wasn't the case. Why couldn't there be a time machine we could hop into and go back a few hours? Just this once.

Eventually Aunt Julie opened the door and came shuffling toward me. She reminded me of a zombie from one of those movies like *Night of the Living Dead*. The big difference was that this zombie had tears streaming down her cheeks.

"I don't know how to break this to you, Benny," she sobbed as she knelt next to the couch. "I'm so sorry, but your father didn't make it."

"Didn't make what? What do you mean?"

"He was in a coma when your mom arrived at the hospital. The doctors informed her there was no brain activity. They took him off the ventilator, and he's gone."

"NO!" I shouted. Looking up, I saw Frank standing at the top of the stairs and rubbing his eyes.

"What's with all the shouting?" asked Frank.

Aunt Julie put her arms around me and whispered, "Benny, I need you to try and hold it together, please, until your mom gets home. Don't say anything to Frank. She'll handle it when she gets here. Please try to stay strong and we'll somehow manage to get through this in time if we all stick together."

"Where's Mom and Dad?" yawned Frank, only half awake.

Julie glanced up the stairway and said to Frank, "They'll be home soon, so you'd better get back to bed pronto."

With that said, Frank wandered back to his room saying he couldn't wait for the morning, because Dad promised to bring him a Blackhawks jersey from the game. I glanced down at my eight-point contract, wadded it up tight, and fired it as hard as I could against the wall.

chapter 3

MELTDOWN

The Morgan Funeral Parlor was a sterile, depressing establishment. Even under better circumstances the interior would still come off as dreary and morbid. The steady line of well-intentioned mourners and relatives all murmured the standard clichés as they passed by, but all the words in the world couldn't change the fact that my father was lying in a coffin twelve feet away and would never again be there for us. In the other main room the visitation for Merv was going on simultaneously. Most everyone who knew my dad knew Merv as well, so these poor souls had to march through two long lines to express their sympathy.

My dad's parents resided in a nursing home down in Boca Raton, Florida, and were unable to travel. My mom's father was deceased. Her mother was in a fairly advanced stage of dementia so it was decided to leave her put in Chicago. Frank was too young to handle the standing at attention through this torturous ordeal so he was in the hospitality room where the parlor had provided sandwiches, snacks, and punch. That left Aunt Julie, her husband Dexter, my mom, and me to face the music.

Among the earliest to arrive was my next-door neighbor, Tara Mangolin, and her parents. Tara was a year older than me and could beat me in every sport except hockey, and that was only because she didn't own a pair of ice sates. She was tall, slender, and a natural athlete. It was a well-known fact that she was the best softball player in the county. She not only was almost unhittable as a pitcher, but could hammer the ball as a batter as well.

"Hey, Dork," she said to me nervously, not really knowing what to say at a time like this.

"Hey, Stork," was all I could think to reply. Her nickname went back years, as she was a spindly, gangly youngster when I first knew her. She'd morphed into more of a swan, with attractive features and flowing blond hair, but the nickname stuck. My nickname was still pretty much fitting, I suppose. Her father, Earl, a heavy drinker and a mean drunk on top of it, offered up to me that he lost his dad at an early age as well. The whiskey on his breath was overwhelming and I could only hope he didn't approach the row of candles next to the casket too closely, or we would all surely burst into flames.

"If there's anything you need, Benny, don't hesitate to ask," added Sara Mangolin, Tara's mother, obviously annoyed at her husband's awkward attempt at saying something helpful.

"Ah, this will toughen him up quickly – he's the man of the house now," slurred Mr. Mangolin. Tara and her mother appeared mortified at this last pearl of wisdom offered up by Earl. Tara quickly moved along the line and out the door in record time. Her mother steered her father the remainder of the way and they made a rather quick exit as well.

When about the fiftieth person patted me on the head and told me to "hang in there, son," I couldn't take it any more. I told my mom that I was going to check on Frank and make sure he wasn't gobbling up all the sandwiches and slurping down the punch till he had one of his world-famous stomachaches. She just looked at me with that blank look she'd been wearing for the last couple of days and nodded. As I walked into the hospitality room my worst suspicions were confirmed. Frank was sitting on a couch with numerous wrappers strewn about, a half empty glass of punch and a sour look on his face.

"I don't feel so good, Benny," he managed to groan. With that he proceeded to hurl right there on the serving table. Between the ham, turkey, peanuts, and fruit punch, it was not a pretty sight. I rushed him off in the direction of the restrooms with the hope that the next person to drop in to the hospitality room for a quick bite wasn't too squeamish, or the scene could deteriorate even further.

The suit Frank was wearing, which was a good one or two sizes too small for him, was pretty much toast. I took his coat and tie off and stuffed them into the waste can. With a couple of dampened paper towels, I was able to pretty much clean off his pants and shoes. He splashed water on his face, dried it off, looked up to me and said, "I feel better now."

"I'm sure you do," I replied. "But we'd better find someone to get that room cleaned up."

"I remember seeing a cake in a pan on one of the tables in there. Can I have a piece of cake, Benny?"

"No, Frank, I don't think that'd be a good idea under the circumstances. Let's just give that bottomless pit of yours a little rest for the time being."

"OK," he said, but I could just see the wheels spinning in his little noggin. Knowing Frank, he wasn't going to completely abandon his quest for a piece of cake. I peeked my head into the room and saw the funeral director, Mr. Marshall, emptying the contents of the serving table into a big trash container, all the while muttering about how he hoped "that little squirt was sick enough to learn a good lesson." Little did he know that the little squirt was already looking forward to dessert.

I loped quickly out of the room, only to bump into Father William Benson, or Father Bill, as he was known to all of us. Father Bill was our parish pastor and was scheduled to conduct the 7:30 p.m. wake service. He'd been an all-state high school basketball player for Rockford Boylan. He could still fire 'em in from all over. I was zero for about ten in games of horse against him on the playground. Even the high school boys rarely gave him a close game.

"How're you doing?" asked Father Bill.

I looked down at my shoes and mumbled, "Fine."

He motioned Frank and me over to a little bench in an adjoining alcove. "Benny, nobody goes through what you're going through right now and is fine."

Frank asked, "Father, do they have football games in Heaven? Dad loved to watch football games and yell at the TV. Can he still do that in Heaven?"

"Well," Father Bill replied, "I'm not sure there's a lot of yelling going on up there. It's a little more of a peaceful atmosphere, I suppose."

"Don't tell me they just stand around chanting and singing. Dad can't sing worth a darn. He told us one time in school a nun told him to just mouth the words in a school play so he wouldn't ruin the song for the rest of the class. I'm afraid he'll get tossed out of Heaven if they make him sing."

Father Bill assured Frank that being unable to carry a tune wouldn't count too heavily against him.

"The way I understand it, there isn't much tossing out of Heaven going on these days anyway," he said.

That seemed to satisfy Frank and he immediately stood up and headed back into the hospitality room. No doubt in search of the cake. Father Bill turned back to me and asked, "How do you really feel, Benny?"

"I'm really, really ticked off right now with God," I answered. "Life isn't fair. All of this religious nonsense is maddening. What did we do to deserve this? What did he do? This whole rotten deal stinks."

He nodded gently and told me that was a perfectly normal reaction. He then surprised me by relating how he got ticked off from time to time with "the Man upstairs" as well.

"Don't worry Ben, He can take it. I'm sure He's heard a fair amount of grumbling over the years." Father Bill then asked if we had family pictures and home movies around the house. I told him we had plenty of each. He asked me to look through all the old pictures and movies and be thankful for all the great times we shared together.

"You'll be better served in life to appreciate the things you do have, rather than resenting the things you don't have, or that were taken from you. There'll always be plenty of people who have more than you in this life, but there will be even more with far less. You still have a wonderful mother who loves you and a brother who adores you, a roof over your head, plenty of food to eat, and clean drinking water any time you're thirsty. There are millions of people in this world who would settle for any one of those things that we take for granted sometimes. Good luck trying to convince them that life doesn't seem fair. And if anyone ever tells you that life is fair, don't believe them for a minute. Your father was a good, generous, happy-go-lucky soul. He possessed a great deal of positive energy. Benny, I want you to grab onto that same spirit of his and run with it. He's counting on you, son, and rest assured he'll be checking in on you regularly. Be strong and don't let him down."

I knew what Father Bill said was probably true, but I wasn't buying any of it right then and I certainly wasn't ready to let go of my anger and resentment. I could be stubborn that way.

"Ben," Father Bill said, "I've been through this often enough in my job to be able to tell you it takes time for the hurt to lessen. One thing that does hurry the healing process along is to help others. Your mother and brother would be a good start. Try to have patience with them and always do your best to cheer them up. That's one of the gifts you've been given in life, Ben. Don't waste it."

"We'll see," was about all I could manage to spit out.

"Trust me, Ben, you'll figure it out."

Aunt Julie came in and motioned to Father that it was time to start the prayer service. I got up to check on Frank, hoping he'd learned his lesson finally on proper eating portions. I wasn't holding out any great hope in that regard, either.

The following afternoon, during the funeral and burial ceremonies, Mom continued to function pretty much in a dazed state of mind. The term "eternally resting" popped up repeatedly but that was just insane. I came to despise that phrase almost as much as the phrase "I'm sorry for your loss." Nothing anyone said or did was ever going to make things the way they were.

The next morning I found myself sitting on my bed staring at the wall. Frank was down the street playing with his best friend, Nicky. He was still sucking his thumb during idle moments, something he hadn't done since he was three. Another disturbing thing that Frank hadn't done in several years—bed wetting—had reared its ugly head. It was hard to tell what was going on it that mind of his, even under normal circumstances.

Mom was at Fosters Health Care Center attending another session with a grief counselor. The night before I had overheard a conversation between her and Aunt Julie that turned into a heated exchange concerning the care of Frank and me. A comment from my aunt chilled me to the bone.

"Suze, are you sure you're up to handling the boys in your present state?"

After a few moments Mom told her she'd think about it. *What was there to think about?* I wondered. Frank and I belonged here and that was all there was to it.

I looked at my baseball glove lying on my dresser, the glove that would never be used in a game of catch in the back yard with Dad. In a fury I marched over, grabbed it, and, opening the window, flung it out into the snow. I shouted some nasty swear words at the top of my lungs out the window to no one in particular, slammed the window shut, went back to my bed, sat down and started to cry. Not just your everyday cry of a few tears, but an avalanche of emotions and a waterfall of tears. I was actually trying to gasp for breath in between sobs. For the first time since "that night," I wasn't angry or distant. What I was, though, was very sad and lonely–and scared. I slumped off the edge of the bed onto the floor and curled up in the corner. A short time later, I heard a noise at my bedroom door. Someone was in my room and here I was, huddled on the floor, having a meltdown. I lamely tried to wipe off the tears with my sleeves, but it was useless. Who'd I think I was fooling?

"You lose something, Dork?" asked Tara. I turned around to see Tara standing there holding my snow-encrusted glove. The thought of her witnessing my embarrassing, obscenity-filled tirade was humiliating enough. I could only hope she hadn't been standing at my door for too long a time during my childish blubbering, which would only make things more horrific. She brushed the snow off my glove, put it down, and walked over to where I was huddled on the floor. She sat down right next to me, held my left hand with her left hand and put her right arm around my shoulders. I tried to apologize for my behavior, but she told me to hush up and bawl all I wanted.

"If you didn't break down and carry on, I'd think there was something terribly wrong with you," she said. "Trust me, I know a thing or two about crying myself. Quite a few times I've locked myself in my room when my father came home after a few too many at Kelly's Bar and Grill. He'd start railing at Mom over some minor problem and I'd run upstairs, lock the door, and hope that some day he wouldn't come home at all. And sometimes, I'd look out my window and you'd be playing ball with your dad or Frank in the yard, and I would get so jealous I couldn't stand it. But then I'd slip down the back stairs and out into my yard trying to act like nothing was bothering me. As soon as your dad or you spotted me, one of you would always ask if I wanted to join in and we'd get a game up. You have no idea what that meant to me, Benny. It helped to take my mind off some of my problems at home and made me feel like I was part of something good. I'm going to miss him, too," she said, and I could see her eyes misting up with tears as well.

"So the next time I see you hurl your glove out the window, I'm going to grab it, march right over here and slap you upside the head with it. Got it, Dork?"

"Got it," I said.

"You know how I've been volunteering at the county animal shelter this winter? I just got an idea, Benny. Why don't you come by tomorrow afternoon and help me out with some dog walking and clean-up? I think it would help to take your mind off some things, and the dogs love having company. They're so lonely it's heartbreaking. What do you think?"

"I'd be glad to come by and help cheer them up. I'm not too sure about the 'cleaning up' part, though," I said.

"Those dogs aren't the only ones who need some cheering up," said Tara. "See you tomorrow, Dork."

chapter 4

VISITING DAY

The following day I took Tara up on her offer and dropped by the county animal shelter. I was amazed at how many abandoned dogs and cats we had in our county. There must have been close to twenty dogs and about a dozen cats caged up in their little pens. I felt sorry for them as they looked out expectantly at me as I entered. It broke my heart to see them in this predicament. Maybe this wasn't such a good idea after all.

"Hey Dork, grab a scooper and we'll bring a couple dogs out to run around and do their business," said Tara. She opened up a cage and let out a Border collie. I looked at an excited-looking beige-colored mutt and decided he deserved a romp outside as well. He was so happy to be going out that I thought his tail would fly off. Once outside, the two of them got into the serious business of sniffing, peeing, and racing about. The yard itself was about an acre in size with an eight-foot chain-link fence surrounding it. Tara told me that the Border collie was named Mollie and the dog I brought out was called Harvey. As we roamed about the yard with our scoopers, I noticed that Mollie continued to circle around us endlessly. I asked Tara if there was something wrong with her.

"No, that's just her herding instinct. They're bred as sheep-herding working dogs, so she's just doing what comes natural to her."

Just then I heard a squeak right behind me and turned to see Harvey intently chomping on some sort of squeaky toy, all the time daring me to try and take it from him. After a little tug-of-war, he let me snatch it from him and I sent it sailing across the yard. He raced after it, grabbed it, and proudly pranced past Mollie in a display of shameless bravado. I must have tossed his silly toy a dozen times, but he didn't seem to tire of the game in the least. I sat on a bench stationed by the building and waited for Harvey to come back with his toy. After taunting Mollie with his prize for the umpteenth time, he galloped up to the bench, dropped his toy, sat down on his hindquarters and stuck out a paw for me to shake. His facial features were that of a German shepherd, but his short hair and body were more Labrador retriever-like. As we shook, he looked up at me with the friendliest big brown eyes imaginable.

"I wouldn't get too attached to him if I were you, Dork. He only has two more days before they euthanize him."

Not knowing exactly what "euthanize" meant, but not wanting to appear stupid, I just shook my head.

"Oh, you mean they're going to neuter him?" I guessed.

"No, Ben, I mean they're going to put him to sleep. As in permanently."

"Why would they do that? He seems like a great dog. Friendly, healthy, and definately playful. You name it."

"There's a sixty-day window at this facility. If a dog isn't adopted out within sixty days, they're put down."

"That's the craziest thing I've ever heard."

As I was scratching Harvey's ears he lay down on his back with his legs outstretched, inviting me to scratch his belly and tummy. I obliged him, all the time trying to figure out what I could do to avert this impending disaster.

"I know, I'll tell my mom that we have to adopt Harvey tomorrow to save his life. I'll put a guilt trip on her and even recruit Frank to help convince her. He's usually good for some serious tears. She won't have a chance."

"Make sure you do your best, Dork, because this is Harvey's last chance."

"How long has Mollie been here?"

"Only a couple of days. Border collies get gobbled up pretty quickly, as a rule. She'll be adopted out within the week, I'm sure."

"Thank God," I said. "Trying to convince Mom into taking two dogs might be a bit of a stretch."

Right then the back door swung open and the massive hulk of a man appeared in the exercise yard. Not the most attractive person, he came complete with a double chin and was in serious need of a decent shave. He glowered at Tara as he bellowed, "Make sure you get all the poop cleaned up this time, Kara. You missed a couple last time you were here."

"The name's Tara with a 'T,' and I think you're mistaken, Martin."

"My name is Marvin with a 'V,' and watch your lip, young lady, or I just might toss you in one of those cages to teach your smart mouth a lesson."

The whole time the big oaf named "Marvin with a V" stood in the yard, Harvey was growling in a low voice and his hackles were standing up on his back. He obviously didn't care much for Marvin, but he also appeared to be a little afraid of him at the same time. As soon as Marvin turned to walk back into the building, Tara shot him the bird.

I commented, "That's not very ladylike, Stork, but don't worry, if the incredible bulk there tosses you in a cage, I'll come out every day to let you run around the yard here. But don't expect me to clean up after you, though."

The gesture directed toward me made it quite clear that Tara didn't appreciate my sense of humor in the least.

"Yeah, and I love you too, Stork."

Before I escorted Harvey back to his cage, I bent down, scratched his ears once more, and told him I'd be back tomorrow to get him. As I looked at those sad brown eyes gazing out at me from inside the cage, my last words to him were, "I promise." For the first time in days I had something to hope for. There was nothing I could do to bring my father back, but I did have an opportunity to save Harvey from a similar fate.

That night when Mom walked in the back door, Frank and I bushwhacked her before she could even put her purse down. I told her about the day's events at the animal shelter, and how we had to save Harvey from the grim reaper. Frank was telling her how we had to adopt the best dog in the whole world, even though he had yet to meet him. Frank even turned on the waterworks to further his case. Mom let us ramble on for another minute or two until she told both of us to sit down. Mom looked tired but she fixed us with a firm gaze. We all sat around the kitchen table while she started in.

"Look, you two, this is not the time to be taking on another big responsibility, which is exactly what getting a dog is. It's a huge responsibility."

"We'll take care of him, Mom, you won't have to do a thing," I argued.

"Just like how you took care of the guinea pigs and the hamster. It seems to me that I was the only one who cleaned out their cages, no matter how many times I threatened you."

"I was younger then," I countered. "I'm more mature now."

That comment produced a major roll of Mom's blue eyes. "It's not just that, boys. Our financial situation is not good at all right now, nor does it figure to be in the near future. Dogs cost a lot of money. There's food and shots and all sorts of vet bills that are inevitable."

"I'll get a paper route and in the summer I can get a lot of extra lawns to mow."

"Benjamin, you know darn well you'll be off playing baseball till all hours of the night while people's lawns you're supposed to be mowing will grow so high they'll look like wheat fields. I'm sorry for this poor dog, but that's not our problem. We have enough to deal with right now as it is. These medications the so-called doctors have me taking are giving me a splitting headache. I'm going up to my room to lie down. You two will have to fend for yourselves for supper again. My final answer is no."

As I tucked Frank into bed that night he asked me if there was a doggy heaven, and if I thought Harvey would make the cut. I told Frank about the promise I made to Harvey, and how I intended to keep it.

"Get a good night's sleep tonight, Frankie. We've got a big adventure ahead of us tomorrow."

"Benny, is this another one of your adventures that's going to land us in a heap of trouble?"

"More than likely, Frankie. More than likely. Now sleep tight and be ready to go tomorrow morning."

chapter 5
THE GREAT ESCAPE

Trying to sleep that night was a waste of time. Numerous plans and scenarios raced through my head as I tossed and turned, until finally at about six o'clock I gave up. Rising, I showered, threw on some warm clothes, grabbed my coat and went off to the animal shelter. It was about a mile and a half away, which was a fifteen-minute jaunt for me. When I got there it was still fairly dark, but the sun was on its way up across the horizon to the east. I walked the fence line that surrounded the dogs' exercise yard. On the west side, next to the building itself, was a muddy low area where the sump pump apparently emptied out onto the yard. It looked as if there had been several unsuccessful attempts by the local residents to claw their way to freedom but the bottom of the chain-link fence was too tight. However, a little digging with a shovel at this spot just might be enough to spring a certain condemned inmate. With the *where* part of my plan in place, I had to return home to work on the *when* and *how*.

After checking our garage to make sure we still had a decent shovel, I called Tara.

"What time do you go in today, Stork?"

"Go in where?" she asked, still half asleep.

"To the shelter," I answered, and went on to explain how my mom had nixed the idea of adopting a dog.

"So if you can't adopt Harvey, what good is it to know when I'll be there?" Tara asked. "I've been working with him the past couple of weeks teaching him tricks and commands to obey me in hopes that it would impress someone enough to adopt him, but no one's even looked twice at him. Knowing that this is his last day, I don't think I can even get myself to go out there. My heart's been broken too many times with these pets and I just can't take it anymore."

"You won't have to, Tara, because I have a plan to break him out today."

"Oh, great, another one of your brilliant schemes. Seems to me your last brainstorm cost you a three-day suspension from school, if I remember correctly."

"It was only two days, and it wasn't my fault, it was just bad luck."

"Well, trust me, Dork, bad luck seems to follow you around like a stalker, so don't count me in on one of your harebrained schemes."

The incident she was referring to happened last September. Along with two of my friends, Derrick and Denny, we decided to call in sick to school. We rode the train into Chicago and took a cab to Wrigley Field for the Cubs vs. Pirates game. It was a beautiful afternoon, we had decent seats and all went well—we thought. During the seventh-inning stretch, two high-school girls sitting behind us unfolded a big sign they'd made professing their love for Cub centerfielder Rick Monday. Unfortunately for us, the TV cameras picked up on it and there we were, right in front of the sign for the entire TV audience.

The following morning at school we were all called into the lion's den. I was quite familiar with the layout of the office and even had a favorite chair that might as well have my name plastered on the seat. Mr. Westmont, the principal of Roberts School, was more than glad to let us know that he had managed to catch the last few innings of yesterday's baseball game.

He asked us if we'd had an opportunity to watch the game in our sickened state while we were recuperating at home. He informed us that his favorite part of the game was the seventh-inning stretch.

"Care to hear what I witnessed, boys?" he asked. By the looks on our faces he already knew the answer. It was a slow death as he kept reliving the scene over and over again—Derrick with his tray of nachos, me with my souvenir helmet, and Denny waving merrily at the camera. Mr. Westmont finally tore himself away from the blow-by-blow description to phone our parents. Needless to say, it was a long and silent ride back home with my mother. When Dad arrived home that evening, I hunched down at the top of the stairs to eavesdrop on them as she informed him of the day's events. As she revealed my misdeeds I thought I heard a couple of chuckles from Dad and his standard line, "Boys will be boys." That comment was rapidly quashed with what I was certain was "the gaze" from Mom.

As my thoughts returned to the task at hand, I knew I had to rely on a guilt trip to entice Tara into joining the caper.

"Well, if you're going to just give up and let Marvin kill poor Harvey, I guess that's it then."

I waited a few seconds to let that soak in and sure enough, after a long sigh, she said, "OK, so tell me what this elaborate 'sure-fire' plan of yours is that's destined to land both of us in deep trouble if not jail."

Tara informed me she was scheduled to go in at one o'clock. I told her I was sending Frank out to get some chocolate custard-filled long johns for her to give to Marvin as a distraction and then to promptly let Harvey out into the yard. I'd be waiting on the west side of the yard next to the building, hopefully with a deep enough trench dug for Harvey to scoot out. She voiced her reservations about my master plan but admitted there weren't any alternate options at this eleventh hour.

I sent Frank to the bakery with a couple of bucks and instructions to pick up three chocolate long johns with custard filling. Meanwhile, I ran out to the pet store to procure a leash and a collar. It wouldn't be a proper escape plan without first-class attention to detail. I was going over final preparations in our garage when Frank returned. I grabbed the bag of long johns and rushed them next door to Tara's. The bag seemed a little light so I peeked in and sure enough, only two pastries survived the trip home from the bakery. Rather than holler at Frank, I simply chalked it up to collateral damage. Thank goodness I didn't send him for just one, or I'd have been left holding an empty bag.

Frank and I left fifteen minutes before Tara so I could get some trenching work in before Harvey was let out. When we arrived, Marvin was out in the yard with a couple of the dogs, one a boxer mix and the other some sort of beagle. There was a pine tree in the corner of the yard and we could observe them without being noticed. Marvin was yelling at the boxer as if it would help the poor dog relieve himself quicker. Marvin looked like he was getting cold or bored or both and stomped over to the boxer, who quickly cowered and slunk back toward the door leading back inside. The beagle gave out a playful yip only to be rewarded with a boot on the rear end from Marvin. Both dogs scurried in without further incident. Once I got Harvey out I was going to make a point of finding a way to alter Marvin's employment status. But first things first.

"Frank, go in and tell that big oaf that our dog ran away and you want to see if he's here," I said. "Don't take no for an answer, because I'm going to need a little time here and I can't have him bursting out that door again into the yard."

Frank was the perfect person to distract someone. By the time Frank was through with him, Marvin wouldn't know if he was coming or going.

The first few inches of damp soil came up easily, but beneath it was frozen earth that was hard as rock. I dug in a frenzy but the going was slow—too slow. I lifted up the bottom of the chain-link fence, which gave a few inches. But that wouldn't be enough. I didn't see any way Harvey could fit under the fence. So I kept clawing away as best as I could and prayed for a miracle. A couple of minutes later I heard Frank behind me.

"Tara's here with the long johns."

Right then the door opened and out popped Harvey and Tara. Tara pointed him in our direction and he raced over to the fence.

"C'mon, Harvey," I urged, and he immediately seemed to sense what the game plan was. He began to dig furiously at the ground as I lifted the bottom of the fence as high as I could. With his front paws digging away and Tara trying to shove his hindquarters out the opening, we were making some real progress. Just then the back door swung open and you-know-who came plodding out, a half-eaten long john in one hand and a cup of coffee in the other. It took him several seconds to register what was happening in our little corner of the world. When he finally put all the pieces together in that walnut-sized brain of his, he came stomping toward us in a hurry. Tara tried to intercept him to give us more time, but Marvin sent her flying backwards with a shove. But before she wiped out, she managed to stick her right leg out and trip him up. Down went Marvin, face-first into the snow.

By the time he stood up again, he resembled a demented version of Frosty the Snowman, complete with a beard full of chocolate and custard. The coffee had splashed all over his face and into his eyes. He was definitely not a happy camper. Sensing the urgency, Harvey continued to claw away as if possessed. His hindquarters finally slid through. It looked as though we were home free. Harvey let out a yelp and stopped in his tracks. I looked behind him and in horror saw that Marvin had managed to grab his tail at the last second. Harvey's tail was the only part of him not outside the fence.

"Not so fast, you little mangy mutt," Marvin spat out. He started to pull on Harvey's tail. It suddenly occurred to me how to fix this mess. I let go of the bottom of the fence and it sprang down on Marvin's meaty wrists, which had been holding Harvey's tail, digging into them painfully while pinning both to the ground. Now it was his turn to let out a yelp. Harvey's tail was safely on our side of the fence and the shoe was on the other foot now.

"Pull the fence up, you little squirt, and let me get my hands out!"

"What's the magic word?" I asked.

Marvin looked like he'd rather be dragged through hot coals than give in, but he really didn't have much choice at the moment.

"Please," he rasped through mud-covered lips.

"See now, that wasn't so hard, was it?" I pulled up the fence and he pulled his wrists out and up close to his body. He writhed in what must have been excruciating pain. Frank had already slipped the collar on Harvey and clipped on the leash. My number-one accomplice was exceeding my expectations.

"Wish we could stay and chat, Marvin, but I think it's time for us to move on."

Marvin stood up and shook the fence with his injured hands, shouting, "You'll be sorry, punk, I'm not through with you yet."

With that, Harvey lifted a rear leg and dampened Marvin's boots with one final parting gift.

chapter 6

THE FUGITIVE

A couple of minutes into our flight, Tara caught up to us. Our intentions were to get home ASAP without traveling through the more-populated portions of town. That meant people's backyards, a little farm property and some wooded areas. There was a creek running through one of the woods and we let Harvey stop for a drink.

"Well, we must make for a pretty sight," Tara offered as the three of us tried to catch our breath. I could only imagine what a ghastly vision I projected. I was covered from head to foot with mud and carrying around a shovel. The first impression one might have had of me was of a homeless grave robber.

We only had one main road to cross, a four-lane highway that was always busy. When we got to it, Harvey stopped dead in his tracks. He wouldn't budge. Tara grabbed the leash from Frank and told Harvey to sit, and he sat immediately. I grabbed Frank's hand and when there was a brief lull in traffic, Tara said, "Heel," and Harvey was up in an instant, walking swiftly right next to her across the highway. Upon reaching the other side I noticed Tara's beaming smile. She was rightfully proud that her training with Harvey had come in rather handy when we needed it. Frank was very impressed and asked Tara what other commands Harvey knew.

"A few others, but now's not the time. We need to get Harvey home and cleaned up first. By the way, Ben, have you figured out your next step yet? He's going to need a home, you know."

"I'm working on it," was all I could offer. When we reached the corner of our street I noticed a white van slowly cruising toward us less than a block away. The big letters on the side of the van read "CACU," and just below them what they stood for was written out: our worst nightmare, the County Animal Control Unit.

"Quick," I half-whispered, half-shouted to Tara and Frank, "behind the huge evergreen." The good news was that the evergreen shielded us from the van. The bad news was that the yard we were in belonged to the Wiswall sisters—two of the oldest, meanest and nosiest spinsters in town. The big dreary-looking dark gray stucco house was a good 100 years old and looked haunted. But that wasn't the scariest part by a long shot. It was the two residents that could put the fear of God in anyone crazy enough to trespass on their hallowed ground. Vera Wiswall was in her early 90s while her younger sister, Nora, was a mere 88. If a kid cut across the corner of their yard on the way home, he could expect a phone call before he even walked through the door. Many a time Frank and I would come steamrolling into the house only to find Mom or Dad on the phone apologizing for our rude manners. And if an errant ball rolled up on their property, you had maybe five seconds to retrieve it before Nora raced out with her cane to claim it or rap the offender on the knuckles. And even if you got away with the ball unscathed, you were forced to endure a lengthy tongue-lashing.

As the van turned the corner and crept by our position, I forced a look at the Wiswalls' side window. There having a hissy fit was the Wiswalls' pride and joy, their beloved cat, Snuffy. Snuffy was not pleased to see a dog in his yard and was more than willing to show his extreme displeasure. Within seconds, both sisters were peering out the window in disbelief, so I scooted to the other side of the pine. The van was far enough away by now that we could risk a run for it. As we raced across the Wiswall sisters' yard, I could hear Nora's cane rapping against the window louder and louder until the sound of breaking glass could be heard. My only hope was that they didn't get a good look at our faces or Harvey wouldn't be the only one whose life was in danger.

As Frank, Harvey, and I reached home, Tara wished us luck and advised us to maintain a low profile for the near future. She entered her side door while Frank and I took Harvey down our basement steps. We had a shower in the basement—both Harvey and I needed one desperately. Twenty minutes later we were clean, dried, and ready for our next step. We had to figure out a new identity for Harvey. I mentioned that with all the digging Harvey had done during the escape that his new name should have something to do with digging.

"How about Digger?" Frank suggested. "What do you think?"

"It sounds a lot better than what Marvin called him—'mangy mutt.'"

Our dog naming ideas were interrupted by the ringing of our front doorbell. Frank ran upstairs and peeked out the window.

"Who is it?" I asked, as he came flying back down the steps.

"There's a police car in the driveway and a big black cop at the door."

This was not welcome news. Why couldn't it have been the Avon lady or an encyclopedia salesman?

"Frank, you stay down here with Digger and do not let him upstairs under any circumstances."

"What do I do if he hauls you away to jail?"

"Grab a file out of the garage and start baking a cake, I guess."

I grabbed my coat and headed out the side door. The last thing we needed was for a cop to start snooping around inside the house, where he would certainly hear Digger whining away in the basement. As I turned the corner to the front of the house, the officer turned toward me. Relief poured over me as I witnessed a familiar face smiling back at me.

"Well, hello, Mr. Woodson, what brings you by today?" Officer Woodson was my friend Derrick's father. "I haven't seen Derrick today, if that's who you're looking for."

"No, Benny. Actually, I stopped by to ask you a few questions."

"Sure, Mr. Woodson. I have a couple of minutes before I have to get to the store to pick up a few things," I fibbed.

"I was just next door to talk to your neighbor, a Miss Tara Mangolin. She's a volunteer at the animal shelter. There was a rather disturbing incident that happened there today."

"Oh, really?" I squeaked and hoped he wouldn't notice my knees knocking together.

"A couple of boys smuggled a dog out of the shelter and assaulted an employee of the facility, a Mr. Marvin Griswold. Miss Mangolin witnessed the abduction while she was out cleaning up the yard. She attempted to help free the dog who was stuck under the fence. Mr. Griswold came out into the yard and he apparently assumed that she was in on the escape plan and pushed her to the ground. She was so frightened of Mr. Griswold that she ran home and seems to be quite shaken up still."

"Did she recognize the two boys?" I asked.

"Said she'd never seen them before."

"That's too bad," I responded, almost a little too quickly.

"Mr. Griswold is bound and determined to press charges against the older lad. He'll probably need stitches to close up a wound on one of his wrists. Says he wants the dog back, too. Has some unfinished business with that 'mongrel,' as he put it."

"Sounds like you have a couple of real desperados on your hands, Mr. Woodson."

"You know, Ben, another unusual thing happened just down the block from here shortly after that. It seems that several kids and a dog were crouching under Nora and Vera Wiswall's spruce tree–almost as if they were hiding from someone. Vera's eyesight isn't what it used to be and Nora's pretty much blind as a bat, so they couldn't identify the 'trespassers,' as they referred to them, but they're pretty upset about the affair. Nora got so excited she shattered a window with that cane of hers. Now they're worried sick that the cat will cut himself to shreds trying to sneak out the gaping hole in the window. I called the glass shop and told them to send out a couple of guys right away to replace the glass before one or both of them had a stroke. Neither of them will probably sleep a wink tonight. It's probably the most excitement they've had in years."

I assured Officer Woodson that I'd be on the lookout for any suspicious dog rustlers in the neighborhood and inquired if Derrick was looking forward to the baseball season yet.

"He sure is, he got a new bat for Christmas and can't wait to try it out."

Derrick was our team's best pitcher and also our clean-up hitter.

"I think we have a good shot at first place this year," I added. If we could just find a way to beat the twin towers. Zack and Zane Bowers were known as the "twin towers" throughout the league not just for their size but for their ability as well. Zack was a tall, lanky southpaw, while Zane was a bulky right-hander. Both of them were intimidating pitchers. On top of that, the two of them were one - two in the home run hitting department last year, with 12 and 11 homers respectively. Even though they dominated the league last year, we were determined to give them a run for their money this summer.

"That's the spirit, Ben. I think we've got a shot at it, too."

I only hoped that our team colors this year would be orange, so that my prison-issue orange jumpsuit might not stick out so much at third base. I started for the front door when Mr. Woodson reminded me of my store errand. Not that he believed a word I'd told him.

As he got to his squad car, he looked back in my direction, but his attention was focused on something over my left shoulder. He chuckled to himself, muttered something as he shook his head and drove off. I turned around to see what he found so amusing. And there, big as you please, with his nose and front paws pressed against the picture window, stood Glidden's number-one fugitive, looking out curiously at the proceedings. Behind Digger, Frank was futilely trying to drag him away by his collar. *Never mind, Frank*, I thought to myself. *It's a little late for that*. Although my number-one accomplice had performed admirably today, he still was in need of a little fine tuning.

chapter 7
DINNER PLANS

We waited about an hour until it got dark enough outside. With Digger in tow, Frank and I headed to the rectory to consult with Father Bill. I figured maybe we'd get lucky and he'd take Digger in as a pet or at least would give us some sound advice. And if worst came to worst and the authorities spotted us, we could take sanctuary in the church. At least that's how it worked in the movies.

Father Bill seemed surprised to see us— who'd blame him, we were two ragamuffins and a runaway dog—but he smiled and invited us in.

"I don't think we've been introduced," he said as he reached down to pet the fugitive.

"Oh, this is Digger–we're trying to find a nice home for him. He's a stray. How would you like to have some friendly companionship here at the rectory?"

Father motioned for us to join him in the living room. "Have a seat and just hang your coats on the coat rack in the corner." When we were seated, he asked us how we happened to come in possession of this "stray."

"Well, Father, it's kind of a long story, you see…"

"Benny, before you go any further, there was an interesting item on the local radio station, WGLD. Their four-o'clock news report included a story concerning an abduction that occurred today at the county animal shelter involving a dog. Authorities are searching for two boys in connection with the dog napping. The newswoman reported that the canine in question was to be euthanized tomorrow morning. Is it just a coincidence that the two of you show up on my doorstep with an unwanted dog the same day?"

"Does this count as confession, Father," Frank asked, "so then you wouldn't have to testify against us?"

Father Bill got a good laugh from that one and answered, "Judging from the calls to the radio station following the news, the townspeople are more likely to give the two a medal than to seek an arrest warrant for saving the dog's life."

I wasn't counting on Griswold or the Wiswall sisters to pin a medal on us anytime soon.

"You know, Ben, your heart was in the right place in this case, but what you did was dangerous, not to mention illegal. When I asked you the other night to reach out and help others while you were coping with your grief, I had in mind the two-legged variety, not the four-legged ones," said Father Bill. Digger hopped up on the couch next to Father Bill to shamelessly pine for head scratches and attention. As Father Bill obliged Digger, I explained how our mother had nixed the idea of adopting a dog at this time, but that I couldn't stand by and let Digger be destroyed. I filled him in on the day's events, including the unfortunate injury to Marvin Griswold.

The doorbell buzzed and Father looked at his watch. "That must be dinner. Just a minute, boys."

Digger followed Father to the door. I heard a familiar female voice but couldn't place it right away. Ms. Dillon, my fifth-grade teacher from a couple of years ago, appeared soon holding a pan of something that smelled good while Father carried a dish of some sort and a bottle of wine out to the kitchen.

"Well, hello, Benjamin," she said. I couldn't tell if her face was red from the winter wind or from blushing.

"Something smells good," was all I could think to reply.

"Bill, I mean Father Bill, doesn't get many home-cooked meals here, so I thought I'd whip up a meat loaf along with a broccoli and cheese casserole." She didn't mention how the wine happened to fit in and I wasn't about to ask.

Father Bill came to relieve her of the meat loaf as well as her coat.

"Would you two care to join us?"

"Oh no, we really should get going, but thanks anyway," I said. Frank looked disappointed but Ms. Dillon appeared relieved. I'm sure the last thing she wanted was the two of us and Digger butting in on their dinner.

"That's too bad," she said, unconvincingly. "Say, I didn't know you had a dog, Ben. How long have you had him?"

"We just picked him up today, as a matter of fact," I replied, hoping she'd leave it at that. Father strode into the room as we were putting on our coats.

"Well, boys, I'm glad we had this little chat. As for Digger, by the way, where is…" Before he could finish, a loud noise came from the kitchen. We all rushed in only to find Digger helping himself to the pan of meat loaf that had mysteriously fallen off the counter.

"Digger!" I scolded, loud enough to send him sheepishly crawling for safety under the kitchen table. He was shaking so badly that I immediately regretted yelling at him. To make matters worse, he was so afraid that he peed a decent little puddle under the table as well. Ms. Dillon got on her hands and knees to try to calm Digger down and assure him that no harm was coming. Frank crawled under the table and gave him a big hug. I handed Frank a few paper towels to clean up the puddle while Father Bill tried in vain to salvage the remaining meat loaf.

Once the mess was cleaned up, I apologized for the ruined supper, but Father was having none of it. "It was my fault for leaving it out on the counter where he could reach it. He was probably starving with all he's been through today."

Ms. Dillon looked puzzled as Father Bill finished. Sensing her confusion, he took a few minutes to summarize our day's exploits. When he had finished, Ms. Dillon walked to the counter, opened the wine and poured herself a full glass. After a couple of generous gulps, she looked at Frank and me and sighed. "So, you two are the source of all those phone calls I received today."

Now it was our turn to look puzzled. Father Bill had poured himself a glass as well and sat down to hear her story.

"A group that I belong to is in the process of raising money to open up an additional animal shelter. It would be a no-kill facility. A local farmer, Joseph Winters, has already donated his barn and five acres for the project. We've spoken to several vets in the area who offered to perform neutering and spaying procedures for us at no cost until we get up and running. We still have a ways to go before it becomes a reality, but with some upcoming fundraisers and a large mailing due out next week seeking donations, our goal is no longer just a dream. And now the two of you may have provided us with some well-timed and much-needed free publicity."

She looked down at Digger thoughtfully. "Perhaps he could even be the face of our campaign ads. The article in tomorrow's *Glidden Gazette* should bring to light the fact that un-adopted pets are destroyed after two months. Most people are not aware of this fact and others just don't want to think about it. This should bring out a better awareness of the situation. If we put an ad in the paper the following day, looking for donations and sponsors, it might hit a nerve throughout the county. Especially when they see how two children had to break the law and put themselves in harm's way to rescue a dog from the needle."

I decided that when I grew up and if I decided to run for political office, Ms. Dillon would serve as my campaign manager. She not only knew how to turn a negative into a positive, but she could really lay it on but good. Another glass or two of wine and there's no telling what she would come up with.

As Father Bill walked us out, Ms. Dillon was scouring the yellow pages for the nearest pizza delivery.

"Sorry again for ruining your supper," I said.

"Sometimes in life I find that things happen for a reason, Ben," said Father Bill. "This might be one of those times. What you and Frank accomplished today might very well expedite the goal Megan's organization has of providing a safe environment for future unwanted pets in this area. Maybe Digger wasn't the only pet you saved today. Besides, between the three of us, her meat loaf isn't exactly what I'd call mouth-watering. It's generally dry as shoe leather, but I don't have the heart to tell her. Now the two of you get right home and tell your mother the truth."

"But she already said we can't have a dog," Frank explained.

"First of all, she'll know that you two could be in big trouble if she returns him and she's not going to let that happen. Second, once she looks into those big brown eyes of his, she'll hardly be able to resist."

As Digger, Frank, and I headed out the door, Father Bill had one last question for us. "How'd you manage to get Digger into the shelter yard in the first place? You must have had someone working with you on the inside to pull this off. Am I right?"

"I'll take that secret to my grave, Father."

"You think so, do you? Well, I'll see you in confession."

Frank looked up at me and laughed. "I think he outfoxed you on that one, Ben."

chapter 8

LOOK WHAT I FOUND

O n the way home from the rectory, Frank asked me a question that I had been dreading, but didn't have an answer for.

"What are you going to tell Mom?"

After all the scheming and craziness of the day's events, it was finally time to come clean. To throw myself on the mercy of the court. Once my mother became fully aware of the high jinks and shenanigans that had taken place, it was unlikely there would be an outpouring of understanding and forgiveness on her part. Time had run out and I was faced with a mortal enemy of mine—the truth. I recalled a phrase from one of my religion classes, "The truth will set you free." I was experiencing great difficulty, in my current situation, fully embracing this concept. *The truth will most likely get me grounded for life* seemed a more appropriate motto in this scenario.

As we tiptoed into the front entryway, we could hear water running in the upstairs bathroom. Mom was taking a shower, which bought us a little time, anyway. I sure hoped it was a warm, relaxing shower that would soothe her and put her in a pleasant, forgiving mood. But just in case, I carefully reviewed all available exit routes.

A few minutes later, we heard Mom in the upstairs hallway, humming a little tune.

"Hi, Mom," we shouted up the stairs to her. "We're home."

"I've got the best news for you boys," she answered back.

Digger was at the bottom of the stairs with his head cocked sideways. He was probably trying to figure out who the stranger was upstairs.

"I heard on the radio this afternoon that the dog you two were so worried about yesterday was saved today. The police are searching for one of the kids involved because of an assault on the custodian of the shelter. It didn't sound like it was gang-related, but you never know."

Digger's curiosity got the best of him, and up the stairs he bounded, toward the source of the voice. The next sound we heard was a blood-curdling shriek. Digger came flying back down the stairs like a bolt of lightning. He ran behind me for protection purposes and then stuck his head between my legs to view the impending chaos. Mom was halfway down the stairs by now with her bathrobe partly undone and a pick comb stuck in her hair. Her right hand was held tightly to her chest, partly to hold her robe together and partly to keep her heart form bursting through her chest. It took her several moments to get her breath back. She kept looking between Frank and me and the frightened head of a strange canine staring up at her through my legs. Mom's appearance and the unfolding scene might have been construed as humorous under different circumstances. However, this was hardly the time and place for hearty laughter and frivolity. Hopefully some day we could look back at it as a family Kodak moment, but right then it was nothing short of a massive train wreck.

After what seemed like an eternity, but was in reality probably only a few seconds, Mom, while staring a hole through me that had more of an effect than a laser beam, simply said, "Frank, go upstairs and take a bath. A long bath. Don't come out until you're squeaky clean."

"But Mom, I just took a bath last—"

"NOW!"

Frank slunk past her on the stairs and chanced a glance back down to me. He couldn't resist one final look at me while I still remained in one piece. I imagined it was the kind of look that a condemned man on his way to the electric chair got while he was paraded past the other inmates. I tried to swallow but the lump in my throat felt like a watermelon.

With the bathroom door closed, Mom walked down the remaining stairs and into the living room.

"Have a seat, Benjamin Thomas."

The use of my middle name had never been good news in the past and I highly doubted that we were starting a new tradition here. Once I was seated with Digger at my side (he seemed to sense the seriousness of the occasion), Mom said, "I want the truth, the whole truth and nothing but the truth."

All that was missing was the Bible and jury. But this was no jury trial—just the accused and the judge/executioner.

While I gave, in great detail, the summary of the day's events, including the role that Tara played in the escape plans, the unfortunate "accident" involving Marvin's wrist injury, the incident at the Wiswall estate, the visit by Officer Woodson, and the visit with Father Bill at the rectory, I could see my mother aging before my very eyes. I purposely left out the meat loaf episode from the rectory. There didn't seem to be any benefit in portraying Digger as an undisciplined houseguest.

"The fact that you defied my wishes about not bringing a dog into our life is bad enough. And to bring our next-door neighbor's daughter into the fray is equally troubling. But to drag your seven-year-old brother down with you throughout this crime spree is unconscionable."

I wasn't sure what that last word meant, but had a pretty good idea it wasn't meant as a compliment.

"I know you only meant well, Benny. Your father's sudden death was traumatic for all of us. But you can't bring him back by saving this dog. If anything were to happen to you or Frank, I don't know what I would do. I can barely keep it together as it is."

As tears began streaming down Mom's cheeks, Digger slowly paced over to the couch where she sat and put his head on her lap. As she softly scratched the top of his head, I witnessed a gradual calm come over her. He raised his left paw and she shook it. While looking into those big brown eyes of his, she suddenly bristled, "Who would ever harm a sweet thing like this? If that Marvin Griswold shows up here looking for any of you, he darn well better make sure his health insurance is paid up. That sore wrist will be the least of his worries."

I sat in amazement. The same human being that had threatened to send me into next week for burping at the dinner table a few nights ago would still protect me to her death from any outside threat. Right then, I doubted that a team of Navy Seals could make it past her if Frank or I were in danger.

"Come on, Digger," she said, "let's get you something to eat."

As the two of them paraded merrily into the kitchen, I couldn't get over this sudden turn of events. In less than sixty seconds, Digger had managed to do something that a week's worth of medication, professional counseling, and well-wishes from friends and family couldn't achieve—putting a smile back on Mom's face.

chapter 9

ME AND MY BIG MOUTH

As the weeks passed, the Davies family finally settled into a normal routine. Frank and I back at school, Mom with her work at the grocery store, and Digger with his house and yard to rule over. We no longer required alarm clocks to wake us up in the morning. Digger took it upon himself to roust the entire household every morning at the crack of dawn. A cold nose and a wet tongue were the first warning. If that didn't get the job done, there was a return visit just as with a ten-minute snooze button. The second visit never failed. Even a dive under the covers was futile. He would just grab the top blanket in his mouth and take off down the hall with it. Upon his return, you either got up, or the next layer was removed until you were left shivering and curled up on the bed while he danced on your back and pawed your head repeatedly. Mom tried closing her bedroom door once, but his incessant scratching was akin to someone scraping his or her fingernails on a chalkboard. I was usually the one who let him out into "his yard" each morning. The squirrels were sent fleeing back up their trees while the rabbits scurried back under the fence and into the safety of their winter burrows. Once the yard was secure he was free to attend to his own needs and concerns.

The doorbell was also of no use to us anymore. From his perch by the front picture window, Digger would joyously announce any approaching visitors to the house. Anyone entering the house had to be sniffed and deemed acceptable before passing through the entryway. A customary head scratch or a bribe in the form of a treat would ensure quick entry into the family room. My uncle Dexter even installed a dog door for him to use while we were at school and work during the day.

It allowed him access to his backyard domain to either relieve himself or just to verify that the other four-legged uninvited guests weren't turning his sanctuary into a playground.

Digger also loved to ride in the car. On his first ride, which was to the veterinary clinic, Frank let him sit next to him in the back seat and rolled the window down for him so that he could stick his head out and sniff away to his heart's content. But in the middle of winter this made for a chilly car ride. So Mom nixed Frank's open-window policy.

The vet, Dr. Carlson, inquired as to how it happened that we'd come to possess Digger. In a carefully rehearsed response, I explained that our out-of-state cousins recently lost their home and were forced to move into an apartment that didn't allow pets. Dr. Carlson suggested that we have Digger's records sent to him to update his records, as to what shots he required and any possible medications prescribed. Mom said that we'd be sure to look into it, but for now, to go ahead and give him whatever shots he needed to get him registered and legal. Fifteen minutes later we walked out with a legal, registered canine, complete with new dog tags. And as previously agreed, Frank and I paid for the visit. When we got the bill, I did a double take. I decided right then and there that I was going to buckle down and try harder in school so that I could make it into this racket someday. By the time we shelled out for the visit, the shots, and the license, Frank and I were officially broke. It was adios to my plans to buy a new baseball bat and for Frank to add to his Legos collection. I whispered to Digger as we neared the car that I was expecting him to get a paper route to pay us back, but he seemed more interested in watering all the trees around the grounds, which I was sure all the other patients had visited in recent days.

Tara and I signed Digger up for a dog obedience class through the park district that was held in the town's new recreation center. He responded very well to various commands such as "stay," "lie down," and "roll over," and got along quite well with his classmates. Some of them, I noticed, were rather unruly and Tara questioned if there was any hope for a couple of them to graduate the obedience class. One poor lady had a huge Saint Bernard named Sir Galahad that dragged her around the gym like a rag doll. His sanitary habits were nothing to write home about, either. The woman, Linda Norcross, mentioned that she doled out $750 for him, and that he came with papers proving he was from some royal bloodlines. From what I could observe, she should have requested a money-back guarantee for the beast. Another of Digger's classmates was a Jack Russell terrier, Mitzie, who looked adorable but was unapproachable. At our first class, a man reached down to pet her and was rewarded with a chomp that made him thankful he got all his fingers back, though a few of them were a little worse for wear. From then on, the other class participants gave Mitzie a wide berth.

The woman leading the class, Siobhan, fell in love with Digger. She frequently used him as an example for the rest of the class when showing a new command or a certain trait to look for. I think I learned more from the class than Digger did. Having Tara there to point out different ways to detect his behavioral habits was a big help, too. I was learning that discipline was as important as reward. If I didn't show him who was boss, he'd just run roughshod over me, if he wasn't already.

Following one of Digger's obedience classes, Tara had a softball practice at an adjoining park district indoor facility that housed both soccer and softball fields. I ducked in to catch some of her team's practice while Siobhan kept an eye on Digger. The team looked pretty good warming up. As Tara was getting loose on the mound, I mentioned to her that it seemed like she had a fine team, but being my usual hilarious self, I added, "for girls, that is." Neither Tara nor the other three or four girls who heard my awkward attempt at humor seemed amused.

Tara shot back, "Why don't you pick up a bat, step up to the plate, and show us how it's done, big mouth?"

I immediately regretted my comment, but by now the entire team was gathering around, awaiting my response. How hard could it be, I thought, to hit a 12-inch softball from a girl throwing underhand when I was used to hitting a baseball, which was 9 inches in diameter? So I grabbed one of the bats, took a few practice cuts, and stepped into the batter's box. I figured I'd drive a few of her pitches into the outfield and walk away with my head up and add a couple of parting remarks on my way out. She whipped her first pitch in and I got around on it a little late, fouling it off to the right. I heard a chuckle or two from the coaches. One of her teammates asked if I wanted a lighter bat. I politely declined and dug in, determined to drive her next fastball to the moon. On her next pitch, I took my "moon" swing, but she crossed me up with a change-up and I twirled around the batter's box like a top. Now it was all-out laughter and howling I was being subjected to. I stepped out of the box for a second to get my thoughts together. My first thought was, *Me and my big mouth.* The next thought was that she'd come back with another fastball. She did, but the best I could do was to barely get a piece of it and foul it straight back. Her next pitch was some sort of sinker or drop pitch that I clumsily drove straight down off my ankle. She had me tied up in knots, and she knew it. Her teammates were having the time of their lives at my expense. After four pitches, I had weakly fouled three off and missed the other by a country mile. She and I both knew I was at her mercy. But Tara had made her point, and was too good of a friend to continue this humiliation. The next pitch was straight down the middle, a little slower with nothing on it. I cracked it on a line over her head and into center field. I ran down the first base and away from that purgatory of a batters box as fast as my legs would carry me. The center fielder tossed the ball into second base as I glanced at the mound. Tara just winked at me as I mouthed a silent "thank you" to her. I wished her team the best of luck for the upcoming season and beat a hasty retreat out of Dodge.

Walking Digger on the way home, I thought it might not be such a bad idea to stop at the Ace Hardware store and get a roll of duct tape for that big mouth of mine. The more I thought about it, maybe purchase two rolls for good measure.

chapter 10

In Like a Lion

There is an old saying that the month of March often roars in like a lion and goes out like a lamb. That year was no exception. It was March first and a foot of snow had already fallen by the time Digger had made his early rounds, with more on its way. We flipped on the radio to get the good news–SCHOOL CANCELLED! Seeing as I'd abandoned my homework assignments in lieu of watching TV and playing tug-of-war with Digger, both deemed highly educational by my wayward conscience, the snow day most certainly turned out to be divine intervention.

Digger raced around the back yard in the fresh snow like a new puppy while Frank tried to pelt him with snowballs. Mom had to leave for work in an hour, so I got busy shoveling the driveway. Most of our neighbors had snow blowers to do their driveways and sidewalks, but Dad had insisted it was better exercise to shovel instead. I always figured it was because we couldn't afford a snow blower but I told myself it would only make me stronger, and that would hopefully translate into more home runs this coming summer. Halfway through the driveway, with the snow piling up to over a foot, I would've gladly traded a few home runs for a brand-new snow blower. By the time I'd finished the driveway and front walk, Mom was backing out of the garage. She got out of the car and motioned me over.

"Great job, Benny," she said as she gave me a big hug. "I made your favorite cinnamon raisin scones for breakfast so hurry in and get one while they're still warm. Keep and eye on Frankie—make that both eyes—and behave yourselves for a change," she said with a wink. As she hopped back in the car, I noticed that Frank was no longer in the back yard, which meant only one thing—he was inside the house, devouring the scones, most likely with assistance from our four-legged vacuum cleaner, Digger. I tossed the shovel aside and raced in, hoping against hope that there would be a few crumbs remaining for me.

Later that morning, I recruited Frank to help me shovel the Wiswalls' driveway. I told him we'd split the twenty dollars, although I didn't mention anything about it being a 50/50 business proposition. I figured five dollars would more than likely be enough to keep him satisfied.

About halfway through the driveway, in the middle of a daydream that had me lying on a sunny tropical beach watching six-foot waves crashing on the shore, I heard laughing and shouting. The Jenkins boys were across the street pelting two younger lads with a barrage of snowballs. The two younger kids were hunkered down behind the Wiswalls' front bushes, tying to seek temporary refuge while they rolled up a couple of fresh snowballs of their own. These two saps had no idea that their biggest problem lay behind them, not across the street. I scurried around to the front to get a better view of the impending rout just in time to see the front door flung open. Nora charged across the front porch with her fiery eyes blazing, a golden cane held high above her head and with a voice even higher as she threatened fire and brimstone to the rascals now trapped in her front yard. But as she neared the top of the steps, she slipped on the ice. Her right leg flew out one way and her left leg the other way as she and her cane went careening down the steps in an ugly twisted mess. There was total silence for a couple of seconds, followed by a faint groaning from the bottom of the steps. The snowball-fight participants scattered in every direction as if the Devil himself were nipping at their heels.

As I approached Nora, I couldn't believe my eyes. Her right arm was bent behind her in an unnatural way—and going the wrong direction from the elbow. Her left ankle was also pointing the wrong way and a bone— or something—was sticking out. When Frank witnessed the carnage he immediately turned an ashen white, doubled over and vomited on top of a two-foot-high snowdrift. So much for Mom's warm, tasty scones.

Much of what I'd learned in Cub Scouts about treating traumatic injuries was a blur, but one thing that did come to mind was to keep the injured person warm. Since lying crumpled up in the snow didn't seem to be the most likely way to achieve that goal, it stood to reason that we needed to get Nora inside. One look at Frank didn't instill confidence that he'd be of much use in carrying her indoors. Seeing his face reminded me of what I must've looked like several years ago when I took a few puffs of Dad's cigar, thinking how cool I was, only to spend the next couple of hours bent over the toilet wishing I was dead. But Frank had recovered nicely and was busy trying to retrieve her cane from the snowdrift.

"Use the cane to prop open the door," I said. "I don't think she'll be needing it anytime soon. Then help me lug her into the house."

I grabbed Nora under her arms while Frank got under her knees and together we were able to haul her up the five steps and into the house. Once inside, we laid her down on something resembling a couch in the front parlor. Luckily, she must have only weighed about ninety pounds. This peculiar couch we placed her on looked so old-fashioned I was convinced it must have come over on the *Mayflower*. Shouting to Frank to find some blankets or sheets to cover Nora up, I heard a scuffling coming from the kitchen.

"Hurry," I whispered to Frank. The scuffling was Vera and her walker making tracks to see what all the commotion was about. When Vera got close enough to witness Nora's dire condition, her knees buckled, and as she tried to compensate for her forward movement, she pulled back, sending herself and her walker stumbling back into the banister leading up the stairs. She conked her head and dropped into a heap on the hardwood floor.

As Frank came down the stairs loaded with blankets, sheets and bed covers, I scanned the room for a phone. I saw what looked like a phone from another century on a desk. Sure enough, when I picked up the receiver, there was no dial tone. I headed to the kitchen, hoping to find a telephone that had been manufactured a little more recently. Hanging on the wall was an ugly yellow one, but at least it worked. Dialing the emergency number, I tried to remember the Wiswalls' address, but came up blank. A pleasant-sounding woman answered and inquired as to the nature of my emergency. I told her to send an ambulance or two to the corner of Locust Street and Monroe Avenue, where there was a big gray house that looked like it was straight out of a horror movie. The woman asked if I was aware of the penalties for making a crank call.

"How old are you, son?" she inquired.

"I'm twelve years old and what difference does that make? There are two old—er—elderly ladies in dire need of immediate medical attention. One slipped and fell down her front steps and has at least two broken bones and the other fainted, hit her head, and is unconscious. Is that enough of an emergency, lady?"

"What's your name, young man?"

"My name is Benny Davies, I'm here with my seven-year-old brother, Frank, and the two injured parties are Nora and Vera Wiswall. I'd love to catch up more with you later, but if you don't start believing me and rush an ambulance over here, you can go ahead and make one more call—to the coroner."

"I'm sending an ambulance, all right, and I'm also sending some police cars, so don't you go anywhere."

"Could you have them bring their snow shovels too, please? I could sure use some help with the rest of the driveway."

chapter 11

HUMPTY DUMPTY

Later that evening, I got a call from Officer Woodson. He had been one of the responding police officers to the morning mayhem at the Wiswalls. He informed me that Nora had undergone seven hours of surgeries, but had pulled through remarkably well in spite of all the complications involved. Vera had sustained a slight concussion and was going to be held overnight at the hospital for observation. He thanked Frank and me for our "valiant" efforts and reported that the paramedics got a particular kick out of Frank's bedside manner with Nora and Vera. Frank had run back upstairs to fetch a pillow to put under Vera's head and retrieved Nora's rosary from the front room table per her request and was reciting the decades with her when the ambulance arrived. He even asked the paramedics if they brought any hot chocolate with them. What a ham.

Mr. Woodson added that the first thing out of Vera's mouth when she came to was, "Who's taking care of Snuffy?" When Nora finally came out of her anesthesia the first thing she wanted to know was if "those snowball-throwing hooligans invading her front yard" had been rounded up and brought to justice yet. The doctor who performed the surgery had no doubt that she'd pull through, mentioning that she was too mean to die.

"Before I forget, Benny," Officer Woodson added, "there's a man that'll be stopping by your house in a little while. The Wiswalls don't have any immediate family. Their emergency contact is Thomas Benton. He's the president of the Glidden National Bank and Trust, and he'll be giving you a key to their house so you can take care of Snuffy until things get sorted out."

"Thanks for the update, Mr. Woodson. I'm glad they're doing better."

"Oh, and by the way, after reviewing the emergency call, the dispatcher's boss wants her to attend a remedial training seminar."

If she wasn't mad at me before, she would be by now. As I glanced out the front window, a shiny black Lincoln Continental pulled into the driveway. Seeing as we didn't know anyone with as nice a set of wheels as this, I assumed it was the bank president.

"I think Mr. Benton is here, so I'll talk to you later."

As Digger announced our guest, I was thinking I could maybe hit him up for the twenty dollars we had coming for shoveling the Wiswalls' drive. After passing inspection by our "butler," Mr. Benton strode into the living room. Mom and Frank came in from the kitchen and introduced themselves.

We sat down and Mr. Benton began, "On behalf of the Glidden National Bank and Trust, in addition to our fine community, I would like to personally thank the two of you fine young men for your quick-thinking action and kindness this morning."

There was a puzzled look on Frank's face, probably because he had never been referred to as a fine young man. Come to think of it, I couldn't remember ever hearing that description and my name used in the same sentence, either. Mom was beaming with pride as Mr. Benton continued with additional praise and superlatives. It was quite a different scene from a couple of months ago in this same living room, when I was trying to explain the acquisition of our new fugitive to a less-than-enthusiastic audience, the same one who was now bursting with pride for her two saintly sons. After another minute or two of shining accolades, Mr. Benton rose and handed me an envelope with a key and crisp ten-dollar bills enclosed. He thanked us once again, slipped me his business card, and excused himself. "Call me if you are in need of additional funds or have any questions."

I liked the sound of "additional funds," as visions of envelopes stuffed with ten-dollar bills danced merrily through my head. As Digger saw Mr. Benton to the door, Frank raced up to me.

"How much did he give us?"

"Frank, it would be rude to count it out now, what with the Wiswalls lying in agony as we speak. We'll check it tomorrow, but for now we should start earning our meager salary by checking in on Snuffy and straightening up their house."

Mom eyed me with her sideways gaze, but she was in such a good mood she decided to let it slide for the time being.

Frank, Digger, and I trudged through the snow to the Wiswalls. Even with the sisters absent, the thought of going into that dark, possibly haunted mansion at night by myself would have been unthinkable. After unlocking the front door, I let Digger lead the way in while I fidgeted for the lights. Upon attaining the proper lighting, Frank and I stepped into the front room. There was Snuffy with his tail puffed up and back arched, confronting Digger, with his tail straight back and a look of bewilderment on his mug. After a few seconds, Digger, sensing a decided size advantage, made his move toward Snuffy. Snuffy side-stepped his initial move, but in doing so, bumped hard into a tall slender table holding a hand-painted porcelain shamrock pitcher. The pitcher teetered back and forth a couple of times before tumbling off and dropping toward the floor. I took a couple of steps and dove head-first across the hardwood floor like a center fielder trying to catch a Texas League pop-up. I almost—the key word being "almost"—made it. Instead, I got a close-up view of the destruction of what was certainly a priceless antique—one that undoubtedly survived decades of turmoil and battles, only to crumble in a matter of seconds under my watch. I was certain there must have been some mistake on my birth certificate because instead of Thomas, my middle name more appropriately should have read "Screw-up." As Digger chased Snuffy up and down the upstairs hallway, I asked Frank if he could search for a broom and dust pan so we could sweep up the evidence. "Couldn't we just glue it back together, Benny?" he asked.

As I surveyed hundreds of broken pieces scattered throughout the hallway and into the kitchen, I told Frank we'd have a better chance of putting Humpty Dumpty back together again.

chapter 12

THE SPIN DOCTORS

The following morning there was a story on the local radio station, WGLD, about how a seven-year-old boy—with help from his older brother—had heroically saved two elderly women from certain death after suffering injuries from falls at their house. It was obvious I needed to hire a publicist in order to receive more favorable press. In the two months since the incident at the animal shelter, numerous opinions had been voiced in the letters-to-the-editor section of the *Gazette*. Most of the letters from obvious animal lovers called my actions heroic. Those letters reasoned that once the boy was identified, a medal should be forthcoming and all criminal charges dropped immediately. But on the other hand, there were some less-than-flattering responses that painted me in darker terms, with the word "scoundrel" being a prevalent theme.

In one of his weekly opinion columns, editor Timothy Norris sided more closely with the scoundrel crowd. He referred to my "taking the law into my own hands" as dangerous and reprehensible behavior, and to the injuring of a valuable employee (Marvin Griswold) as downright criminal. As soon as I looked up the word "reprehensible" in the dictionary, I came to the immediate conclusion that Mr. Norris was off his rocker. Besides, referring to that buffoon Griswold as a valued employee—now *that* was downright criminal.

Ms. Dillon phoned me later that afternoon with some good news—her no-kill facility was up and running. The Helping Animals Together Shelter (HATS) fundraiser had been a gigantic success, and she wanted to personally thank Frank and me (and Digger) for our part in providing awareness throughout the county of the sorry plight of abandoned pets. Ms. Dillon also mentioned that Timothy Norris was currently on a leave of absence from the paper, and that the owner of the *Gazette* had strongly suggested Norris look into a new line of work. I concluded that it couldn't have happened to a nicer guy. She reminded me that in case Griswold ever discovered my identity and I ran into legal trouble, that one of the board members of HATS, Richard Petrino, a prominent lawyer, would gladly take up my case pro bono. When I hesitated, she explained that Mr. Petrino would be offering his services free of charge. I could live with that. Free is always good. She gave me his phone number and although I hoped I'd never need it—you never know. I asked Ms. Dillon if HATS needed volunteers to walk the dogs and help out, but she told me I'd have to wait a couple of years until I was in high school. It was probably a good rule, seeing as I still had plenty to learn about our current resident canine.

After work, Mom drove Frank and me to the hospital to visit the Wiswalls. Nora had casts on nearly every appendage possible and looked rather out of sorts. Vera was seated in a chair next to the bed with her head wrapped in a bandage. They were happy to see us, and immediately inquired as to Snuffy's disposition, what with the both of them being absent from him for the first time ever. We assured them that Snuffy was holding up well under the circumstances but there was one little problem. As the sisters held their breath, I gave them an abbreviated version of the previous night's events. I explained that when we arrived to feed Snuffy and to check on the house, he got spooked—probably because he wasn't expecting us—and rammed into a table. I cleared my throat as I got to the point. "There was a pitcher of some sort that was knocked off the table and we didn't quite get there in time."

Frank broke in, "Yeah, it hit the floor and shattered into a zillion pieces. You should have seen it."

Mom stared a hole through Frank while I kicked him in the ankle. I was hoping to ease into the details of the destruction of their priceless antique a little more delicately, but Frank had let the cat out of the bag.

"That old eyesore," commented Nora, "I can't remember how many times I wanted to take my cane to that monstrosity myself."

"Did poor Snuffy get hurt by the flying shards?" asked Vera.

"No, he was too busy flying up the stairs because—ouch!" Now Frank's other ankle was going to be sore, too.

"Because," I continued, "he was probably scared of the noise from the broken vase. It was pretty loud. But we finally got it swept up and he came back down after a while and ate his food. When we left, he was curled up on a sofa by the side window, sound asleep."

Both Wiswalls were delighted with the good news—or at least my version of it. Frank looked to be somewhat skeptical of my view, but knew that any account he might offer would only lead to sore shins to go along with his bruised ankles. Mom just shook her head as she excused us and cautioned the Wiswalls to get plenty of rest and not to worry about a thing—the house and Snuffy would be in good hands while they recovered. Whether or not she believed what she'd just said was a different story.

On the way down the hospital corridor Frank looked up at me and commented, "Boy, are you full of it."

When we arrived home, there was a man and a woman hovering near our house. As we got out of the car, they rushed over and introduced themselves. The woman, Janet, was a reporter for the *Gazette* and the guy, Phillip, was a photographer for the paper. Mom invited them in. Janet asked us questions, mostly of Frank, who was the obvious media darling, and finished with Phillip getting a few shots of Frank and me together. On the way out, Janet mentioned that Frank appeared to be limping and wondered if it stemmed from his heroic deeds at the Wiswalls. "Yes, I must have bumped my ankle while I was racing upstairs to get blankets for Nora. She was shivering so much, I knew if I didn't hurry, there was no telling what might happen to the poor dear."

As Janet jotted down this last piece of nonsense, I gazed at Frank in wonder, trying to imagine exactly what kind of monster I had created.

chapter 13

THE PURSE

The next morning before I headed out the door for school, Mom called out excitedly, "Benny, take a look at this."

As I entered the kitchen, she was reading aloud from the newspaper to Frank as Digger paraded around the room with a sock in his mouth, trying to entice one of us into a game of tug-of-war. It was the article Janet put together on the Wiswall affair with the major focus on Frank, naturally. The picture accompanying the article was a good one of Frank with his bright shiny eyes, happy-go-lucky smile and Irish freckled face. But as usual, a dreadful head shot of me. I normally took bad pictures, but this one was especially hideous. My eyes were half-closed and my mouth was twisted in a way that made it look like I just bit into a lemon. Mom proudly cut out the article and put it up on the refrigerator—probably more to scare the mice away than anything.

As I reached the sidewalk, dreading the beat-down I was in for at school, Tara came rushing up to me.

"Are you crazy, Dork?"

I was expecting a certain amount of verbal abuse at school, but was hoping for a kinder reception from Tara.

"My picture wasn't that bad, was it?"

"Not bad enough so that Griswold won't recognize you, dummy. What were you thinking?"

A sickening feeling reached the pit of my stomach as I realized what she was getting at. If Griswold saw the picture on the front page of the *Gazette*—and how could he not—I was sunk.

"Is this your idea of keeping a low profile that we talked about?"

I was too numb to answer, but was thinking to myself that Jamaica or Barbados would sure be nice this time of year. Maybe if I hurried, I could get an advance from Mr. Benton at the bank for my cat sitting duties and hightail it out of town on the double.

"Forget it, Benny. I can just picture that mind of yours concocting some elaborate escape plan. It was bound to catch up with you sooner or later. Besides, you might not look so bad in an orange jumpsuit after all."

"Gee, thanks for all the encouragement, Stork. You really know how to make a guy feel good. Be sure and have a nice day."

Sure enough, that afternoon, about ten minutes after I got home from school, a county sheriff's police car pulled into the drive. My first instinct was to dash out the back door and make a run for it. But with my luck, some trigger-happy rookie would plug me in my tracks.

Two policemen got out of the squad car and started for the door. With each step my apprehension turned quickly to nervousness, then fear, until I stood ten feet from the door frozen stiff. When the doorbell chimed, I was in full panic mode and visibly shaking. Sensing my extreme anxiety, Digger went into an attack mindset, lunging at the door and snarling viciously at whatever awaited on the other side. Not only was I worried about what they had in mind for me, but what if they were also here to take Digger away? For all I knew they considered him stolen property. That sealed it. I clipped a leash on him and out the back door we flew as the pounding on the front door grew fainter. My thoughts flew to a scene from a movie I had watched a couple of weeks earlier, in which a Los Angeles SWAT team prepared to ram through a door while a Clint Eastwood-type yelled from a bullhorn, "Come out with your hands up, we've got you surrounded!"

Even knowing this was hardly such an intense situation, I still managed to get a chuckle out of it. And if anyone needed a laugh right then, it was me.

We cut through some back yards, front yards, and vacant lots until we reached the rectory. Father Bill would know what to do, although it probably wasn't every day that a wanted twelve-year-old boy and his faithful runaway canine companion on the lam showed up at his doorstep.

"Well, to what do I owe the pleasure of your company today?" Father Bill asked as he opened the door. As I stood, still shaking and gasping for breath, he continued, "Let me guess. That wonderful photo of you and Frank on the front page this morning brought some undue attention your way."

I nodded and he invited us in.

"You look like you've just seen a ghost, Benny."

"No, two ghosts, Father, and they were wearing police uniforms."

I explained to him my predicament and how we fled out the back door.

"We didn't know where else to go."

Father Bill got a glass of water for me and a dish of water for Digger while he dialed up a number on the phone. He ducked into the other room, coming out once to ask what time my mother got home from work.

"Six o'clock," I told him. A minute later, he came back.

"Have your mother bring you to the police station tonight at seven o'clock. Did Megan Dillon give you a phone number for a lawyer?"

"Somebody named Petrino, I think, Father."

"Good, call him as soon as you get home. I'll give you two a lift home now."

"What about Digger?"

"He's safe for the time being—but don't forget to call Petrino first thing."

As Digger and I walked into the house, a racket could be heard coming from the kitchen. It came as no surprise to find Frank grazing away at the table with peanut butter, jelly, bread, a half-ripped-open bag of potato chips, and a glass of chocolate milk heaped in front of him. I explained to him my dilemma and how Mom and I had an appointment at the police station at seven.

"How about me?" he asked.

"No you're safe, it's me they're after."

This seemed to satisfy him and he went back to devouring his sandwich.

"I'm worried about Digger, though. They might be able to take him away from us."

"I got it. Let's paint some stripes on him and if they come for him, we can tell them we don't have a dog, just a pet tiger."

"Yeah, that's sure to fool them, Frankie."

I grabbed the phone number for Petrino and called his office. His secretary informed me that he was out of the office and inquired if this was an emergency. I assured her that it was indeed an emergency–at least to me–and she took down my name and number. Several minutes later, Petrino called back. I told him the police wanted to see me at seven o'clock along with my mother. He took down our address and told me to be ready at 6:30. He'd pick us both up then and drive us to the station.

"Don't worry, Benjamin, everything is going to be all right. Just make sure to take a shower and wear something decent. Not too nice, or they'll portray you as a spoiled rich kid. But we don't want you coming off as a slug, either. We're looking for that everyday, next-door-neighbor-boy type, with a clean, wholesome attitude. And a hero to boot."

I asked my new pro bono mouthpiece who "they" were that I was trying to impress, and he said simply, "Leave that to me, you'll see."

When Mom arrived and was informed of our seven o'clock tête-àtête with the county police, she panicked. I was able to calm her down somewhat with the news of our free representation, compliments of Mr. Petrino and the local HATS organization. She ran upstairs to clean up, change, and "look presentable."

On the way over to the station, Mr. Petrino cautioned us to keep quiet and let him do all the talking. "Only if I give you the OK can you answer any questions" was his final piece of advice.

Not in my wildest imagination was I prepared for the scene that greeted us upon our arrival to the station. The front yard and parking lot was filled with young and old, carrying signs. Many of the signs had pictures of dogs or cats sitting helplessly in cages. Others had messages written on them such as "DROP THE CHARGES NOW," and "LET JUSTICE PREVAIL." One sign in particular was aimed at Sherriff John Low: "HOW LOW CAN YOU GO?"

Janet and Phil from the *Gazette* were setting up shop at the front door. As we filed past to enter, I noticed a TV van pulling up with bright letters on the side door proclaiming WREX–ROCKFORD, CHANNEL 13. Richard Petrino might have been taking my case at no cost, but he was pretty shrewd about conjuring up some free advertising in the meantime. With the media circus he'd managed to drum up in a few short hours, I half expected to see the governor's limo pull up next.

When we entered the main lobby, a very unhappy-looking Sherriff Low greeted us rather coldly and immediately ushered us into a meeting room. He did not appear to be enjoying all the attention.

With the door closed he spun around and addressed Petrino directly.

"I don't appreciate this grandstanding maneuver of yours one bit."

"These fine citizens are simply exercising their rights to peacefully express their opinions. We still live in a free country, don't we? And may I remind you, John, that this is an election year."

Petrino opened the blinds for more effect. More people were arriving by the minute. The crowd had swelled to well over two hundred strong.

"If you choose to pursue this, John, need I remind you what a political disaster you'd be inviting? Why, you'd be lucky if your own mother voted for you. In fact, isn't that her in the front row standing by the statue of Lincoln?"

Low glimpsed out, and sure enough, holding up a sign with a picture of a malnourished, flea-infested puppy, was Mrs. Florence Low. She seemed to be leading some sort of chant at the moment. The sheriff pulled the blinds closed, stumbled back, collapsed into his chair and began massaging his temples. He appeared to have suddenly developed a pretty wicked migraine.

Mom fished in her purse for some aspirin and offered some to Sheriff Low.

"Thanks, just the same, but unless you've got a bottle of Jack Daniel's in there to wash them down with, I don't know that it'd do any good," he answered.

There was a knock on the door and a young deputy poked his head in. "Excuse me, sheriff, but there's a man that's been waiting to speak to you for an hour in room five, and he's getting pretty upset about it." Before Low could respond to the intrusion, the deputy went lurching forward, the door flew open, and there standing in the doorway was none other than Marvin "Bad News" Griswold.

His menacing gaze immediately focused on me and he took two steps toward me muttering, "There you are, you little squirt." Just as he reached down and grabbed me by my shirt collar, a big black purse smashed into the left side of his face, followed by a return visit to the right side of his mug. The third and final blow directly connected with his nose and sent him reeling backwards through the door and out into the lobby, where he collapsed in a heap. Because Mom's purse was opened in search of aspirin, half of its contents lay strewn about the room and lobby. A pocket organizer struck the deputy and cut his lip. The aspirin bottle smashed against the wall and sent dozens of tablets flying all over. Several feminine hygiene products lay out in the lobby at the feet of Griswold, who was lying flat on his back holding his bloody schnoz. Low cursed harshly at the deputy for his ineptitude. Two officers rushed from behind the front desk to restore order—or what was left of it.

Petrino was furious. "Sheriff, this is an outrage. To have that maniac loose in the same building where my client was a sitting duck is inexcusable. Not only the health of this young man was at risk here, but also his peace of mind. How's he supposed to get a good night's sleep with 'Big Foot' stalking him? Would you endanger your son in this way? I should think not."

A groggy Marvin Griswold began spewing more insane comments. "I want to press assault charges against the lady with the purse."

"One more word out of you, Griswold, and I'll turn you over to that mob out front," countered Low. "I can't imagine they'd be likely to greet you with open arms."

Griswold stuck his head out the door and quickly retreated back inside.

"Sheriff, is there a back way out of here?"

"There sure is, and you'd be wise to take advantage of it right now. Anything to get you out of my hair."

Low assigned one of his deputies to escort Griswold to his car. As Griswold exited the building, Low muttered, "Good riddance."

"I demand a complete investigation into the handling of this case. If charges aren't dropped immediately, you can expect to see a civil lawsuit filed against the department first thing in the morning," said Petrino.

Sheriff Low's master plan, whatever it was, had blown up in his face. He was in strict damage-control mode.

"We'll have to review the assault and theft charges against Mr. Davies in lieu of the recent developments. I'll contact you personally when I reach a decision."

"That's assuming you're still sheriff, John. The way things are going, I wouldn't count on it."

Upon reaching the steps outside, with TV cameras running, the radio people elbowing their way to the front and the *Gazette* staff poised for some juicy tidbits, Richard Petrino was primed to not disappoint anyone. He strode confidently to the microphones.

"I wish to personally thank each and every one of you for your enthusiastic support of this exceptional family. A possible travesty of justice was hopefully derailed tonight. Thanks in part to this wonderful display of community togetherness, the sheriff has decided to review these outlandish charges. Thanks again for your prayers and support. May God bless all of you."

On the way home I thanked my lucky stars that Mom had remembered her purse. I made a mental note to never wise off to her in the future if that purse was nearby. I pictured poor Sheriff Low down on his hands and knees, scooping up the wayward aspirins and returning to his desk, where he more than likely kept a bottle of medicinal bourbon on hand for just such an occasion.

chapter 14
SURPRISE!

When we arrived home following the debacle at the station, Tara, who was sitting for Frankie during our absence, met us at the door, eager to hear all the gory details. By the time we finished filling her in, she could only sit back and mutter, "No way." She asked if there was a chance the TV cameras caught any of the thrashing Mom handed out to her old nemesis, Griswold.

"No, I'm afraid all the cameras were outside on the front lawn," Mom said. Actual footage capturing the chaos and ineptitude during our visit this evening would not be something Sheriff Low would be eager to share with the general public.

I told Tara that I still wasn't off the hook, and explained how the department was reviewing the charges.

"I have an idea that might help you out of this jam, Benny. I have softball practice tomorrow night, but first thing Saturday morning, be ready for a little 'field trip.'"

Shortly after Tara left, Frank and Digger came bounding down the stairs.

"We were watching *Escape from Alcatraz*," he announced. "Are they going to ship you off to 'the Rock,' Benny?"

"Not likely, Frank, but I guess it wouldn't hurt to work on my long-distance swimming this summer."

"They don't use that awful place for a prison anymore," Mom offered. "I think it's only used as a tourist attraction these days."

"Can we go?" begged Frank.

"We'll talk about it some other time. Now get to bed, both of you."

That was Mom's way of saying, "Forget about it."

The following afternoon, Petrino called and relayed to us an offer from Griswold: Give back the dog and he'd drop the charges against me. Mom politely refused, but asked the lawyer to relay a message back to Marvin.

"Tell him if he wishes to stop by the house to discuss any further options, I have a couple of other purses that I've been dying to try out."

Just about sun-up Saturday morning, Tara showed up with a black case of some sort slung over her shoulder.

"What's that?" I asked. "Binoculars?"

"No, Dork, better than that. It's a video recorder. I borrowed it from my coach. He tapes our batting practices and then we go over them to see what we need to work on. I asked him if I could use it to tape my pitching mechanics."

"That's all fine and dandy, Stork, but how will that help me out of this mess?"

"Remember how you told me Marvin was treating the dogs when you spied on him the morning we busted Digger out?

"Yeah, he was smacking them and even kicking at them if they didn't hurry up and do their business quick enough to suit him."

"Well, I've noticed similar treatment myself a few times. Especially early in the morning before he's had his coffee and rolls. If we can capture some of that abusive behavior on film, maybe we can bring that fat slob down once and for all."

On our way there, Tara related to me that when she first started helping out at the shelter, the director, Alicia Montoya, was in charge.

"Alicia was a wonderful boss. She loved the animals as if they were her own. The person that served as her backup, Victor Sorbin, was exceptional in handling the pets. He made sure they all got plenty of attention and care. But Alicia had back surgery in December and won't be back until May. Victor's father took ill right before Christmas and he had to take a leave of absence to care for him. That left Marvin temporarily in charge. Everything at the shelter has rapidly deteriorated with that lout running the show."

"Well maybe we'll get lucky and turn things around for our furry little friends. If anyone's due for some good luck, it's them," I said.

When we arrived at the shelter, we positioned ourselves in the former escape corner where we could use the pine tree for cover. The spot where Digger had clawed his way to freedom was now filled in with gravel. The bottom of the fence had been reinforced to discourage any repeat occurrences.

About ten minutes elapsed before the back door swung open. Three dogs came scampering out and began sniffing and shuffling about the yard. A moment later, the main attraction appeared, looking a little ragged. He had a piece of white tape across his nose and a multi-colored bruise on his right cheek. His top lip was still split open. Marvin wasn't a particularly handsome man to begin with, but with these freshly added features, he was downright hideous. Tara had to stifle a chuckle as she began filming. Two of the dogs—a lab mix and a Rottweiler—began playfully wrestling about on the ground and taking turns chasing each other around the yard. Marvin stomped after them in disgust. *How could these two have the audacity to enjoy their short time out of their cages?* he must have been thinking. He got a hold of the lab first and shook it violently while yelling at him to hurry it up. The Rottweiler was next. A few socks to the jaw and he whimpered off to a corner of the yard. When the beagle mix came running up to Griswold, barking and snarling at him in frustration, Marvin promptly picked her up, raised her to eye level, smiled, and proceeded to drop kick her toward the fence. Tara gasped as the beagle limped away in retreat. Griswold spun around at the sound and Tara jumped back behind the pine and smacked up against me, pinning me to the side of the building. We remained motionless for a full minute while we waited to see if he was aware of our presence. Normally, it would be unpleasant to be stuck in this awkward position, but for some reason I was enjoying this close encounter immensely. The smell of Tara's hair and the warmth of her body was something I would not soon forget. When she pulled away, finally, I was sorry it had to end. I was hoping that she didn't notice my face. It felt flushed and must have been red as a beet. Luckily, her attention was on the door where Marvin was re-entering the shelter.

"I think we've got enough right here, Benny. Let's get out of here."

I could only nod in agreement, for my voice had deserted me.

Tara and I raced the damaging footage to Petrino's office. No one was there. It was Saturday, after all. Following a brief debate, we decided to turn it over to the county police. When we arrived at the station, a female deputy, Betty, greeted us with a nervous smile.

I started to introduce myself but she quickly raised her hand to cut me off.

"I'm well aware of who you are, Mr. Davies." Turning toward Tara she inquired, "And who might you be, young lady?"

"Tara Mangolin."

"The same Tara Mangolin that initiated those harassing telephone calls last fall that questioned our diligence in regard to the alleged inhumane treatment of the turkeys at Bronson's Turkey Farm?"

We weren't off to a very good start with Betty. "Is Sheriff Low in his office today?" I asked.

"Yes he is. But he's busy. Is there something that I can help you with?"

"No. We need to see him personally," Tara insisted. "It's very important."

"Well, this should make his day," she scoffed, as she ushered us toward his office door.

Upon entering Sheriff Low's quarters, it was apparent he wasn't about to summon the Welcome Wagon committee to celebrate our arrival. "Oh great, just what I need," he said. "A visit from the Glidden Humane Society. Let me guess. The two of you have been out all morning rustling abused and neglected cattle."

Tara calmly replied, "We'd appreciate it if you gave the sarcasm a little rest, Sheriff. We have brought you valuable evidence in regard to the mistreatment of animals at the county shelter."

"Why am I not surprised?" he laughed. "Please enlighten me. I suppose one of the cats has been keeping a journal."

"Very well," Tara shot back as she stood up and started for the door. "We'll turn over the film to Mr. Petrino. He'll be more than eager to release it to the TV stations so that everyone will be able to witness the abuse that's been going on right under your nose."

"Hold on there. Just a minute, young lady. Are you telling me you two have a recording of animal abuse? This I've got to see."

A few minutes later, the three of us were seated in a separate room with a projector. Low quickly sped through the batting practice part of the film until he arrived at the scene unfolding in the shelter yard. The sickening recording was almost too much to stomach. By the time the beagle was sent spiraling through the air, the sheriff had spun away from the screen in disgust.

"It appears as though I have seriously misjudged the two of you," he said. "Please accept my apology and rest assured that this behavior won't go unpunished. Thank you both for your efforts. We'll take it from here."

On the way home, Tara and I laughed about how things turned out at the station.

"We definitely didn't get off on the right foot with Betty or the sheriff," I pointed out.

"Yeah, well you noticed when I brought up Petrino's name, Low sure changed his tune. I don't think he much cares for your lawyer, Benny."

"It's probably a safe bet that they're not on each other's Christmas card list," I added.

Shortly after I walked into my house around noon the phone rang. It was Betty. She informed me that due to recent developments, the sheriff's department was not going to pursue criminal charges against me. Now that was what I called good news.

To celebrate, I invited Frankie, Tara, and Digger to Hank's for ice cream. They had the best desserts in town, and I felt we certainly deserved some. Frankie chose the double-chocolate waffle cone, Tara went with a root beer float supreme, and I pigged out with the super-duper chocolate-and-Butterfinger parfait.

I felt bad ordering Digger a small dish of vanilla ice cream, but he didn't seem to mind until he scarfed it down in about ten seconds and saw what we were devouring. It was all we could do to fend him off while we tried to finish our treats in peace. Frankie wasn't as successful with the fending-off part, and by the time we left, he was wearing a sizeable amount of chocolate on his jacket. Mom wasn't going to be pleased about that, but I figured we had all afternoon to think of a good excuse. We were all in agreement that additional dog obedience courses for Digger were in order.

On the way home we stopped at Prairie Park, a ten-acre area with a fair amount of shrubs and a small woods on one end. Digger loved it there, especially if Duke, a black lab, was present. Duke was there that day, and the two of them went chasing and tumbling after each other until they were worn out.

Frank and I tossed a Frisbee around while Tara roamed through the park, making friends with the other less rambunctious canines. She probably missed her volunteer job at the animal shelter. Tara sure loved animals. Hopefully some day she could work with animals, either as a vet or a trainer of some sort. Tara was a strict vegetarian, which is one of the reasons I didn't hold our little celebration at McDonalds.

Eventually Digger tired of his roughhousing with Duke and set his sights on our Frisbee. As soon as he got his jowls on it, he paraded around the park for a victory lap. Following a brief tug of war with Frank, he carted it off into the woods, where he was distracted by a squirrel. With our game of catch effectively over, it was time to head out. On our way home, we heard thunder in the distance. Digger began barking at the invisible noise, and when a bolt of lightning appeared overhead he nearly pulled my arm off trying to race to the house. We arrived home in record time. He scampered about the house in a frenzy until the storm blew past. Digger didn't appear to be a big fan of nasty weather. It was a good thing we didn't live in Kansas.

Mom got home a little after 4:30 and was eager to catch up with all the gossip concerning the day's activities. When we got to the point about how the charges were dropped against me, she raced out to grab a celebratory glass of wine from the pantry. I was a little confused when I noticed her deliberately pour not only the glass, but the entire bottle into the sink moments later. Must have been a bad batch, I guessed. We collectively decided that ordering a pizza was a perfect dinner option. I was hunting for Papa Luigi's in the phone book in anticipation of ordering their meat lover's special when the doorbell rang.

It was Tara at the door and it was obvious that she'd been crying. I glanced over to her driveway and could see her father's pickup truck parked at an odd angle. The rear of his truck was on the driveway but the front cab was resting in the front yard. I was pretty sure that his return from Kelly's had triggered this visit. Noticing how upset Tara looked, Mom welcomed her in with a hug before ushering her into the kitchen for a private talk.

While Mom tried to get Tara settled down, I called Papa Luigi's. When asked what kind of pizza I wanted, I hesitated briefly. With Tara joining us for supper, I decided to go with an extra-large cheese and green pepper with a side order of bread sticks. Frank, who was counting on the meat lover's special, began to protest mightily, but I hushed him quickly.

A short time later, Tara and Mom emerged from the kitchen. Whatever Mom said to her must have worked. Tara seemed quite a bit calmer and more relaxed. While waiting for the delivery guy we switched on the TV to see if the five o'clock Rockford news would be carrying the Griswold story. Sure enough, the lead story was focused on Marvelous Marv's troubled day. The camera showed him being led into the police station in handcuffs.

The on-scene reporter, Carrie Dorland, was busy explaining that when police arrived at the shelter to question him, Marvin became aggressive and shoved one of the officers. That earned him a quick introduction to the double silver bracelets and a free ride to the station. Carrie asked Marv if he had any comment to offer, but the majority of his response was bleeped out. Good ol' Marvin, what a classy guy. We all got a kick out of it but Frank wanted to know what happened to the microphone.

"I could hardly understand a word he said," complained Frank.

It's just as well," Mom explained, "but I'm sure any lip readers watching the clip got an earful." Digger could only growl at the sight of Marvin crossing the screen.

The pizza arrived, but we were at a stalemate as to the choice of TV shows. Mom voted for the Saturday night movie, *The Sound of Music*, Frank voiced his preference for Channel 6, which was running a cartoon marathon weekend, Tara wanted to see a PBS special on wolves, and I campaigned for the Blackhawks vs. Redwings hockey game. Tara believed that Digger would side with her on the wolf choice so that her vote really counted as two. Guess who won?

The gray wolf documentary focused on a particular pack in Yellowstone that struggled to make a go of it under very difficult circumstances. They managed to survive by sticking together and working as a team. I looked around the room. Digger was front and center, hanging on every howl. Mom sat in the middle of the couch, one arm draped around Tara's shoulders, while Frank dozed with his head on her lap. I came to the conclusion that humans and wolves had a lot more in common than you might think.

Following the wolf pack exposé, Mom walked Tara back to her house while I marched Frank upstairs. Failing to wake him up so he could brush his teeth, I gave up and let Digger escort him to bed while I hurried downstairs to see if Mom had returned from next door. I was curious—or to be honest, just plain nosy—about what had happened at the Mangolin residence.

Trying to drag any information out of Mom was never easy, so I attempted to ease my way into her confidence.

"So, I guess the wine turned out to be a little stale, huh?" I started.

She glanced at the living room wall almost absentmindedly and I heard her mumble to no one in particular, "No, there was nothing wrong with the wine."

Setting her eyes directly upon me she announced, "The reason I poured the wine out, Benny, is because I'm three months' pregnant."

chapter 15
OPENING DAY

Baseball season was finally upon us. My coach that year, Al Sanders, called one day to inform me that our first practice was the next night at five o'clock. Just the day before, I had purchased a new "war club" at Helton's–the El Diablo. The El Diablo was decorated with green bolts of fire and lightning shooting out from its name. It was a heavier bat than I was used to, but I figured being a year older and stronger that I'd be able to handle it all right. And it sure looked impressive in my hands. I even paid for it myself with the money I earned from the Wiswalls.

Mom was beginning to show rather prominently as we moved into the later stages of the spring season. The neighborhood was abuzz with rumors of another unruly Davies child being unleashed upon the world. But Mom calmed most of their fears when she related that her maternal instinct told her that this one was a girl. A collective sigh could be heard throughout Glidden following her announcement.

The Wiswalls were back in their house again, but needed a live-in caregiver. The woman, Ksenia, was Ukrainian, but spoke English fairly well. She didn't have a driver's license, so it was up to me to get most of their groceries and household needs. Small orders I could handle on my bike, but the larger orders required me to enlist Mom as my official chauffer. I also mowed their lawn and trimmed the numerous hedges and bushes scattered throughout the grounds. In addition to the Wiswalls, I managed to pick up three extra lawn jobs in the neighborhood from advertising flyers that Frank passed out. Frank assisted me with my grounds keeping duties, mostly by trimming around trees and shrubs with his handy grass clippers. Whenever he'd complain, I'd assure him that the strength he was building up in his wrists would be responsible for numerous home runs this year during his tee-ball season. Digger accompanied us on most of our jobs and served as a pleasant distraction for Frank, who became bored quite easily and often lost focus on the job at hand. With Digger there to toss the tennis ball to and chase after, it helped to keep morale high for my assistant. The lawn care business kept us pretty busy, but also managed to put some decent spending money in our pockets as well. Unfortunately, we weren't able to blow any of it at Hank's—at least not for another week, when our suspension ended.

When Mom found Frank's wadded-up chocolate-covered coat in an old bureau on our back porch, she had hit the ceiling. Not only did she issue a two-month ban on Hank's, but in addition we were forced to endure her annual tirade concerning our general lack of acceptable housekeeping habits along with improper hygiene practices. Her recent development into expectant motherhood didn't seem to be mellowing her demeanor.

"I'm not your personal maid," she scolded. "You two have a dresser and a closet for a reason. The floor is not a proper resting place for your clothes. I can't even tell your clean pants and shirts from the dirty ones half the time." When I offered that I could differentiate between the two either by seeing if they were still folded or else by smelling them, I thought she was going to grab her purse and come after me.

The HATS organization, on the other hand, had an enjoyable and prosperous spring. With Alicia Montoya back in charge of the county animal shelter, there was renewed cooperation between the shelter and the HATS facility. The two combined their resources and established a common goal—to house abandoned pets in a safe, friendly, no-kill atmosphere. Volunteers from HATS even drove several vans down to Tennessee to rescue more than two dozen dogs and cats that were stuck in overcrowded shelters following a terrible flood. The adoption and foster care networks they utilized meant that precious few furry friends were left lingering in cages for very long. In fact, Tara was currently fostering a spirited beagle-mix dog rescued from Nashville. Rufus and Digger became instant buddies as well as partners in crime. On a couple of occasions, Frank failed to latch the gate properly, thus allowing the dynamic duo full access to the neighborhood. The first time they raced about digging up freshly planted vegetable plots and trampling through flower gardens before chasing Mrs. Delanbach's cat up a tree. Frank eventually coaxed them back to the yard with the help of some raw hot dogs. Another time they converged on the mailman after stealing a soccer ball off the Pearsons' front lawn and puncturing it while trying to wrestle it away from each other. Luckily, Ron, the mailman, didn't resort to his pepper spray but instead lured the two ruffians back into the yard with some dog biscuits. The flattened soccer ball was returned to the Pearsons' front lawn, where hopefully a raccoon or opossum would shoulder the blame.

The last couple of months had gone by somewhat smoothly, considering the circumstances, in the Davies household. There were a few rough patches, though. Opening day for the Cubs was a tough one without Dad. The two of us had always managed to catch most of the opening day game together and to review our high expectations for the season. Each year was finally going to be season the Cubs made it to the World Series.

That year, after school, Digger, Frank, and I watched it together. We munched on hot dogs and peanuts and washed them down with root beers. Frank was old enough by then to understand most of the ins and outs of the game and he really got into it. I was sure that in no time he'd be a know-it-all, just like me.

As much as I missed Dad during the game, I had a feeling he was watching over us somehow. He would be mighty proud of his two sons keeping this tradition alive. During the seventh-inning stretch, I teared up remembering how Dad would always belt out the words to "Take Me out to the Ballgame" way off key. He actually had a worse singing voice than me. When Frank asked me what I was crying about I blamed it on showering my hot dog with too many onions.

The Cubs ended up beating the New York Mets 6-4 to start off the season on a high note. We celebrated by taking Digger out to the "north forty," a large open area that used to be a nine-hole golf course, where he ran to his heart's content while Frank and I rambled on about how the Cubbies were going all the way this year..

At three o'clock the day of our first practice, Mom called from work to remind me that my room needed to be presentable before I left. I assured her that my room was in immaculate condition, which of course it wasn't. My focus, in reality, was on the Cubs game. The Atlanta Braves had the bases loaded with two outs with Dusty Baker up to the plate. The Cubs had a 7-0 lead coming into the inning, but it was now 7-3. On a 2-0 count, Rueschel hung a slider and Dusty sent it out of the park, across Waveland Ave. and up against a house. I clicked the Off button and stomped out of the house, hopped on my bike, and took off to cool off.

By the time I got back from my cool down, it was almost 4:30. I switched on the TV in my room as I got ready for practice just in time to see a Jose Cardenal walk-off home run that gave the Cubbies a nerve-racking 10-9 victory. My joy suddenly turned to panic as I perused my living quarters, a disaster area second only to a toxic waste site. With Mom due home any minute, I had to resort to emergency measures. Virtually shoveling empty potato chip bags, candy wrappers, and dirty clothes under my bed at breakneck speed and stuffing encrusted glasses and plates into the bottom drawer of my dresser, I was able to assemble a normal-looking twelve-year-old boy's room in record time. I grabbed El Diablo, my glove, and my ball cap and raced down the stairs, determined to be on time for our season-opening practice. Mom was coming in the back door as I breezed by her on my way to my bike in the garage. A quick kiss and a promise to be careful got me past her. I gathered my equipment together, hopped on my bike, and started down the driveway. Halfway down, I glanced up in time to see a disturbing sight standing at the intersection of the sidewalk and the drive. Standing with legs spread apart and both arms outstretched in the stop position was Mom, and I could think of only one word: BUSTED.

I screeched to a stop and asked her if she was auditioning for a part-time job as a traffic cop. Not amused, she calmly relieved me of El Diablo, baseball glove, and cap while pointing up to my room.

"But Mom, I can't be late for my first practice," I started.

"You should have thought of that before you crammed your entire wardrobe and messy food containers under the bed."

I knew it was useless to argue. Racing back to the house, I was reminded of last year's embarrassing first practice. After promising Mom that my homework assignment was finished, I raced off to practice, not thinking that she would actually check up on me. But her mother's intuition must have kicked in, and she rifled through my top desk drawer. There she discovered my term paper on the Civil War, which consisted of two sentences and a series of doodles and Cub logos. As she dragged me off the practice field, my explanation that I was suffering from writer's block fell on deaf ears.

On my way to the garbage dump that doubled as my bedroom, I snagged Frank and promised him five bucks to help me clean up. He took care of the food items while I concentrated on the clothes. In ten minutes, we had things under control. I paid Frank his five bucks and headed out the door.

"Benny," Mom shouted from the kitchen, "did you know that your new bat, El Diablo, means 'the Devil' in Spanish?"

No, I didn't, but it sure seemed to go a long way in explaining why I chose it.

Arriving at practice a few minutes late, I noticed some familiar faces as well as a few new ones. Derrick, Denny, Alejandro Del Toro, Alan Gresh, and Jimmy Patterson were all on my team last year. I recognized Rakeesh Patel and Jeremy "Knuckles" Brannigan from school. Most everyone at school had a nickname and no one earned it more than Jeremy. Seldom did a week go by when Knuckles wasn't involved in a fracas of some sort. With his fiery red hair and nasty disposition, he was a walking poster child for the "Fighting Irish."

I also remembered Milosh Petravick from last season. He played with the Elks and had a rocket for an arm. The only problem was that when he pitched no one had any idea where the ball would end up. Know as "the Muslim Missile," Milosh was unhittable when he got the ball over the plate, but too often he didn't and ended up walking most of the batters. When that was the case, opposing teams were able to form a conga line waltzing around the bases.

After warming up, I was introduced to three kids I'd never met. Jesus Morales was new to Glidden, having just moved there a week before. Billy Sanders, Al's son, was homeschooled, as was Andre Moreau, a Haitian refugee whom the Sanders had adopted following a devastating hurricane several months before.

A lot of people in Glidden weren't sure what to make of Andre. He spoke some broken English with a heavy French accent, which really stood out here in the heartland. His passion was skateboarding and he was very talented in that area. A popular hang-out in Glidden for boarding enthusiasts was a section of Frontier Park with sloping sidewalks and nasty curves. A couple of regulars at the park apparently became jealous of Andre and began teasing him, using some rather mean-spirited names, including "Voodoo Boy."

Then one day Andre showed up at the park with two sock dolls. Each doll had several pins sticking in various parts of its anatomy. Andre muttered a few phrases in French, placed a doll at the feet of each boy, and walked off. The two boys thought it was funny—until the next day, when one of them fell off his board doing a flip and sprained his wrist. The following day the other kid came down with a severe case of laryngitis, and an urban legend was born.

Following practice, Coach Sanders sat us down and mapped out his vision of our season's goals. Strangely, very little had to do with winning baseball games. Most of what he covered dealt with healthy karma, building lasting relationships, and displaying top-notch sportsmanship. More than once during this endless rambling I was able to catch Derrick's and Denny's raised eyebrows as they stared back at me in disbelief.

Coach Sanders' last comment would have been considered comical if it hadn't been delivered with such passion. "I don't care if we win a single game," he pleaded, "just as long as we lift the Stan Brophy Memorial Trophy at the end of the season." The trophy he was referring to was a prestigious award to the team exemplifying the finest sportsmanship throughout the season and was given in honor of the late founder of Glidden's Little League.

Al Sanders seemed like a nice guy, but in looking around at the mugs on this team, it was rather obvious that his bubble was sure to be burst on the sportsmanship issue. There was a far better chance that some of the players on this team would end up with their names on a police blotter before they'd be engraved on a sportsmanship trophy.

chapter 16

CLASSROOM CHAOS

The day of our opening game, I was busy daydreaming my way through Mr. Lundborg's seventh-grade science class when I was distracted by the classroom door opening. In swept the school secretary, Mrs. Dineen, affectionately known to generations of school kids as "Old Ironsides." Mrs. Dineen's visits usually preceded a painful death march to Principal Westmont's office. After whispering briefly into Lundborg's ear, she shifted her gaze right at me. My mind immediately began racing, desperately attempting to recall possible recent indiscretions. Was it the thumbtack I put on Shannon Bloom's seat yesterday in history class? Could it have been the day before, when Denny and I bushwhacked a couple of sixth-graders in the hallway with our super-soaker squirt guns?

Old Ironsides motioned to me with her index finger to follow her out into the hallway. I grudgingly picked up my books and, with the entire class focused on my red face, began the slow walk to the door. Several of the girls were giggling away in obvious enjoyment over my predicament. I glanced back at Denny, who was suddenly very interested in his shoelaces. Boy, it sure was comforting knowing he had my back.

On the torturous trip down the hallway, I decided that whatever charges Principal Westmont brought against me, I was going to offer complete denial. Any attempt to pry information out of Old Ironsides would be fruitless. I'd have had a better chance of getting the combination to Fort Knox than of getting her to divulge any useful hints to aid in my defense. No, I was going to have to go in cold and wing it.

We entered Westmont's office, and before I could begin denying any charges as vicious lies and outright slander, I was taken aback by what caught my eye. There, sitting in a chair with his lip puffed up and his shirt torn half off, was Frankie.

"What happened to you?" I finally spat out. Before he could answer, a determined-looking Westmont motioned for me to take a seat.

"Your brother was involved in a disturbing fight this afternoon involving Steve Nestor. Steve made some rather unflattering comments pertaining to your late father, and Frank here responded with his fists. Our school has a strict policy involving violence, and while we certainly don't condone Francis's actions, the extenuating circumstances in this case dictate that we allow for some leniency. I'm going to ask you to escort Francis home now. And since tomorrow is Friday, I'm going to give him the day off. By Monday, things should have cooled down sufficiently so that we can resume our normal schedule. Have your mother call me tomorrow with any questions or concerns."

I looked over at Frank, who was still steaming. He had a look on his face that I knew only too well. When he was this mad the only one to have any success in calming him down was our four-legged butler. It wouldn't take Digger but five minutes to have him back to his old self.

Seeing as the principal was giving me a free pass to blow out of school two hours early, I was only too willing to take him up on his offer. Westmont was as eager to get Frank out of his hair and not have to deal with Mom as I was to escape Lundborg's constant droning in science class. It was a win-win situation, and I had Frank under wing and out the door before Westmont could change his mind.

On the walk home, Frank explained the circumstances leading up to the room-clearing melee. Mrs. North was going over the list for the second-grade boys who were participating in the next day's Take Your Son to Work event. Steve Nestor, who sat in front of Frank, turned around and said, "So it looks like you'll be spending the day at the cemetery, Davies." Before Ms. North could step in and restore order, two rows of desks had been rearranged, Jennifer Brown's glasses had been dislodged and subsequently broken, and the pride and joy of Mrs. North's class, the dinosaur exhibit, had been reduced to a pile of rubble.

"I hope Nestor looks worse than you, Frank."

"A lot worse, but I'm not through with him yet. The next time I see him, I'm going to…"

"No, Frank, let it go," I said. "You got your point across." I wished I could believe it myself, but I knew better. Steve was the youngest of three brothers, each one meaner and ornerier than the next. The oldest, John, was an eighth-grader and the middle one, Freddy, was in fifth. The three of them managed to keep the Band-Aid company in business, the E.R. doctors busy as beavers, and the local dentists rolling in dough. When you took on one of them you took on all three. The way the Nestors conducted business, it was only a matter of time before John would be coming after me. Enrolling in a self-defense class began making sense the more I thought about it.

Seeing us arriving home a couple of hours earlier than usual, Digger was beside himself with joy. Opening the front door and seeing him with a stuffed animal in his mouth, whining playfully with his tail wagging a mile a minute never got old. He beckoned us to follow him out back, where he pranced about the yard proudly, thus assuring us that all was well with the property and there was no need to worry. As Frank chased after Digger in a vain attempt to snatch the stuffed beaver away from him, I went back into the kitchen in search of provisions. I opted for Popsicles and dog biscuits. A Popsicle would be just the thing for Frankie's swollen lip and soured disposition. As I walked back out the door I stopped short. Heaped together on our backyard hammock swing were Frank, Digger, and the beaver. Frank was busy unloading his angst on Digger as tears rolled freely down his cheeks. He obviously had a lot to get off his chest. Digger was not only a good listener, but also periodically licked the tears off Frankie's chin. Some people might feel better lying on a couch while they divulge their worries and concerns to a psychiatrist. But lying on a hammock in the shade while you bare your soul to the family dog sure made a lot more sense to me. I returned Frankie's Popsicle to the freezer, thinking it would be better to wait until after his "session." Flipping on the TV to the Cubs game, only to see that the score was 8-1 in favor of the Phillies, who were easily on their way to a three-game sweep, I could only hope that Digger wasn't booked up for the entire afternoon.

chapter 17

STRATEGY

I was feeling a little nervous anxiety as I checked out my new uniform in the mirror. The dark green shirt with the white letters spelling out "Moose" went well with the white cap that displayed a giant M on the front. It reminded me of the Oakland As' jerseys. I flew down the stairs hoping that Mom was ready to take me to the field, but she was still lecturing Frank on the evils of resorting to violence. I was on Frankie's side on this one, but getting into a debate would only delay our departure further.

Frank asked Mom, "What does 'bane' mean?"

"Where did you hear that word, Frank?"

"Mrs. North told me that I was the bane of her existence."

I started to crack up, but was immediately silenced with an unpleasant sideways glance from Mom.

"It means she thinks you're a pain in the... neck," she answered. "I can't imagine where she'd get that idea."

Eventually it was determined that we'd continue the conversation later, and that I would stay home from school tomorrow to keep an eye on Frank. Mom was going in to have a face-to-face meeting with Principal Westmont. The knowledge that Westmont wasn't getting off the hook easily with just a phone call did my heart good. Maybe she'd even bring her purse.

Our opening-night opponents were the Knights. The Knights were a decent team but lacked an outstanding pitcher, which usually spelled doom for any Little League squad. Coach Sanders batted me third in the order. In our half of the first inning, I came up with Denny on first base and one out. The first pitch was right down the middle and I jumped on it. The ball sailed over the left field fence and I jogged around the bases certain that this was just the first of many for El Diablo and me.

Derrick shut down the Knights for two innings and Milosh pitched the next two, with a plethora of walks and strike-outs that sent a nervous Coach Sanders pacing back and forth in the dugout until he wore a deep rut in the dirt. But despite nine walks in the two innings, the Knights managed only three runs. I pitched the last two frames allowing one run on three hits as we coasted to a 9-4 victory. My last two at-bats didn't go as well. I popped up to short and grounded out to third. With an opening-night victory and a home run to boot, the minor disappointment of my final at-bats was soon forgotten.

Mom decided that an opening-night victory was deserving of a trip to Hank's to celebrate. Frank and I were in full agreement on the matter. As we waited in line for our order, I caught sight of a familiar face. Sitting on a picnic table with a couple of other troublemakers was John Nestor. He spotted us and slowly made his way to where we were waiting in line. As he neared, I wished I had El Diablo handy. Mom was busy ordering as he walked by, purposely shouldering me as he murmured, "See you soon, dead man." I only hoped he didn't notice the grapefruit-sized lump in my throat. Instead of replying, I simply stood there frozen scared. Frank looked up at me in semi-confusion and I was utterly ashamed of myself.

Oblivious to what had just happened, Mom turned and handed us our waffle cones. Seeing the look on my face, she asked, "Are you feeling all right, Benny? You don't look so good."

"I'm fine," I managed to squeak out. But I wasn't fine. I was mad and scared at the same time. The double-chocolate cone did little to soothe my mood. I had a new worry on my mind and probably little time to figure it out.

The next morning, Mom headed off to her conference with Principal Westmont. Frank and I decided to take Digger to Hogan's Park. He loved to chase the squirrels, making them scurry back up into the trees— where he felt they belonged. Since it was a school day, we pretty much had the park to ourselves. As Digger splashed about in the river (one of his favorite pastimes) Frank asked me what I had in mind in regard to John Nestor. Nestor was in Tara's class and seemed to have a "thing" for her. The fact that she detested him did little to discourage his awkward advances. On more that one occasion, I heard her scream at him to leave her alone when he showed up at her house. He was as stubborn as he was dense, so it did little to deter him. Since he knew that I lived next door to her, it was only a matter of time before he came calling on me.

Finally Digger began to tire out, so the three of us headed home. On the way there, we passed by the rectory, and Father Bill was out in his mini-garden planting a couple of tomato plants. When he saw us approaching, he looked perplexed.

"Don't tell me you two are playing hooky."

As Digger sniffed about the garden, we told Father Bill about the episode that led to our unscheduled holiday. I added the embarrassing moment at the Dairy Deluxe the night before and asked if he had any suggestions.

"You two would have been better off picking a quarrel with a nest of rattlesnakes than to stir up the Nestors. Those kids have a miserable home life, as I understand it. It's no wonder they're so mean and ornery. John has always been the consummate bully. If you let him push you around you'll never be rid of him."

Father Bill led us into the rectory and down a flight of stairs to the basement. Hanging in the middle of the room was a big punching bag.

"Put these on, Ben," he said, as he handed me a pair of boxing gloves. They were a little large for my hands, but supplied plenty of padding.

"The thing to remember about the likes of John Nestor is that bullies are not used to smaller kids fighting back. They normally use intimidation tactics to scare the person. But if you can get the first punch in and hurt him, the fight'll be over before he knows what hit him."

For an hour he briefed me on proper footwork and weight shift in order to deliver maximum force with my punches. The element of surprise was burned into my memory as he coached me on how to sucker him into a false sense of security by pretending to want no part of a fight with the obviously bigger and stronger foe.

"Let him think you're afraid of him. When he lets his guard down or gets distracted, that's when you light into him. His over-confidence will be his downfall."

Over and over I practiced Father's two-punch strategy. The first, a left jab delivered to his right collarbone, had a two-part goal. To render useless my foe's right arm, and to get his left hand—which would instinctively go to the right shoulder—out of the way, leaving his face unprotected.

"Aim for the bridge of his nose with your right fist," instructed Father. "If you deliver those two blows properly, it'll be 'good night Irene.' Not only will this most likely get him off your back, but just maybe in the future he'll think twice before picking on someone else. Never pick a fight, Ben, and try to avoid violence at all costs, but when you're backed into a corner and not given a choice, sometimes you have to take a stand."

I was receiving some excellent strategic advice. Whether or not I could execute it under pressure was another thing.

"So much for the turn-the-other-cheek sermon I got from Mom yesterday," offered Frank.

"Your mother was right to give you that advice, Frank. Steve Nestor was only using words to insult your family. There's no reason to respond to that type of behavior by striking out with your fists. In Ben's case, it's apparent John Nestor is determined to make it a physical attack."

When my pugilistic lesson had ended and we were leaving, I asked Father Bill, "What if I miss and he doesn't go down?"

"Benjamin, that's why the good Lord gave you two good legs. Run like hell."

chapter 18

RABBIT ON THE LOOSE

Frank and I were finishing up a game of lawn jarts when Tara strode by on her way home from school.

"You two have a tough day? Playing games all day while the rest of us mortals were stuck in school?"

With that she grabbed a jart from Frank and tossed it dead center into the circle.

"I win," said Frank, "that's twenty one."

"That doesn't count," I protested. "She's not on your team."

"Don't be cheating your little brother, you cheapskate! Pay up."

Grudgingly, I pulled out a dollar bill and Frank snapped it out of my hand before I could taunt him with it. Off he raced into the house to celebrate his tainted victory with another Popsicle. The twenty-four pack was dwindling quite rapidly.

"So, that blowhard Nestor's been bragging all day how he's going to take you apart. Is that right?"

"We'll see. Time will tell."

"Benny, please tell me you're not seriously considering taking on that gorilla. He's got twenty pounds on you and he's meaner than a junkyard dog. Don't even think about it."

"Don't worry. You know me. I always have a plan."

"That's what scares me, you and those grand schemes of yours. Well, this one's bound to get you killed."

"Not to worry, Stork, I'll leave my baseball card collection to you in my will. You'll be well taken care of."

"Always the comedian, aren't you? Benny. I've got softball game tonight at McDougal Field at seven, in case you're interested in seeing what a *real* team looks like. Bring Digger along, though, just in case that oaf Nestor shows up. Even he's not stupid enough to try anything if your bodyguard's with you."

"Let me check my busy social calendar and see if I have an opening tonight."

After a few unanswered calls, I got the impression my "friends" were avoiding me like the plague. With Nestor and his posse of troublemakers looking to send trouble my way, I could hardly blame them.

Tara's team, the Diamonds, were playing the Sidewinders, a squad from Aurora. Digger and I were stationed down the right field line, trying to stay back in the shadows. The Sidewinders were up 3-2 in the fifth but the Diamonds had two runners on with two out. Tara stepped up to the plate. With my attention focused on the action on the field, I failed to notice an impending disastrous situation developing right behind me. A rabbit wandered out into right field and decided to do a little grazing. Digger noticed this totally unacceptable behavior at the same time Tara lofted a fly ball to deep right center field. As the center fielders and right fielders converged on the fly ball, they were quickly joined by a pair with a different agenda. The bunny zigzagged in front of the right fielder, causing her to freak out and spin around until she landed on her knees. The center fielder was on a dead run, with her outstretched glove reaching for the ball, when she clipped Digger's hindquarters and did an impromptu somersault before landing flat on her back next to her traumatized teammate. The hare escaped unharmed by scooting under the fence. Having finished his job to his satisfaction, Digger fetched the ball from the warning track and dropped it at the feet of the dazed center fielder. He appeared disappointed that no "good boy" or "thank you" was forthcoming from either player.

By this time, I'd finally reached him and quickly slipped on his leash and took off down the right field foul line. I glanced back to view the bedlam back in the infield. The Diamonds were celebrating what they hoped was an inside-the-park home run while the umpires were besieged by the entire Sidewinders coaching staff and irate fans. The public-address announcer was trying to restore order and calm down the crowd until an official ruling was made. A couple of unhappy parents came jogging out toward right field, shaking their fists in my direction.

"Well, Digger, I think that's our cue. Adios."

As we slipped off into the cover of darkness I chanced one last look back at the chaos on the field. From all appearances, the fun and games were just getting started.

On our trek home, I realized we hadn't eaten supper yet, so we stopped at White Castle for a couple of sliders. As we were dining at an outdoor picnic table, who should come traipsing up the sidewalk but my arch nemesis, John Nestor. Not noticing Digger, who was under the table finishing up his burger, the doofus walked right up to me and without a word jabbed me square in the chest with his index finger. He almost didn't get his finger back. In a flash, Digger sprang up. After inflicting a decent-sized gash on Nestor's finger, he lunged for his arm as the startled Nestor stumbled backwards down the grassy incline behind the tables. With Nestor flat on his back and a look of pure terror on his face, I pulled a snarling and teeth-bared Digger by his leash and eased him off his prey.

Finally, collecting his wits and standing back up, Nestor cursed at Digger and vowed to put him out of his misery. I noticed a stain his jeans. Tough guy John Nestor had wet himself.

"You know, Nestor, you're the second person who's sworn to do mortal harm to my dog. It didn't work out particularly well for the first one." Looking at his bloody finger I added, "Don't worry, John, you still have three good fingers and a thumb to pick your nose. Things could be worse."

The White Castle shift manager came dashing out, and recognizing Nestor, he lambasted him, saying, "You again! I'm telling you for the last time, stay away from here. The next time I see you lurking about our grounds, I'm calling the police. Now scram."

Nestor flipped him off and started walking away. He turned back to me and snarled, "I'm going to mess you up bad, Davies—real bad."

"You sure talk a lot," I shot back as I sat back down to finish my burger. Digger's only goodbye retort was a low growl as Nestor faded away into the night.

"I agree, Digger, good riddance."

chapter 19

SHOWDOWN

Saturday morning started slowly. My game was at ten o'clock, so that gave Frank and me plenty of time to goof around with Digger at the dog park. One of his "sweeties," Sophie, a German shepherd, was in attendance, so he was doing his best to show off and draw her attention. He always managed to have a little more hop in his step when she was around. After finally dragging him away, we drifted by the pastry shop, where the aroma of fresh-baked cinnamon rolls and chocolate donuts forced us to stop in to devour our share.

Arriving back at the house a little after nine, I figured I still had plenty of time to throw on my uniform and bike over to the field. Today was picture day so we were supposed to be there by 9:30. Unfortunately, my uniform was nowhere to be found. I checked all the usual places— under my bed, in the clothes hamper, my closet, even in the clean laundry pile, but it was missing in action. Desperately shoveling through my closet floor, I located it all crumpled up in a corner of the jam-packed labyrinth, hidden beneath an avalanche of other discarded wardrobe items and pizza boxes. I might never have found it if it weren't for a sliver of green protruding through the mess. The uniform top was wrinkled to the max. The once-white pants were stained with pizza sauce and the hat looked as though it had been run over by a semi. I took a few moments trying to smooth out a few wrinkles—to no avail. With time running out I slipped on the crumpled ensemble and headed down the stairs.

Waiting at the foot of the stairs was a less-than-pleased-looking mother.

"Did you imagine that your uniform was going to magically wash itself? If you don't put it in the clothes hamper, it doesn't get washed.

Do you think I have enough money to hire a rescue team to comb the depths of that room in search of your belongings?"

I hated it when she asked questions there were no reasonable answers for. But I was hardly in a position at the moment to protest.

I handed her the form from Naples Studio, detailing prices for the team and individual photos.

"Today's picture day? Thanks for the heads-up. You hand me this on your way out the door looking like you just climbed out the back of a garbage truck. I'm not paying eighteen dollars for these pictures just to be reminded of what a terrible mother I am."

"It's not your fault, Mom, I'm the one who forgot about the pictures. Don't worry about it, I'll be fine."

She looked as though she had a few more things to get off her chest, but then her look softened and she gave me a hug and said, "Maybe we both learned a lesson here, Benny. Between the baby and this mortgage business, I get so distracted that sometimes I don't pay enough attention to what matters most—you and your brother."

"What mortgage business?" I started, but she cut me off immediately.

"Never mind, forget I mentioned it, and don't repeat a word of this to anyone. It's probably nothing anyway. Just go out and have a good game."

Something was definitely bothering Mom and her little pep talk at the end was not very convincing.

The photography session turned out to be an interesting situation. I was able to borrow Denny's hat for my individual shot, while strategically placing my glove over the largest of the pizza sauce stains on my pants. For the team shot, the photographer stationed me in the back row, where my crumpled hat would be less obvious.

Finally it was time for baseball. Today's opponent, the Lions, were a scrappy squad with a couple of speed demons at the top of the order and several decent spray hitters scattered throughout their lineup. The key to beating the Lions was to keep the first two off the bases and make the rest of them earn their way on base—in other words, no walks. Their two main pitchers—Lance Calhoun, a righty, and Malik Brown, a southpaw—were solid but not overpowering.

We jumped off to a 2-0 lead in the second on a two-out double by Andre Moreau off Calhoun. Derrick's solo shot in the third made it 3-0 and things seemed to be going our way. But in the top of the fourth, Milosh walked the two roadrunners on close pitches to start the inning. The home-plate umpire, Robert "Magoo" McGruder, was known for a couple of reasons. First was his thick, Coke-bottle glasses that were reminiscent of the cartoon character Mr. Magoo and which contributed to very questionable vision. Second was his penchant for a frosty ale beverage or two—sometimes before, some claimed during, and always after a game. His Jeep Cherokee was famous for making a beeline to Kelly's within moments of the final out. Tuesday evenings were the worst. With a two-for-one special at the watering hole on Tuesdays, Magoo was in a particular hurry to get the game over and claim his favorite stool closest to the TV, where his limited vision could best make out the figures on the screen. He was a pitcher's best friend on Tuesdays, when anything the catcher could reach was a strike and games were over in record time.

But this was Saturday and Milosh was out of luck. The more he squeezed the strike zone, the more frustrated Milosh became. With the score tied at three apiece and a man at third, I fielded a two-hopper and fired home to Knuckles. The ball and the runner got there at the same time, but Knuckles had the plate blocked and the runner never got to it. Knuckles tagged him out but Magoo signaled safe. Our fans screamed bloody murder while the Lions fans howled with laughter. The runner sidled back to the dugout with a smirk on his face as Knuckles berated Magoo while pointing to the plate and telling him he was blind as a bat. That got Knuckles tossed, and when Milosh told Magoo what he thought of the blown call, his day was over, too.

I took over for Milosh on the mound and finished up the inning with Alejandro donning the catcher's gear, but the damage was done. It remained 4-3 going into the last of the sixth. With two on and two outs, I came up with the game on the line. I had a walk and a strike-out in my first two at-bats so I was due. I was determined to blast one over the wall. Brown's first pitch was on the outside corner and I went for it. Unfortunately, all I could manage was an easy bouncer to short and the game was over.

I spent the entire bike ride home mad at the world. Mad at myself for going hitless and failing to drive in the potential tying and winning runs. Disappointed with myself for showing up for picture day looking like a dumpster diver. And furious with Magoo for being himself and blowing the call at home plate. The madder I got, the faster I pedaled, perhaps subconsciously thinking that the faster I went, the more I could outrun the demons that seemed to be nipping at my heels.

Arriving home in record time, I was greeted in the front yard by Frank's innocent question, "What happened to you, man? You don't look so good."

"It's a long story, Frank. Let's just say it's not my day."

Frank and his buddy Nicky were enjoying a leisurely game of catch while Tara sat on her front porch keeping one eye on the boys and the other on a book.

"From the look on that mug of yours is it safe to assume that the mighty Moose squad took it on the chin?" she shouted out from her perch.

"We lost 4-3—no thanks to me and Magoo."

"They're still letting him umpire games? He must be either related to the league director or be working dirt-cheap. By the way, did you catch the license number of the truck that ran you over? You're looking a little rough around the edges today, Ben."

"Like I mentioned to Frank, it hasn't been my day."

"It doesn't look like it's going to get much better, either. Your new best friend is getting ready to pay you a visit."

Sure enough, right when I figured things couldn't get any worse, I turned around to witness John Nestor strutting down the sidewalk as if he owned it.

"We have some unfinished business, puke-head," he spat out. "I see you don't have that ugly mutt of yours handy to watch over you this time."

For once he was right. Digger was in the back yard playing with Rufus and oblivious to my impending crisis. I started backing up, desperately trying to recall the instructions I had received from Father Bill yesterday.

"Leave him alone, you big ape," Tara shouted as she dropped her book and started down her front porch steps.

"Don't worry, sweet cakes, this won't last long," he boasted as he smirked in her direction.

This was the opening I was counting on. Overconfident and distracted, he was right where I wanted him. With the day's frustration building to a crescendo, I drove my left fist into Nestor's right collarbone. Predictably, he raised his left hand to his injured shoulder and I stepped into a hard right cross to the bridge of his nose. Nestor dropped to the ground like a sack of potatoes. As he blubbered and moaned pitifully, I actually felt sorry for the big lug. Blood gushed out of his nose. Grabbing an old rag that Frank had been using for a base, I handed it to Nestor.

"Keep your head back, John."

"You broke my nose," he muttered as tears continued to fall down his cheeks.

"Well, you know, when you stick that big Pinocchio schnoz of yours in other people's business all the time, bad things are bound to happen to it eventually," Tara offered.

"I'm going to get even with you, Davies, just you wait and see."

"I don't think so, big shot," replied Tara. "I'll be more than glad to share with everyone in school about this whole 'butt whooping' if you ever come around here bothering us again. I guarantee you everyone in our class will be hearing all about your pathetic performance."

Mortified to think how thoroughly humiliated he would be if word of this debacle were to be broadcast throughout the school, Nestor's flickering spirit was finally extinguished. Helping Nestor to his feet, I offered up one last piece of advice.

"You know, John, maybe it's time you got out of the bullying business and found a safer line of work."

"Shut up, dipstick," was his only response as he started down the sidewalk. With his head tilted back, the dirty blood-soaked rag covering his nose, and his right shoulder tucked in tight against his neck, his departure was a sight for sore eyes.

Looking at Nestor staggering out of sight, Frank walked over and slapped me on the back, saying, "And you thought *you* were having a bad day."

chapter 20

DIVINE COUNSELING

M om got home a little after four o'clock, and before she could put her purse down the phone was ringing. On the other end was our nosy neighbor from across the street, Mrs. Harper. Mom was obviously getting an earful, and the look she shot in my direction got me thinking it just might be time to go for an extended bike ride. Like maybe as far as Indiana or even Ohio. Just before I reached the back door, however, my plan was scuttled with a resounding, "Where do you think you're going, young man?"

"I thought I'd go for a little..."

"March your fanny right back in here this minute."

From the sound of Mom's voice, Mrs. Harper must have exaggerated today's incident on the front lawn to the extent that it was on par with the shoot-out at the OK Corral. I sat next to Frank on the couch, figuring maybe we'd have strength in numbers.

"Over the last three days, the two of you have managed to get involved in separate violent fist fights. If you think I endured a couple of torturous labors to produce a brood of barroom brawlers, you've got another thing coming. I pray to God that I'll be delivering a girl this time."

"Having a baby sister would be cool," Frank said.

Trying to distract Mom further I chimed in, "Mom, can Frank and I name her? I have some great names picked out."

"No, you can't. And quit trying to change the subject. Now both of you get cleaned up and look presentable. We're going to pay a little visit to the rectory. Maybe Father Bill can talk some sense into the two of you."

Frank and I exchanged knowing glances and I thought to myself that this could turn into an awkward situation, to say the least. Hopefully Father Bill wouldn't bring out the boxing gloves and punching bag. If he did, there'd be three of us in Mom's doghouse.

"Mom, I don't see any reason to drag Father Bill into our problems. I'm sure…"

"My mind's made up. I'll call and make an appointment while the two of you get ready. A peaceful man of the cloth's words of wisdom just might be what the two of you need to hear."

"Well, this promises to be an interesting meeting," I mentioned to Frank when we got upstairs.

"Are you going to tell Mom about the boxing gloves?"

"No, I don't see any sense in making life miserable for Father Bill. It's not his fault we're in this mess. Let's just keep quiet and see how this plays out."

Forty-five minutes later a nervous-looking Father Bill answered his door and welcomed us into the front room.

"Your mother explained to me on the phone that you've each had an unfortunate incident recently involving fisticuffs. Perhaps we can figure out a plan of action to avoid future reoccurrences. Suzanne, if you wouldn't mind stepping out of the den for a few minutes while I counsel these two lads. They tend to be a bit more candid when a parent isn't present, which should help us get to the root of the problem."

"Certainly, Father, take all the time you need. They're really good boys at the heart, but I just don't want to see them heading down the wrong path."

With Mom out of the room, Father turned to me and asked, "Well, how did the strategy work?"

"Like a charm—it was over before he knew what hit him."

"Good, but let's make that the last time, OK? From now on I

want both of you to use your heads and look for ways to avoid these situations."

"Are we supposed to run away and hide when someone insults us or bullies us?" I asked. "You told us yourself that sometimes you have to take a stand."

"And you did. You were backed into a corner and you showed him he couldn't intimidate you. Now it's time to move on. He'll think twice before pestering people in the future. You probably did him a favor because sooner or later, if he keeps it up, he's going to run into someone with a gun. And I have yet to meet anyone who can outrun a bullet. If he does change his ways, who knows, you might even have saved his life. An injured collarbone and a sore nose might be the best medicine for someone like John Nestor."

Turning to Frank, Father asked him, "Why do you think Steve Nestor said those mean things to you?"

"Because he's a stupid jerk, that's why," Frank shot back.

"My guess, Frank, is that the real reason he wanted to hurt your feelings is because he's been hurt so often by his own father. People who come from loving, happy families don't go out of their way to make others feel miserable. But people from troubled home lives often look to bring seemingly happy people down to their level. The old misery-loves-company concept. The next time someone says something mean to you, take a minute and try to figure out what's hurting them so bad that they feel they have to lash out and bring you down. Then say a little prayer that they get the help they need to feel better about themselves. When Jesus said to 'turn the other cheek,' what he was saying was don't react to insults with violence. Refuse to let someone's harsh words or criticism bring your spirits down. React with love, patience, and prayer. Besides," he added, "there's nothing that'll drive your enemies crazier than a smile."

Frank and I both got a laugh out of that thought. Though I didn't expect Frank to give Steve Nestor a big hug in class on Monday, or for me to "high five" John in the hallway between classes, I think we both came away with a better understanding of why some people act out the way they do.

On the way home, Mom asked us what we learned.

"Turn the other cheek," I answered.

"And what did you learn, Francis?"

"If some jerk makes me mad, I'm going to smile at him. Father says that'll drive him crazy."

Mom shook her head and looked skyward, as if for help. I couldn't help but think that the one thing Frank was truly best at was driving people nuts. And now he had another weapon for that arsenal—his smile.

chapter 21

BOOT CAMP

It was Tuesday evening and our opponent in our third game of the year was the VFW. The VFW's record was even at one win and one loss, the same as the Moose, so this game was important to both of us. On top of that, our next game, on Thursday night, was against league favorite the Elks, featuring the twin towers of Zack and Zane Bowers, so a loss tonight would be devastating to our chances of capturing the pennant this year.

The VFW had a strong lineup but questionable pitching. Our best bet was to pile up some runs and hope our pitching could hold them in check. Unfortunately, we didn't come up with clutch hits when needed and fell 8-5. No thanks to me and El Diablo, either. I got a walk, a stolen base, and scored a run my first time up but popped out and grounded out my last two chances, each time with runners in scoring position. To make things worse, Tara picked this rotten game to attend. After bragging all spring about how good the Moose were going to be, and how El Diablo and I were going to shower the field with hits, I spent the post-game coach's talk searching for a good-sized rock so I could slither under it and hide.

On the bike ride home, I couldn't even raise my head up to look at Tara, and when we reached the trail that ran along the Blackhawk River, I stopped my bike, got off and flung El Diablo toward the river. With the way things were going for me, the bat hit an old tree stump and bounced back up the bank.

"Boy, you really are in a slump. You can't even hit the river with your bat," said Tara.

I stormed down the embankment to retrieve El Diablo and finish off the tree stump with it. After about twenty whacks it was still intact but I was exhausted.

"Feel better now, slugger?"

I was so mad I felt like jumping in the river and floating away forever.

"What's wrong with me? Why can't I hit anymore? I don't have a single hit since that homer to start off the year."

"If you're done with that stump, follow me back to my house and I'll show you what's wrong. That is, if you don't mind taking advice from a girl."

"Right about now I'd consider taking advice from that tree stump."

Twenty minutes later we were in her back yard with my old bat, the Silver Streak, in tow.

"You're not big enough for El Diablo yet, Benny. The Silver Streak served you well last year."

She had a point. I had a .412 batting average last season with "the Streak."

"It's not the size of the bat—it's the bat speed that makes all the difference, Benny. You're a good singles and doubles hitter with great speed and base running smarts, along with a good eye. Don't try to be something you're not."

For the next half hour Tara broke down the plate and how to control it. She emphasized that the plate was 17 inches wide. She tossed Wiffle balls to me, getting me to turn on the ones toward the inner part and drive them to left. The tosses on the middle part I worked to drive up the middle or to the power alleys. The tosses on the outside corner were the major point of emphasis.

"Take the outside corner pitches to right," she scolded time after time. "And don't drop your right shoulder, numbskull. Right now you're trying to pull everything over the left field wall. In doing so, you're rolling your wrists over—hence all the grounders to short and third."

This went on for quite some time, but I definitely felt a lot better and more comfortable with each repetition. If Tara was undecided about her future career, I thought I knew what she'd be great at—a drill sergeant for the Marine Corps.

"What're you doing tomorrow, Benny?"

"I've got yard work all morning for the Wiswalls."

"At two o'clock we're heading for the bating cage. We'll have you ready for Thursday night's showdown with the Twin Towers."

I felt like saying, "Yes, Sergeant Mangolin," but instead thanked her for all her help.

"No need to thank me, you'll be getting a bill in the mail." She winked at me and headed toward her back door. I felt like reaching out and hugging her but the Marine Corps probably frowned on that sort of behavior toward superiors.

The next afternoon found Sergeant Mangolin and Private Davies hard at work in the batting cage. We picked the "fast" speed for the pitching machine because both of the Bowers threw heat. Tara was much more patient and complimentary with me than last night. I figured that's the way the Corps worked. By the time we went through three buckets of hard balls, I had my old confidence back. We stopped by Hank's on the way home. I treated the sergeant and myself to turtle sundaes and all was well with the world again.

As we warmed up Thursday night before the big game, I noticed Milosh seemed a bit out of sorts. I glanced over to the Elks' bench and noticed their third baseman, Elston Branch, with a towel wrapped around his head in a spiraling upward way. He was pointing out toward Milosh and laughing out loud.

"What's that all about?" I asked Milosh as he threw down his glove and started for the Elks' bench.

"He calls me a 'towel head' because I'm Muslim. All last year he taunted me when the coaches weren't looking. That's why I switched teams."

"Don't let him get to you." I stepped in front of him and guided him back toward the diamond. "He's stupid and he thinks he's funny. Don't get mad—get even. He has to bat against you, right? If one of your fast balls accidentally happens to sail up and in on him—well that's baseball, right?"

Milosh seemed to relish that thought, and a smile returned to his face. I wouldn't have wanted to be in Branch's shoes right then. Milosh threw major heat. Milosh and I both agreed not to bring up this subject during our next team sportsmanship lecture.

I glanced at the starting lineup before the game and noticed that I had been dropped to the number-eight spot. That hurt, but I couldn't blame Coach Sanders. We had a game to win and that's all that mattered.

Derrick pitched well the first two innings, but Zane Bowers blasted one well over the center field fence and it was 1-0 Elks going into the top of the third.

Zack Bowers sailed through the first two frames but lost Jimmy Patterson on a 3-2 pitch to start the third inning. I came up to the plate with Tara's words ringing in my head. "Just relax and hit the ball where it's pitched." Bowers' first pitch was a little inside—his way of keeping me off the plate. I was pretty sure the next one would be on the outer edge, and it was. I drove it over the first baseman's head and down into the right field corner. Jimmy was off like a bullet. The relay throw came into the plate but Jimmy beat it easily and I romped into third with a triple. Zack stomped around the mound in disbelief that the bottom of the order could actually get to him. The next batter, Jesus Morales, on a 1-1 pitch hit an easy one-hopper back to Bowers. He bluffed a throw to third to drive me back but it wasn't a very good bluff. As soon as he turned toward first, I took off digging for home. The first baseman was a little surprised I was trying to score and his hurried throw home was a little high. By the time their catcher, Walter Burgess, got the tag down, I was across the plate and the Moose had a 2-1 lead.

Milosh walked two batters in the bottom half of the third but struck out the side with no damage. In the bottom of the fourth he retired the first two batters and up to the plate came poor Elston Branch. I almost felt sorry for him. Almost.

The first pitch rode right in on him and plunked him in the ribs. The ball rolled halfway down the line to me. I got a good look at Elston's face. Tears had immediately welled up in his eyes. He was definitely hurting big-time. Milosh remained on the mound admiring his handiwork. I jogged up to Branch and put my arm around him as if the comfort him.

"Maybe you can use that towel of yours to dry your tears, wise guy," I whispered to him. He was too busy trying to catch his breath to answer as the coaches whisked him away to the dugout. I tossed the ball back to Milosh, gave him a wink and mumbled softly, "Paybacks can be painful."

The top half of the sixth started off with a single by Alan Gresh off Zane Bowers. Jimmy laid down a decent sacrifice bunt to get Alan to second and I came up with a chance to get us an insurance run. The first pitch was right down the middle and I smacked it past Zane's leg and out into center field. The center fielder tried to get Alan at the plate but his throw was late and up the third base line, which allowed me to scamper into second. On the first pitch to Jesus, I took off to steal third. Burgess's throw skipped in past the new third baseman for the Elks. By the time the left fielder retrieved the ball and threw it home I was in the dugout.

With a 4-1 lead in the bottom of the last frame I felt a little less pressure but still had to navigate through the meat of the order. Zane was first up and I was able to get a pitch in just far enough so he hit off the handle and spiked a can of corn to left fielder Billy Sanders. Next up was Zack and I wasn't quite as fortunate. The left-handed hitter drove an outside corner fastball over the left center field fence. Oh well, it was still 4-2. I got the next hitter to bounce out to Alejandro for the second out but Burgess singled sharply to left. Up to the plate came the potential tying run, Gavin Morris. Gavin was certainly capable of hitting one out. I was beginning to get a little nervous until I glanced at the on-deck batter. Morton Leese was standing there with drooped shoulders and a bat that looked like a telephone pole in his smallish hands. Morton was the first person you'd call if you were having trouble with your science or math homework. But his extraordinary ability in the classroom didn't extend to athletic endeavors.

Knuckles must have read my mind. He sauntered out to the mound and we agreed to throw four wide ones to Gavin before going to work on Morton. After ball four to Gavin, a pitch at least a foot outside, the Elks' head coach, Miles Fromke, slammed down his clipboard and glared out at the mound. He knew exactly what we were doing and there wasn't a thing he could do about it. By league rules every player had to have a chance to play in the field and bat at least once. It was his own fault for not putting Morton in earlier when the game wasn't on the line. Three pitches later the game was over and the Mighty Moose were back in the hunt. At 2-2 we were only a game back of the now 3-1 Elks.

It was an eight-team league, so we played the other seven teams twice for a fourteen-game schedule. Our fourteenth game was against the Elks, so if we could keep our noses clean it could set up a huge rematch in the season finale.

On the way through the line after the game—when the two teams shook hands and said meaningless clichés to each other, like "good game"—coach Fromke called me "Bush League" and referred to Milosh as the "little assassin" to his assistant coach. If Coach Sanders were counting on some support from the Elks staff in his quest for the sportsmanship trophy, he was out of luck. Not seeing Elston Branch in line, I looked over to the Elks' bench. Elston was holding an ice pack on his bruised ribs and wearing a major scowl on his face. All in all, it was plain to see that from the Elks' perspective, there was no joy in Mudville.

chapter 22

Pass the Hat

It was Sunday morning and Mom was all wound up. Today was Frank's first Communion, and I was to be one of the altar servers during the Mass. Mom had cleaned and pressed Frank's best outfit for the ceremony. The Bishop was coming down from Rockford to preside over the event, so Mom was leaving no stone unturned. Since my altar boy robe would be covering my clothes, she wasn't too concerned with my choice of wardrobe, but when I tried to sneak past her in my tennis shoes, she would have no part of it.

"You're not serving Mass with the Bishop in attendance wearing sneakers, young man. Now find your dress-up loafers and let's get going."

I knew the last place I put my good shoes was by the back door, but when I checked the little nook by the back door, only one shoe was accounted for.

"Where's the other one?" I hissed, and immediately Digger slunk around the corner. Scouring the back yard, I soon located the missing shoe—or what was left of it—under the pine tree. By all appearances, the shoe had been the target of a serious tug-of-war contest between Digger and Rufus. While it was unclear as to who won the tug of war, it was very clear who lost—the shoe.

When I reported back to Mom with the mangled shoe in hand, she let us have it. Digger quickly scurried up the stairs and under my bed, leaving me to catch the brunt of the lecture. Following the brief tirade, Mom settled down and suggested I phone Denny, who lived just up the street and was about the same size as me in everything from head to toe.

"See if he'll lend you a decent pair of shoes for the morning and we'll pick them up on the way to church."

A few minutes later, we pulled up to Denny's house and I ran in to grab the shoes. Denny's dad met me at the door, handed me the shoes, and told me to keep them.

"Denny's outgrown those shoes, Benny, so why don't you just keep them. And if there's anything else you need, just let us know."

Being in a rush, I didn't think much of what he said right off the bat, but the more I thought about it, the more it bothered me. Did he think we were too poor to buy a pair of shoes? Were we?

Just before we pulled into the church parking lot, Frank announced to us that he wasn't sure he was cleared to receive his first Communion.

"Of course you are, Francis, you had your first confession yesterday so you're all set."

"That's just it, Mom, I didn't really carry out all the penance for my sins. Father told me to say five Hail Marys and five Our Fathers in atonement for my sins."

"So what's the problem, then?" Mom asked, as she nervously looked at Frank, afraid of what the answer might be.

"I only know one Hail Mary and one Our Father. What am I supposed to do about the other four?"

I burst out laughing while Mom tried hard to suppress her mirth. She shooed me out of the car as she explained to the confused Frank that he simply had to say the one Hail Mary and Our Father five times each. That seemed to satisfy him and they hopped out of the car and proceeded into the church. I looked back at the two of them, convinced that Mom or Dad must have dropped Frank on his head when he was a baby.

I kept zoning out during the readings at Mass, not an unusual occurrence for me as my mind jumped from one thought to another on a regular basis. But as I thought about what Denny's father had said to me, and the way he said it, I began to worry more and more. Come to think of it, there was seemingly less and less food on our shelves as well as in the fridge. I couldn't remember the last time we went out to eat, for that matter. And a lot of the times Mom opened the mail, she appeared worried and distracted and she usually went upstairs to lie down with a headache.

But for now she was a proud mother, sitting in the third row and beaming away. During the Gospel I stood to the Bishop's side holding my candle upright in front of my face. This time, my lack of attention led to an embarrassing situation. Bishop Hardy paused in the middle of the reading as if he were trying to smell something. He looked over at me and his eyes turned as big as saucers. He quickly removed his giant hat—I think they refer to it as a miter—and began swatting the top of my head. At first I thought he'd lost his mind, but suddenly the smell and heat on top of my head made me realize I'd gotten the candle too close to my hair and it was smoldering away. Quickly reaching for his holy water sprinkler (I'm sure there's a fancier name for it), the bishop generously doused me with enough holy water to protect my soul for eternity. My scalp was a little sore but not burned, fortunately. My hair didn't fare so well, however, and it appeared a buzz cut was in my near future. Bishop Hardy's miter didn't come through the ordeal unscathed, either. It was partially burned on the inside and noticeably smudged on the outside. I hoped he kept a spare one handy or I might find myself on the diocese excommunication list. Mom was no longer beaming but had that look on her face that was a combination of worried, embarrassed, and disappointed. Frank was fighting hard to suppress laughter but was losing the battle. As Frank's mirth became more and more noticeable, the bishop, upon finishing the reading, glared down from the pulpit at him before returning to his chair. With the lasting impression Frank and I managed to make on our esteemed guest, it seemed highly unlikely he'd be visiting our fair parish again any time in the near future.

Mom wasn't too impressed with our performance either. The entire ride home she kept repeating over and over, "Where did I go wrong?"

Tuesday evening found the Moose taking on the Masons. Magoo was behind the plate, which was good news for the pitchers. For the first time ever, Milosh didn't walk a batter in his two-inning stint. With two runners on and two out in the bottom of the sixth inning, I knew Magoo was dying to race down to Kelly's for his frosty mug. I threw three pitches about three or four inches off the plate and Magoo promptly rang up all three as strikes and the Moose had a 4-0 victory.

Thursday night found us matched up against the Fire, appropriately adorned in red jerseys. They had a 4-1 record with their only loss to the Elks. They had the best offense in the league, averaging ten runs per game, and we had to find a way to cool them off. While the Fire was taking its pregame infield/outfield practice, our right fielder, Andre Morneau, wandered over to the Fire's bat rack. I couldn't help but wonder to myself, *What's he up to now?* He took some sort of powder or dust out of a leather pouch he was carrying and sprinkled it generously over their bats as he recited some words in a foreign language that I assumed was French. Just as he was finishing his little ritual, a couple of Fire players noticed Andre and started shouting at him. He casually walked away and stuffed the pouch back in his pocket. A few minutes later, when the whole Fire team was in their dugout, what began as a low murmur turned into a loud dialogue with fingers being pointed in Andre's direction while the coaches inspected the bat rack area for the mysterious powder.

The entire Fire team was now in an uproar, certain that what with his reputation stemming from the incident at Frontier Park involving the two unfortunate skateboarders, Andre had put some sort of curse on their bats. The head coach, Bernie Richardson, stormed out to protest to the home-plate umpire that all their bats had been hexed.

The umpire just looked at him and said, "You know, you really shouldn't be drinking before the game, Bernie. Now quit this ridiculousness and play ball."

Flustered, Bernie stomped back to their dugout in a huff. The dusting of the bats definitely had an adverse effect on the Fire, as they never did get in sync. Andre had a base-clearing double in the second inning and by the time Knuckles ripped a three-run homer in the top of the sixth, the Moose was home free with a romp. The final score was 10-3 and I wouldn't be surprised if the Fire decided to toss their "cursed" bats in the dumpster and go out to buy some new ones before their next game. I asked Andre after the game what was in the pouch of his that he sprinkled on their bats.

"It was just some dirt I scooped up from the warning track before the game and put in my marbles pouch."

"Yeah, but did you put some sort of voodoo hex on it before dusting their bats?" I asked.

Andre laughed.

"Benjamin, I wouldn't know a voodoo hex from an Egyptian mummy curse. I'm Lutheran."

Well, I guess the Fire didn't get the memo. Andre managed to get inside their heads and use that urban legend nonsense to confuse and distract them. Proving once again that all is fair in love and war—and of course, baseball.

chapter 23
OUT-FOXED

Saturday morning arrived with gray skies and blustery winds. Since Frank had his first tee-ball game at one o'clock in the afternoon, we decided to take Digger and Rufus for a morning jaunt along the river and to the north forty. Tara and I kept the dogs on leashes until we got past Walnut Street and then let them go loose, while Frank, who trailed slightly behind with his ball and glove, tossed the ball endlessly into the air while he imagined himself making the game-winning catch. Whenever he dropped the ball or misjudged it, he always had an excuse. "The sun was in my eyes." "The wind took it." "A dragonfly zapped me in the face."

"You'll fit in perfectly with the Cubs, Frank, with those alibis," I told him. "Yeah, but he'll never make it with the Sox with those lame excuses, Benny," said Tara.

Tara was a White Sox fan who seldom missed a chance to get a dig in on my beloved yet bumbling Cubbies. I was about to hand her a nasty retort when Digger and Rufus began a furious barking and snarling duet in the high grass on the bank of the river. We raced down the embankment to see what all the fuss was about. Not knowing what to expect, Tara parted the tall grass and the three of us set our eyes on the source of the commotion. Lying on the ground with his leg caught in a steel trap was a fox. He had a hopeless look on his little face and seemed near death. His body was emaciated and he could barely lift up his head. With a wound above the part of his leg that was trapped, it appeared he had attempted to gnaw his leg off in order to escape his doom. Tara and I were able to free his leg from the trap while Frank tried to calm down Digger and Rufus. It was apparent that the fox didn't have the strength to escape as Tara scooped him up and cradled him in her lap. I braved a squadron of mosquitoes at the river's edge to scoop up some water to offer the little guy. He hardly had the strength to lap up the tiny bit that didn't spill out of my hands. Things weren't looking too promising for him at the moment.

Tara raced over to the nearby Shell station to call her mother. Five minutes later the six of us piled into Mrs. Mangolin's sedan and we were off to Oaken Acres, a wildlife rescue center for injured and abandoned wild animals that was a few miles north of town. The entire way there, Digger and Rufus curiously poked their noses under the blanket Tara had wrapped the fox in. Under normal circumstances, the fox would probably have died from fright, but he didn't seem to even have the energy to be scared.

Upon arrival at Oaken Acres, Tara and her mom raced ahead with the patient while Frank and I leashed the hounds and allowed them to drag us into the main building. They were on full alert with all the smells to sniff. It was almost too much for them.

The woman in charge, Marylyn, seemed equally concerned about the fox's degree of dehydration and leg wound. Tara had already taken it upon herself to name the fox Freddy. I was hoping that she wouldn't get too attached to Freddy in case he didn't pull through.

Marylyn and Tara started right in to get Freddy rehydrated with a glucose and electrolyte solution. As they attended to Freddy, we took Digger and Rufus on a tour of the facility. Most of the residents were housed in a barn-like building attached to the main building. I was amazed at the number and variety of wildlife on site. Most of the borders had little placards near their cages explaining how they happened to be taken in and what hopes existed for their release back into the wild. A red-tailed hawk eyed us curiously from his cage. A screech owl was caged up not far from the hawk. He had endured a car collision in which he suffered neurological damage that made his release impossible. A great horned owl was the next one in line. She had been rescued with a broken leg caused by a 50-foot fall from her nest in an old tree. Her future seemed a little brighter as the leg was healing rapidly. There were baby squirrels, baby opossums, and baby raccoons. Digger and Rufus were mildly interested in these little rascals but their alertness reached a fever pitch when we stepped out of the building to the outdoor enclosure. A beaver kit was busily constructing a den in a transformed chicken coop. She had a large horse trough to swim in, plenty of branches to build her den, and a couple dozen ears of field corn that she had instinctively stockpiled for future use by neatly stacking them in a corner.

"I'm getting tired just watching her work so hard," said Frank as the dogs moved on to check out the fawn who was hobbling along the back fence. Rescued as a two-pound baby after her mother was killed by a car, the fawn was still a little wobbly but was progressing well and was on track to be released in a couple of months. In a separate section lay a sleepy coyote pup that had suffered spinal trauma when she was hit by a car. The placard indicated that she, too, was on the road to recovery and if all went well, she would be released sometime in the fall.

Digger was growling at the coyote pup and Rufus began barking at the fawn. It was apparent the two of them were making some of the denizens increasingly nervous, so we decided to walk them back to the car. I left Frank and Tara's mom in charge of the two mischief-makers and went in to see how Freddy was holding up. The fox was fast asleep in a makeshift crate. His damaged leg was bandaged up and Marylyn explained to me that she intended to continue with the glucose solution until he was stabilized.

I looked for Tara, and found her in another room, an office of some sort. She was seated in a chair, cuddling a baby woodchuck as it nursed from a bottle. Already volunteering at the county shelter and the HATS facility, she informed me she had signed on to work every other Saturday at Oaken Acres.

"Well, it looks as though you've hit the trifecta," I offered.

She just smiled broadly at me for a moment before returning her attention to her patient. For the life of me, I couldn't remember ever being upstaged by a woodchuck before.

chapter 24

DIAMOND DISASTER

I went to Frank's tee-ball game that afternoon. Fortunately, they still enforced the five-run-per-inning limit, or the games would never end. Frank's team, the Orange Crush, triumphed 30-28. In the fourth inning, Frank, who played shortstop, snagged a liner and stepped on second base to double up a runner, or the game would certainly have ended 30-30. On the way to Hank's for a postgame celebration, Frank bragged about how he went five-for-five with two doubles and a triple. I tried to tell him that at least two of his so-called hits were really errors, but he was having none of it.

"They were way too hot to handle, Benny. Anyone could see that," he shot back.

Not wanting to rain on his parade, and knowing it was fruitless to argue, I patted him on the back and congratulated him on his heads-up unassisted double play. He was beaming all the way to Hank's. I had a feeling, with his generous scorekeeping, that he was on his way to a 1.000% batting average for the season.

The following afternoon, I checked with Tara to see how Freddy was coming along. She assured me that the prognosis was favorable for a full recovery, but that he would be lodging at Oaken Acres for a month of two until he was healthy enough to be released back into the wild. But then she began her rant against the "scumbag" who was setting traps along the river.

"The police told me that this was the third report of illegal trapping along the river this week. In the other two cases, the animals were already dead by the time anyone found them. The first poor critter was a beaver—second one, a raccoon."

"Do the cops have any suspects?" I asked.

"They have a couple of leads, according to Derrick's father. He stopped by an hour ago to inform me nicely that it would be best if I didn't call the station anymore in regard to this issue."

"How many times did you call them?"

"About fifteen. On the last call, the dispatcher, or whoever, hung up on me. So I called back. The lady barked at me about how only emergencies were to be called in on that number. I asked her if innocent animals being murdered for their fur wasn't an emergency, then what was? About five minutes later, Officer Woodson stopped by with a cease and desist order."

I had little doubt that if Tara were chief of police, a SWAT team would have been called in to deal with the illegal trapping culprits.

"If they catch this cretin, I'm going to suggest the cops pin his leg in a trap and leave him to deal with the elements. See how he likes it."

"I'm all for your solution, Tara, but I have a feeling his or her lawyer just might object to your idea."

"Well fine. We'll get two traps and the lawyer can join the client."

Tuesday evening found us up against Helton's Sporting Goods. After this game, we would be at the halfway point in the league season, having played each team once. Coach Sanders admonished us in a pregame talk to begin showing better sportsmanship and fewer shenanigans. He reminded us that the prestigious Stan Brophy Sportsmanship Trophy was still within our reach. Who was he kidding? Looking over Sanders's shoulder, I noticed that the league commissioner, Lloyd Deverman, was in attendance this evening. No wonder we were getting a lecture on sportsmanship. Deverman had probably been tipped off to some of our alleged shortcomings in this area. With the exception of Knuckles Brannigan, we all assured Coach Sanders that we would be on our "best behavior" that night. Knuckles didn't possess a "best behavior" personality. Also in attendance was Knuckles' father, Henry "Hammerin' Hank" Brannigan. He had been a pretty fair ballplayer in his day, according to my dad, but it was suspected that the nickname had more to do with his beer consumption than his baseball prowess.

The game progressed fairly well early on for the Moose faithful. Derrick went yard for two runs in the first. Alan Gresh doubled Denny and me home in the third and we tacked on another two runs in the fourth. We led 6-2 but Helton's walked their way to two runs in the top of the fourth inning off Milosh. We owned a 6-4 lead with two on and two out in the top of the sixth when all the fun started.

Riley Slager bounced an easy two-hopper to short and the usually sure-handed Alejandro gobbled it up. With the Moose ready to celebrate, disaster struck. Alejandro's throw to first was wide and up the first base line. Derrick couldn't catch it and it bounced off the fence and out toward right field. The runner on second scored easily and the runner on first, Gary Burton, was waved in by Helton's third-base coach. The throw had him beat by a mile, but Knuckles took his eye off the ball for a second to see where Burton was. The throw skipped through his legs on its way to the backstop. Burton kept on coming and Knuckles just stood there blocking the plate—but without the ball. Burton crashed into Knuckles and dropped to his knees. The umpire immediately called the runner safe for interference. The score was tied and all hell was about to break loose.

Behind us in the stands, Jimmy Patterson's father, Ralph, yelled at Knuckles for missing the throw. That's all it took for Hammerin' Hank to turn around and send a couple of haymakers Ralph's way. The two of them proceeded to topple all the way down the bleachers, in the process knocking over several spectators, including Alan Gresh's grandma, who was recovering from recent hip surgery.

Meanwhile, back on the playing field, things were disintegrating at a rapid pace as well. Gary Burton got up and shoved Knuckles—a huge mistake. A couple of socks to the jaw and a body slam later, Burton was in serious need of medical attention. Burton's coach, Maury Shenberger, came running out of the dugout to protect Burton from further abuse. Coach Sanders arrived at the same time, attempting to separate the two combatants. Both coaches inadvertently bumped heads. Shenberger mistook the bump as intentional and grabbed Sanders by the shirt collar and began shaking him forcefully. Sanders responded by getting Shenberger in a headlock and the two of them tumbled to the ground in a heap. Witnessing the carnage from the safety of the mound, I had a notion Abner Doubleday would be spinning in his grave at this spectacle. It was hardly what he envisioned when he invented this gentlemen's game back in the 1800s.

With Alan's grandma screaming in pain, Hammerin' Hank and Ralph exchanging blows, and the chaos on the field, I noticed league chairman Deverman desperately racing over to a pay phone near the entrance of the complex. "The Commish" looked so panicky it wouldn't have surprised me if he was calling out the National Guard. I was beginning to get a sense that Coach Sanders's quest for the sportsmanship trophy was rapidly slipping away.

chapter 25

THE TROUBLE WITH EARL

It was some time before things got sorted out and order was restored. Alan's grandma was whisked away to the hospital in an ambulance. Mr. Brannigan and Mr. Patterson were escorted to the police station to face misdemeanor battery charges. Knuckles and Gary Burton were ejected along with both head coaches. Our assistant coach, Felipe Morales, Jesus' father, took over, as did Helton's assistant coach Marty Buerlin. Two outs remained in the top of the sixth inning with a runner on second and the score knotted at six. I retired the next batter on a lazy fly to center to end the longest half inning in the history of Glidden Little League.

In the bottom half of the frame, Denny led off with a sharp single to left. I followed with a bloop single to right center. Derrick roped a liner to the left center gap, Denny waltzed home easily and the mighty Moose escaped with their fourth straight victory. The postgame shaking-of-hands lineup with Helton's was a bit awkward, but we managed to get through it without further incident. As we were bagging our bats and equipment after the game, I looked into the stands and noticed Lloyd Deverman gazing into our dugout with a wicked snarl on his face. If looks could kill we'd have been dead meat. Lloyd looked as though he'd aged ten years during tonight's game. If he decided not to return as commissioner next season, I didn't think anyone would have blamed him.

Upon returning home I was in a hurry to run in and tell Mom the good news about the Moose victory (luckily she hadn't attended tonight's fiasco). But before I reached the door, my attention was drawn to a ruckus of some sort next door at Tara's. Digger came flying around the corner of the back yard and looked at me with nervous anticipation, his ears standing straight up. He was obviously perturbed and began barking madly to be let out of the yard for some reason. Just then Tara's front door opened and Tara and Rufus came running out. Tara was weeping hysterically while Rufus growled back toward the house. That was all it took for Digger to scale his way over our fence and dart over to Rufus and Tara. Seconds later, Tara's mom came scurrying out the front door as well. Her blouse had been ripped, her lip was bleeding, and she had a red welt on her cheek. Following close behind was the source of all the commotion—a rather intoxicated-looking Earl Mangolin.

"Get back in here, you," he said, pointing at Tara's mom. "I'm not through with you yet."

"Well, I'm through with you," she shot back.

He started toward the steps, where he was greeted by the canine welcoming committee. Rufus had his teeth wrapped around his right ankle while Digger was busy tearing a hole in the seat of his britches. By now the neighbors were out on their front yards. Mom rushed over to Tara and her mother and whisked them across the front lawn and into our house. Mr. Mangolin recovered enough to send Rufus tumbling down the front steps. He wasn't having as much luck with Digger, though, and he fled back into the safety of the house, banging his head on the door jamb on his way in. Frank showed up with a leash and a belt, which enabled us to drag the dynamic duo back to our yard and get them settled down a bit. Eventually a couple of squirrels got their attention and they were off on another important mission.

Shortly after that, Tara came out into the back yard. Frank ran up and hugged her. I didn't know what to say and figured for once I'd keep my big mouth shut and try not to put my foot in it.

A visibly shaken Tara finally blurted out that her mom was calling the police to have her father arrested for battery. In addition to that she had decided to file a restraining order against him.

My first thought was, "It's about time," but in keeping with my intentions, I managed to keep the 'mouth that roared' closed for a change.

Frank asked me about our game and I was more than glad to move to another subject. Giving them the blow-by-blow description in great detail got their attention temporarily away from the domestic disaster of the past ten minutes. In no time they were roaring with laughter as I described the chaos that took place in the sixth inning. Tara stopped me to ask if Magoo had been umpiring, because she felt that was the only thing that could make the situation even more bizarre.

"No, thankfully, Magoo wasn't behind the dish tonight. If he had been, the game might have been forfeited and martial law would have been declared."

It was good to see Tara laughing again. Frank suggested a game of pickle, in which we took turns with one person being the base runner while the other two were the fielders. We used a tennis ball along with two cushions substituting for bases. During the game, I heard Digger growling by the fence and noticed two cops escorting a handcuffed Earl Mangolin to a squad car parked out front. Fortunately, Tara had her back to the scene and was spared the sight of her father being led off to the slammer. Sara Mangolin's decision to press charges was a long time coming. Knowing my mom and how she felt about the situation, she probably had an influence in the decision. Mom was always more than willing to share her opinion on such matters. Sometimes her opinion wasn't welcomed, but that never seemed to hold her back.

Tara and I purposely missed a few throws, enabling Frank to arrive safely to his base several times. The game was winding down when Mom and Mrs. Mangolin strolled out back with three Popsicles held high. Frank immediately declared himself the winner and raced ahead of us to claim an orange Popsicle (his favorite) before we could react.

It was a beautiful evening. We savored our Popsicles, Digger and Rufus gnawed on their meat bones, and the stars twinkled away over a cloudless sky. Little did I know that severe storm clouds were brewing just around the corner.

chapter 26

BAD NEWS ON THE HOME FRONT

Saturday morning arrived with my four-legged alarm clock frantically pawing at me to let him out to answer nature's call. Figuring that the possible consequences of not letting him out to do his business were not pleasant, I forced myself out of bed and down the stairs toward the back door. While Digger took turns relieving himself and investigating possible breaches in yard security, I attempted to focus on my day's plans. The Moose were scheduled for a one o'clock tilt with the Knights because of a rainout on Thursday. Frank and I had fallen behind on our yard duties at the Wiswalls, so that chore would have to be tackled this morning. Whenever I fell behind on lawn and garden responsibilities, I felt it necessary to include Frank as a member of my landscaping enterprise. Customers were less likely to come down hard when a seven-year-old was involved. When he balked at helping me out at my last tardy job, I promised to promote him to assistant landscaping engineer. He was so delighted with his new title that he didn't even bug me for a raise.

Commissioner Deverman had placed a one-game suspension on Knuckles and Coach Sanders for their behavior in our victory over Helton's. Mr. Brannigan and Mr. Patterson were forbidden to attend future games until they attended two anger-therapy seminars. Alan's grandma was out of the hospital and vowed to attend our game as long as "those two neanderthals" weren't present. Derrick's father, Officer Woodson, was scheduled to replace Mr. Sanders for the game. I wasn't sure if it was because of his knowledge of baseball or due to the fact that he was licensed to carry a firearm.

When I had talked to Tara the night before, she seemed upbeat about the situation with her father. Mr. Mangolin had moved in with his brother, Michael, who was an AA member and had agreed to be his sponsor.

It was after eight o'clock by the time I dragged Frank out of bed. We were heading out the door when the phone rang. Mom answered it on the third ring. She looked very nervous as she spoke into the phone.

"Are you sure there's nothing else I can do?" she pleaded. "Well, what am I supposed to do?" she started, but when she saw me looking at her with a worried look on my face, she stopped and held the phone at her side.

"Ben, you and Frank hurry along now."

"Mom, what's going on?" I asked.

"Don't worry, everything will be all right. I get off at two o'clock today, so I can probably catch the end of your game. Now run along, you two, and have a good day. I'll be OK."

On the way to the Wiswalls', Frank asked me who it was that called.

"It was probably just a wrong number," I lied. Mom was good and worried, and now so was I.

It took us over three hours, but we got the Wiswalls' yard and garden looking pretty decent again. Ksenia, their live-in caregiver, came out into the yard with a couple of glasses of lemonade and a tray of chocolate-chip cookies along with our pay. Accompanying Ksenia was Snuffy, who seemed intent on inspecting the grounds before payment was rendered.

Frank began attacking the cookie tray with a vengeance. Ksenia looked at Frank's assault and turned to me.

"Don't you ever feed this young man?" she asked. "It looks as though he hasn't eaten in weeks."

"Oh, he gets plenty to eat, trust me. When it comes to snacks and desserts, his eyes are usually bigger than his stomach. You'd better get those cookies back inside before he devours the whole tray."

Just as Ksenia reached for the platter, Frank snatched one last cookie for good measure. After finishing off the lemonade, we headed back to our house. Frank was already moaning about a stomachache.

Our game that afternoon against the Knights started off well. We scored four runs in the top of the first, two more in the third, and another four in the fourth. With a 10-3 lead in the fifth, I was able to coast the final two innings on the mound and we walked away with an 11-4 victory. I had three singles; Denny added two doubles and Andre blasted a home run. All in all, I was feeling pretty good on the way home. Frank had brought Digger along to keep him company during the game, and as we walked home we took turns tossing a Frisbee to him. He enjoyed chasing it and was pretty good at catching it too, but sometimes he got distracted on the return trip and forgot to bring it back. I remember Tara mentioning that most dogs tend to lose focus from time to time because of all the sights and smells of the outdoors. I'm not sure what my excuse is but that same lack of focus sounded like something I suffered from during the majority of my science classes.

By the time we reached the front door both Frank and I had our hearts set on the two remaining fudge bars in the freezer. Ready to make a beeline through the living room on our way to the kitchen, we both came to an abrupt stop. Sitting hunched over on the couch was Mom, and she was sobbing hysterically.

"What's wrong, Mom?" asked Frank as he hopped up next to her. "Did you hurt yourself? Can I get you a Band-Aid? You can have my fudge bar if you want."

"No thanks," Mom finally managed to spit out.

"What's the matter?" I asked, even though I had a feeling it wasn't something I really wanted to hear. I sat in a chair facing her for what seemed like an eternity until she could gather herself to answer me.

"We're going to lose the house, boys."

I sat in stunned silence as I felt the world come crashing down around me for the second time in the last half year.

"Your father had everything invested in his business. He didn't even have a life insurance policy. I've been praying for a miracle for months now, but it's just not happening. We're sunk."

"Can't we just promise to pay for the house when Benny and I get to be grown ups and have real jobs?" Frank asked.

"I'm afraid it doesn't work that way, Frank."

"Well, that stinks," said Frank.

"That sucks," I blurted out.

"Benjamin, watch your mouth."

I could think of a few other choice words to throw in, but now wasn't the time or place. This was the only home I'd ever known. The only neighborhood I was used to. And Tara was right next door. Having to move was unthinkable. I wouldn't allow it. I felt like I was going to be sick to my stomach.

Frank asked, "When do we have to get out, Mom, and where can we go?"

"I've spoken to your Aunt Julie. She and Uncle Dexter have agreed to let us live with them in their condo. It wouldn't be until school starts up in September. They have two extra bedrooms so if you and Benny were to double up in one, we could squeeze in. The baby and I can share the other bedroom. And it's only fifteen miles away."

It might as well be on the other side of the moon, I thought to myself. A different town, a different school, crammed into a different house. They didn't have a fenced in yard, either—what little yard they did have.

"What about Digger?" He wouldn't even have a yard to patrol.

"Well," Mom managed to whisper, "that's another thing. Their condo association doesn't allow pets."

That was the final straw. I erupted like a volcano. Ranting and raving, I began throwing magazines and newspapers around before knocking a stack of coasters across the living room. By the time I finished my whirling dervish, Mom had returned to crying, Frank had a petrified look on his face, and Digger was upstairs hiding under my bed.

I stormed out of the house, making sure I slammed the front door as hard as I could. Pedaling madly down the street on my bike, I made a vow. No matter what, we weren't going to move to a condo that didn't allow pets. Having to get rid of Digger wasn't an option. September was two months away. Not much time to come up with a plan to throw a wrench into that lame idea of condo living—with no Digger. The condo association probably wouldn't be turning back flips about the likes of Frank and me trying to exist within the framework of their covenant restrictions either. I needed to calm down and start thinking clearly. Two months, huh? *Tick tock, tick tock.*

chapter 27

PLAYGROUND CONFESSIONS

Eventually I calmed down somewhat, but the more I pedaled around the more confusing everything seemed. I was in serious need of some experienced counseling and direction. Cruising past the church parking lot, I spotted just the ticket. Holding a basketball under one arm as he bent over talking to someone in a silver Chevy Malibu was Father Bill. Not wanting to appear nosy, I took a couple of spins around the block until I saw the Malibu exiting the lot. Behind the wheel was Ms. Dillon. She seemed preoccupied and didn't even notice me as she sped off down the street. As I pulled closer to Father Bill his mind seemed to be elsewhere too, but when he spotted me he smiled and challenged me to a game of horse. He must have figured that I stopped by for some reason other than a social visit, so after I clunked a couple of bricks off the rim he asked me how things were going.

"Not too good. We've fallen hopelessly behind on payments to the bank for the house so we have to vacate. My mom's making plans to move in with relatives in another city. On top of that, the place we'd be moving to doesn't allow pets. I made it clear that I wasn't in favor of that plan at all and would not be accompanying them anywhere that didn't include Digger."

"You've become quite attached to that dog, haven't you?"

"It's not just me, Father. After my dad died, Frank had nightmares and began wetting the bed at night. Mom was a total wreck and I was basically a zombie. Bringing Digger into our home seemed to settle everyone down. He was like a guardian angel for us—even though he wasn't always exactly angelic. But with him aboard, things calmed down. With Digger at the foot of his bed, Frank stopped having nightmares and there were no further accidents at night. Mom came out of the doldrums and became more like herself again. I don't know what we'd have done without him. He's not just a pet. He's a member of the family now. We can't just ship him off somewhere. What kind of a place doesn't allow pets?"

"Probably the same kind of place that won't be too tolerant of a spirited pair like you and Frank. I can understand why you're worried. I have to agree with you that this initial option of your mother's might not be a good fit for your family. But keep in mind that this is a very difficult time for her as well, and she'll need all the help and support you can give her. There are several possibilities that we can explore right here in Glidden. Let me make some inquiries and I'll give your mother a call next week and we'll set up an appointment to go over them. Just maybe we'll be able to keep you all together right here in town. I just wish I could figure out a way to simplify my life. I've got an either-or situation to straighten out myself."

I had a feeling that "either" was continuing on in the priesthood, and "or" just drove off in a silver Malibu.

Our game of horse was struggling along and it became apparent that neither of us had brought his A game with him that day. There were too many distractions for both of us to concentrate fully on basketball. We decided to call it a tie at HORS. Out of the blue, Father Bill confided in me about his calling to the clergy and how he loved serving God in this manner. But, he added, "The sacrifices endured for my commitment are not only challenging but overpowering sometimes."

"So being a priest isn't as easy as it looks, Padre?" I joked.

Father Bill broke out into a hearty laugh.

"Just for that crack I'm going to tack on some extra penance for your next confession. I've been letting you off way too easy lately. And by the way, you're long overdue for one."

"Isn't that what we're doing now?"

"I suppose we are, aren't we?"

I always felt better after a talk with Padre Bill. Since Dad died, I had to lean more on him than ever before. It was just now that I realized that it must be difficult for him as well when he had a problem. I suppose talking to someone, anyone, even a twelve-year-old bonehead like me, was better than holding it all inside.

"So how about we pray for each other," I offered finally. "Sounds like we could both use it."

"It's a deal, Ben, but don't forget to include your mother in those prayers, too. She's going through a trying time. With financial problems and a baby due in a few months, she'll need your support more than ever. I'll make calls to some people and organizations that could prove very beneficial to your housing situation. Just hang in there and maybe we'll be able to work something out."

"I'm worried sick about the thought of losing Digger. I just can't allow that to happen."

"Look at it this way, Benny. You and Frank plucked Digger from the jaws of the grim reaper. The two of you saved the lives of your elderly neighbors. You managed to get theft and assault charges against you dropped. And you even took on the school bully and lived to talk about it. Certainly a little thing like the banking industry shouldn't prove to be an obstacle you can't handle. I'm pretty sure you have more friends in this town than you think. Where there's a will, there's a way. You definitely have the will. Now you just have to find a way."

chapter 28
MAGOO

Tuesday evening arrived with storm clouds and a blustery wind out of the north. The Moose were scheduled to battle the Lions, weather permitting. The Lions had edged us 4-3 earlier that summer, so we needed to turn the tables on them and stay right on the heels of the front-running Elks. Mom and I had declared a truce on our future living arrangements and Father Bill was scheduled to stop by our house the next night with some alternate options that Mom promised to consider.

As we loosened up in our pregame ritual it was good to see Knuckles back on the squad following his one-game suspension. Coach Sanders was also back at the helm. He spared us the usual sportsmanship pep talk, thankfully. He'd obviously given up the quest for the Brophy Trophy—that ship had sailed. Sanders did apologize to the team for his embarrassing role in the fiasco during our game against Helton's. He seemed to have shifted his focus more on winning the league title. That was a good thing. A 'no more Mr. Nice Guy' coach seemed to be a better fit for our particular gang of roughnecks.

Magoo was behind the plate that night, which was good news for pitchers and also gave us a better chance to get an official game in before the weather worsened.

Derrick retired the Lions in order in the top of the first. In our half, Denny singled, I followed suit, and Derrick drove us both in with a drive off the left center field fence. Knuckles dropped a bloop double down the right field line and we had a quick 3-0 advantage. Raindrops began falling during the third inning, but not enough to delay the action. Magoo was determined to avoid any talk of a rain delay. Batters were duly warned to be up there swinging away. Walks promised to be an extremely rare occurrence this evening. That worked well for Milosh. More than one Lion batter grumbled to Magoo on his way back to the dugout after watching a head-high fastball called strike three. Magoo ignored their grunts as he hurried the next victim into the batter's box. The frosty mugs down at Kelly's were calling his name and he wasn't about to disappoint them.

We added two more runs in the fourth and I got my second dinger of the year, a two-run shot in the fifth, to make it 7-1. The Lions picked up a run in the top of the sixth to make the final 7-2. By the time the third out was recorded, an easy two-hopper to second, the rain was starting to get real serious. As we began to line up for the traditional handshakes, I heard the sound of squealing tires coming from the parking lot. Sure enough, there went Magoo's red pickup truck peeling out of the lot on its way to the watering hole.

Frank and Mom met me as we filed off the field. Luckily I wouldn't have to ride my bike in this increasingly nasty weather. After throwing the bike in the back of the station wagon, we took off for home. Frank asked me if I'd closed my eyes on my home run so I felt compelled to drill him in the shoulder. Mom quickly pulled the car over and gave us "the gaze." The gaze was all it took in most cases, and when I saw the purse on her lap, I figured it was time to back off.

"Sorry, Frank, my hand must have slipped."

"Well if it 'slips' again, you won't think you're so funny," said Mom. "And I can always call off our appointment with Father Bill tomorrow evening and you can start packing your bags for Aunt Julie and Uncle Dexter's."

We rode home the rest of the way in silence.

The following evening we picked up Father Bill at the rectory. He had a list of three addresses to check out. The first one was an older house on the north side of town that was split into two apartments. The available one was an upstairs flat with three bedrooms (if an over-sized closet could be considered a bedroom), a small kitchen, a family room, and one bathroom. There was a decent-sized back yard, but it wasn't fenced in. There was an alley that ran behind the back yard, but no garage.

Our second visit took us to the south side of town to what was once known as Southtown Trailer Park. It now bore a new name: "Heritage Modular Estates." Most of the modular units were privately owned but there were two available for rent. One was pretty small, but the other one had three bedrooms and two bathrooms. There were no yards to speak of but there were several green areas within the confines of the subdivision that would allow Digger to stretch his legs. The biggest drawback I could think of was that if we did move here, we'd most likely bring the average resident age down by twenty percent.

As we approached the third possibility on the east side, we got some pretty bad vibes from the onset. It was a federally subsidized group of duplexes. Broken glass was everywhere, the predominant lawn decorations appeared to be empty twelve-packs of beer, and two separate gang signs in bright red and purple paint were plastered across a wooden fence next to an alley. It was quite evident by the messages that the two rival gangs weren't about to get together for a love fest anytime soon.

Frank was staring at the signs and started to ask, "What does… " but I cut him off with, "Never mind, Frank. I don't think you'll have to memorize any of those words for your next spelling bee."

Mom didn't even slow down.

"I think we'll take a pass on this one, Father."

"I'm sorry, Suzanne. I should have checked this one out more. The brochure photos and information pamphlets painted a much cheerier picture than this."

"No need to apologize. We're grateful that you took time out to show us what's available. This gives us a better picture of our options. The first two places were decent possibilities."

When we got home, we asked Mom what she thought about tonight's two possibilities.

"I don't know boys, we'll see."

The "we'll see" answer she gave in trying to avoid an argument was not a positive note to end on.

A little later I was out back with Digger when Tara and her mom came pulling in their driveway. Tara had her bright green Diamonds jersey on.

"How'd you do tonight?" I asked, as Digger and I walked over to her yard.

"We beat the Naperville Cougars 7-2. We're two wins away from going to Nationals."

"When's your next game?"

"Saturday afternoon in Madison. We play the Beloit Snappers. They're undefeated but I think we have a decent shot at knocking them off."

"I'm driving up to the game, Ben. If you and Frank want to go, I can take you," Tara's mom offered.

"Yeah, that'd be cool, thanks. I could use a road trip. It's been a rough week so far."

"Why—what's been rough, Benny?" Mrs. Mangolin inquired.

I told them about our dire financial situation and the current options we were exploring.

Tara looked at me and asked, "You're not giving up on your house, are you? You can't move!"

I noticed her eyes glistening over as she spoke. It appeared to me that she just might miss me as much as I'd miss her. That made me more determined than ever to not allow this travesty to occur. If I had to crawl on my hands and knees into the Glidden Bank and Trust Company president's office to save our house, I was prepared to do so. Of course, if there was a less humiliating way to avoid eviction, I was all ears.

"No, I'm not giving up," I answered with newfound confidence. "If we do get the boot, it won't be without a fight. I promise you that."

"That's more like it, Benny," Tara announced as she gave me a hug. "You'll come up with something, slugger. You always do. Just try not getting arrested this time, though, OK? See ya Saturday for our road trip. But this time, you might want to leave Digger home. The last time you brought him to my game, he caused quite a ruckus."

Looking down at Digger, I noticed his hackles were raised as he inched toward Tara's side hedge. A low growl was starting in his throat. The light from the front porch shone just enough on the bushes that we could make out a shadow with a pair of eyes glowering in our direction. I tried to grab Digger, but it was too late. He dashed headlong toward the visitor who in turn rushed off between the houses with Digger in hot pursuit. Getting a pretty good look at the intruder as it sped through the open area, we could see that our uninvited guest was a coyote. Remembering the coyote we saw at Oaken Acres a few weeks ago, I felt sorry for him or her. It couldn't be an easy life, that's for sure. A minute later, Digger came bounding back into the yard with his hackles still up while he did some serious sniffing about the hedge. Inside the house, Rufus was barking madly at the window, bound and determined to join in on the action.

"We'd better get in and settle old killer down before he destroys the house," laughed Tara as they hurried up the steps. "See you and Frank Saturday."

Walking back to our yard, I shook my finger at Digger. "What do you think you're doing, Digs?" I scolded as I shut the gate. "You could have been injured, you big clown."

Digger shot me a puzzled look as if to say, "I was just doing my job, that's what."

Looking at it from his perspective, it made perfect sense. We were his pack and he was protecting us. I bent down, scratched his ears and pulled out a few burrs that had settled in his tail.

"Let's go inside, buddy, you deserve an extra treat." Hearing the word "treat" was all it took as he rushed past me on his way into the kitchen. As I was closing the back door I took one last look out into the darkness. I wondered what would become of the coyote, hungry, with no real home and an uncertain future. I could only hope that this wouldn't turn out to be our fate in a couple of months.

chapter 29

IN THE LAND OF THE CHEESEHEADS

Thursday night's game against the VFW promised to be a good one. They beat us 8-5 earlier in the season. In fact, they were the last team to beat us. The Moose had a six-game winning streak and we weren't about to let up now.

The game seesawed back and forth through the first five innings and was tied 6-6 going into the last frame. The VFW picked up an unearned run in the top of the sixth when our center fielder, Rakeesh Patel, dropped a routine fly ball with two out and a runner on second.

Alejandro led off with a single in the bottom of the sixth. Denny bunted him to second. I came up trying not to think of the last time I was in this situation against the VFW when I'd grounded out to end the game. But that was with El Diablo. Now I had the Silver Streak and a great deal more confidence. On a 2-1 pitch I lined a double down the third base line to tie it up. Standing on second base I heaved a huge sigh of relief. It sure felt a lot better being a hero than a goat.

I was certain Derrick would drive me in for the game winner, but unfortunately he tried to kill the first pitch and ended popping out to third base. Knuckles was next up but they walked him intentionally to get to Jimmy Patterson. Jimmy was in a bit of a slump with only one hit in his last fourteen at-bats. His body language showed his lack of confidence as he trudged to the plate. Sanders called a time out and called Jimmy back for a little pep talk. Whatever he said must have worked because Jimmy jogged back up to the batter's box and pounded his bat on the plate determinedly. On the first pitch he scorched a hard grounder to the right of the shortstop and into left field. I didn't even look at the third-base coach as I dug around third. There was no way I was stopping. The throw from the left fielder was a pretty good one, but a little up the first base line. I dove head first with my left hand reaching for the plate while the rest of me was on the third base side of the box. By the time the catcher could control the one-hop throw and reach back toward the plate, I was across. The team and the Moose faithful erupted at once. Some of the more boisterous parents even spilled out onto the field. Jimmy had a grin on his face a mile wide and the mighty Moose winning streak was now at an impressive lucky seven.

The white-knuckle victory had helped to take my mind off our housing dilemma. Life was good again and I was determined to enjoy the weekend and not allow our financial woes to bring me down.

Come Saturday, Frank and I rode up to Madison with Tara and her mom for the game. I took a little extra out of my landscaping fund and told Frank this would be our little vacation.

While Tara and her Diamond teammates went through their pregame ritual, Frank and I walked down toward nearby Lake Minona to toss the ball around. There were dozens of boats on the water. The sailboats were particularly fascinating to watch. Mom had packed us some sandwiches so we sat on a picnic bench and took in the entire lake experience while we wolfed down our lunch.

We noticed a sandy beach area about a quarter mile down the shoreline so we took a walk over to check it out. It was at least 90 degrees out as we strolled along the sand. Before I knew it, Frank had ditched his tennis shoes, socks, and shirt and was running along the pier that jutted out about thirty yards. I yelled for him to stop but it was to no avail. He dove off the end of the pier despite my pleas. Normally I wouldn't mind, but he forgot to take his baseball cap off before diving in. Oh well, it was getting pretty musty and a good soaking would probably do it good. Of course, Frank was furious with himself for forgetting to remove his cap before the plunge, convinced that its fine-tuned shape was now ruined.

"That'll teach you to ignore your older, wiser brother, Squirt. Next time maybe you'll listen to the voice of reason."

"If you're the voice of reason, we're in big trouble," Frank spat out as he flipped his soggy hat to me.

As much as I wanted to jump in myself to cool off, I didn't dare take my eyes off Frank for a second. I settled for taking my sneakers and socks off while I sat at the edge of the pier soaking my feet in the refreshing lake water. About the third time Frank dashed out on the pier to dive in, the lifeguard whistled for him to stop. Too late—he flew off the end of the pier and proceeded to do a cannonball right in front of an elderly gentleman wearing a Panama hat and sunglasses. The man's hat was drenched and he looked none too pleased about it. Meanwhile the lifeguard had climbed off her stand and was jogging out to the water. Blowing her whistle repeatedly, she waded out toward Frank with a rather stern look on her face. As Frank swam back to her, she let him have it.

"What's the matter with you? You're a menace to the beach. Can't you read?"

She must have been referring to the sign with bright red letters on a white background that read NO RUNNING ON THE PIER—and just below that NO DIVING. Frank looked up at her sheepishly and answered, "No, Miss, I'm afraid I can't read."

That major fib caught the teenager off balance. "Well," she finally blurted out, "running on the pier is strictly forbidden and there is no diving allowed off the pier."

"I'm sorry," Frank said, in his innocent-yet-earnest voice. "It won't happen again. I should have known better."

The lifeguard shook her head as she walked back to her perch, still trying to figure out how the little imp had managed to squirm his way out of a well-deserved lecture.

On the way to the softball game from the beach, I suggested Frank might want to allow for a little extra time on his next visit to the confessional.

We were a little late by the time we got back to the softball field. Our view from the stands was a picturesque backdrop behind the outfield fence of pine trees and rolling hills that left a favorable impression of the Badger State. But my attention was drawn to the hurler toeing the rubber. Tara was wearing her bright green Diamond jersey, her blond ponytail flapping in the breeze and that determined look on her face as she delivered pitches. It was becoming increasingly obvious to me that she wasn't just the girl next door anymore. This was uncharted waters for me. A little confusing at times, but in a good way.

With two outs and two on, an easy grounder went right through the legs of the second baseman and the Snappers took a 3-0 lead. It reminded me of watching the Cubs. In the bottom of the fifth, though, the Diamonds loaded the bases with one out. Tara strode to the plate as the crowd was buzzing with excitement. Frank even took a break from his second order of nachos and cheese to take in the moment. The Snappers' pitcher, a tall slender redheaded southpaw, got ahead of Tara 1-2. But when she tried to slip a fastball past her, Tara was ready. She sent a high arcing fly ball to straight away center that cleared the wall by about five feet. The crowd went wild. Tara's grand slam gave the Diamonds a 4-3 lead. With all the jumping and high-fiving, Frank's hat got knocked off and onto his cheese nachos, which in turn got kicked under the bleachers. It was turning out to be a rough day for Frank's hat.

The slam held up and the Diamonds 4-3 win put them just one win from Nationals. The only thing between them and a trip to Denver was the Cedar Rapids Crushers. That game was scheduled for next Friday in Moline.

We were able to retrieve Frank's beleaguered ball cap from under the stands but his cheese nachos were toast. His temporary depression was replaced with glee with the purchase of a fudge bar from the concession stand. Frank was on a first-name basis with Jenny, the girl behind the counter, by the time we left. Keeping Frank's appetite satisfied was putting a serious dent in the landscaping funds. A few more road trips like this and our enterprise would be belly-up.

A couple of Tara's teammates rode back with us. Bridget and Monica were taken with Frankie's charm and beach stories. When he told them about his run-in with the lifeguard, they roared with laughter. Tara, quite used to Frank's antics, looked at me and rolled her eyes. We both knew he'd be retelling this story for months—and each time he'd add a little extra to the tale. In fact, Frank was enjoying himself so much on the ride back to Glidden that he only took time out twice to moan about his self-induced stomachache.

chapter 30
GHOSTS IN THE GRAVEYARD

It was almost dark by the time we got home. Bridget and Monica were spending the night at Tara's, so I suggested a game of ghosts in the graveyard, a nighttime version of hide and seek. I got a hold of Denny and Derrick. Frank recruited his friend Nicky to join in. We were having a blast—even Nicky, who was a little afraid of the dark. The only problem was the gate. It kept getting left open, which allowed Digger access to the neighborhood. All I had to do when I was the seeker was to follow him and every time he'd lead me right to Frank's hiding spot. Digger seemed to have a natural instinct to protect Frank and Nicky, probably because they were smaller and he felt they were more vulnerable. Of course, Frank didn't see it that way and scolded him for repeatedly giving away his hiding spot.

As I was hiding behind Mrs. Delanbach's enormous pine tree I noticed Digger out on our front lawn with his nose in the air and his tail pointed straight back. At first I figured he was going to cross the street and give me away to Bridget, who was the seeker. But then, he took off in a flash right past me and up the block toward the Wiswalls. This didn't look good, so I took off after him to see what he was up to.

I heard loud noises coming from the back yard as I approached the Wiswall mansion. The first thing I saw was Snuffy frantically clawing at the side door. He looked like he'd been dragged through the brambles. There was what appeared to be some blood on his neck and back. Ksenia opened the door and Snuffy bolted past her and into the house. Ksenia and I exchanged puzzled looks before she closed the door. By now, Nora and Vera were stationed at the large picture window, peering out into the darkness. Just then, Digger came bounding around the corner of the house from the back yard. He also appeared to have been involved in some sort of skirmish. For the life of me, I couldn't figure out what had just happened. Surely Digger didn't gallop down the street and into the Wiswalls' back hedge to attack Snuffy. He'd been known to chase an occasional feline up a tree or to the safety of a front porch. But to actually viciously attack Snuffy—no, I couldn't bring myself to believe that scenario.

I marched Digger home while Tara came rushing out to see what all the commotion was about. As I tried to explain what I heard and saw, she glanced skeptically in Digger's direction. Rufus came bounding toward Digger. He began madly sniffing and examining Digger. I took a closer look at Digger under the streetlight and noticed a scrape across his nose. There also appeared to be some additional abrasions on his right ear and the back of his neck. There was no longer any interest in our ghost in the graveyard game as we retreated into the house to tend to Digger's wounds. Monica and Bridget started right in with some warm washcloths and hydrogen peroxide. Digger squirmed with every swipe of the cloth. He particularly railed against the introduction of the peroxide on his fresh wounds. He did not make for a cooperative patient. The worst of his injuries was to his right ear. It had a nasty slice on it and was bleeding the most. Any attempt to clean it was met with an angry snarl. It was 9:30, so it was too late to bring him to the vet. We did the best we could with our ornery patient. Mom would be home any minute. She'd know what to do.

The whole time, though, I couldn't stop my mind from racing to all sorts of negative conclusions. Nora and Vera might assume that Digger attacked their cat, and have him taken away by the animal control unit to be locked up and tested for rabies. This development could also make Mom reluctant to keep a dog that could be viewed as unpredictable. I knew deep down that this wasn't the case, but things weren't looking too rosy right now. Rufus seemed intent on licking Digger's fresh cuts. He seemed to prefer Rufus's tongue to soothe his wounds rather than the nurses' continued assaults.

While the mounting worries scrambled my overworked cranium, the phone rang. I answered it on the third ring with a weak "Hello." It was Ksenia on the other end.

"Benny, we need to see you and Digger at once."

I put the phone down and quickly reviewed my options.

1. Take Digger, my sleeping bag, our pup tent, and head for the hills;
2. Come up with an elaborate story involving another dog that resembled Digger and claim that it was this lookalike dog that was involved with Snuffy; or
3. March over to the Wiswalls and face the firing squad.

As I reviewed my options in desperation, Tara offered to accompany Digger and me to our showdown.

"Benny, this is no time for one of your harebrained schemes. I'll go with you and we'll plead our case. Maybe there's a good explanation for all this."

I hoped she was right. As we were leaving the yard, Mom was pulling into the driveway.

"Where are the three of you off to in the dark?"

"Uh... Hi Mom! How was work?"

"Fine, but you didn't answer my question."

"We were playing ghosts in the graveyard and Tara thinks she lost her house keys up near the corner when she was hiding in the Wiswalls' hedge."

"Don't you think it might be a good idea to bring a flashlight?" she asked suspiciously.

"Why didn't we think of that?" Tara answered, poking me in the ribs. I raced back into the house to grab one as Mom looked skeptically at Tara. Once I secured the flashlight, I instructed Frank to call Mom inside with a bogus semi-emergency as a distraction. The last thing I needed was for her to come traipsing after us and catch wind of the impending slander to be rendered against Digger—not to mention the little white lie about Tara's lost keys.

I reached the front curb just as Mom was interrogating Tara.

"What's that bulge in your jeans pocket? Isn't that a key chain sticking out the top?"

Tara shot me a panicked look.

"Mom, hurry up, you gotta see this," came our bailout from Frank as he leaned out the front door. Good ol' Frank. Where would I be without him? Mom rushed into the house as Tara and I breathed a sigh of relief.

"That was close," she said. "I'm not in your league when it comes to faking a story on short notice."

"Yeah, well, you haven't had near as much practice as I have. Stick with me. With all the tight spots I end up in like this, it becomes second nature."

"That's what scares me, Benny. Some people develop addictions to drugs or alcohol. Some to gambling. You, on the other hand, I think you're addicted to chaos."

I supposed she had a point. It would be hard to argue with her on that matter. And now, the impending wrath of Nora and Vera Wiswall awaited us as we approached their dark, gloomy estate.

"You know, those two are pretty fond of that cat, Benny."

"Don't I know it. Do you think they might try to have Digger quarantined? Or even locked up? Or worse?"

"It's very possible. They have a lot of clout in this town. And a lot of money. Plus, if your mom finds out, she might be more inclined to part ways with him."

I crouched down and wiped away a little more blood from his snout.

"Don't worry, buddy, we've been through worse. It'll be all right," I assured him. I only wished I could believe it myself.

My stomach felt as though it was tied up in knots as we sidled up the driveway. The side door opened and out came the Wiswalls' backyard neighbor, Eric Swanson. He waved goodbye to Ksenia and strolled across their yard toward his house.

Oh great, I thought to myself. *The whole neighborhood's going to be in on this lynch mob.* But the next thing that happened was the last thing in the world I expected to see. Ksenia stepped out onto the porch and, with a big smile on her face, held out her hand. In the bad light, I thought at first it might be a gun. As I began to think about diving behind the bushes, I heard Ksenia coaxing Digger up the steps. Digger nearly pulled my shoulder out of its socket as he jerked me toward Ksenia. The source of Digger's excitement was a ham bone she held in her hand. The ham bone was a definite upgrade from a gun.

Tara and I looked at each other in astonishment. Tara leaned over and whispered, "I hope it isn't poisoned."

As we both tried to digest this unexpected turn of events, Vera's voice floated out from inside the house.

"Bring our little hero inside. Nora wants to see him, too."

Tara and I were totally confused as we trudged into the foyer. "Maybe it's a trap," I mumbled to Tara.

Ksenia began to explain. "At first, we thought that Digger had attacked Snuffy, and we couldn't understand why. Needless to say, Nora and Vera were quite upset. I called you up to get your version of the story. After I hung up, Eric stopped over and asked how Snuffy was doing. As it turns out, Eric was taking the garbage out to his garage when he heard noises coming from the hedgerow. At first, he thought it sounded like a catfight, so he walked over to the commotion, hoping to scare them away. He was shocked to see a coyote dragging Snuffy into the brush. He froze for a couple seconds when suddenly Digger came bounding across the yard and headfirst into the hedge. Digger and the coyote went at each other while Snuffy scurried back to the house. The coyote soon realized it was overmatched and retreated through Eric's yard and off into the darkness. Digger gave a halfhearted chase but eventually gave up and headed back to the house."

I was so proud of Digger. I went over to him and gave him a big hug. "I told you it'd be all right," I whispered into his injured right ear. But he was oblivious to the hug and praise. The ham bone was the only thing that mattered to him right then.

Just then a car pulled into the drive. Out of the car stepped Dr. Butters, a veterinarian. *Wow*, I thought, *a vet that makes house calls.* Tara was right. The Wiswalls definitely had plenty of clout in Glidden.

Dr. Butters went to work on Snuffy first. Some of Snuffy's wounds concerned him and he told Ksenia to bring him in tomorrow morning—a Sunday, no less—at eight o'clock for additional treatment.

I took the ham bone from Digger while Dr. Butters looked him over. Digger never took his eye off the bone the entire time he was being poked and prodded. Finally when the torture was over, he was reunited with his new favorite treat. Dr. Butters wasn't too concerned about Digger's injuries but told me to bring him in on Monday for a checkup in case of infection.

Following Dr. Butters' departure, the conversation turned to small talk and the various maladies affecting the sisters' health. Vera then mentioned how wonderful the grounds looked that summer and praised the job that Frank and I had done. I wasn't sure how much of her observation was warranted and how much was a matter of her declining eyesight. Either way, I thanked her for her kind words. I then felt it best to mention that our landscaping arrangement might be coming to an end shortly.

"Why is that?" Nora asked. "Aren't we paying you enough?"

"No, no, it's not that at all. You've been more than generous. I'm afraid the problem goes deeper than that. We're losing our house. The bank's foreclosing on us so we're going to have to find somewhere else to live. Finding an affordable apartment that allows pets in Glidden is turning out to be harder than we thought, though."

"It wouldn't be the same in the neighborhood without you, Benjamin," said Vera. "The peace and quiet would probably kill us. We'll be praying for you every day. Don't give up the ship just yet. Stranger things have been known to happen."

An unpleasant odor wafted through the room. I wasn't sure if it was Digger or one of the Wiswalls, which made things a little uncomfortable. Of course, in these cases the dog usually gets the blame. And this was no exception. Excusing Digger's lack of manners, we made our way to the door. The sisters thanked Digger again for saving Snuffy's hide, and invited us to stop in any time. Ksenia walked us to the door and gave Tara and me a big hug.

"I'm so thankful things turned out OK. They would have been crushed if Snuffy had been carried off by that coyote. And I would have blamed myself for letting him out. We all owe Digger a lot."

"Ksenia, could you bring me the phone?" came Vera's voice from the living room.

"I wonder who she plans on waking up tonight," Ksenia asked. "There's never a dull moment around here."

"I know what you mean," Tara said. "Try living next door to Benny and Frank. It's like living on the edge of a cyclone."

chapter 31

GOOD NEWS

Tuesday afternoon was hot and humid. On top of that, the mosquitoes in our back yard seemed particularly hungry. Frank and I were trying to play a little warm-up game of pepper but between the humidity and the pests we quickly abandoned our futile attempt and headed inside to the friendly confines and comfort of air conditioning and lemonade. Digger had positioned himself in the shade but was quick to follow us to the cooler environment. His ear was looking better every day and he didn't seem to have any other lingering health issues from his Saturday-night TKO. The coyote had most likely moved on to greener pastures where there wasn't such a strict neighborhood watchdog in effect.

We flipped on the TV to catch the last two outs in a 3-2 Cubs victory over the Giants. Mom was off work early and was excited to be able to attend my game tonight against the Masons. But the phone rang and I heard her mumble into the phone, "Now what?" Following a brief conversation, she worriedly hung up.

"That was Mr. Benton from the bank. He needs to see me at four o'clock. I'll try to make it as quick as possible and meet you boys at the field. While I'm downtown, I might as well stop and pick up someone's birthday present."

That got Frank's attention. He was turning eight on Sunday.

"What is it? Can I have it tonight?"

"You're just going to have to wait until your party Sunday afternoon. We're cooking out, and Nicky's mom is letting us borrow their big blow-up castle. Between that and the Slip and Slide, it should wear you rascals out but good."

Frank was in seventh heaven envisioning his party—and of course, the presents. He was counting on a train set from Mom. I didn't have the heart to break it to him that he might want to set his sights a little lower.

Mom took off for her appointment while Frank and I rode our bikes to the game. On the way, Frank asked me if he'd still need a babysitter now that he was turning eight.

"With you, Frank, Mom'll probably go right from a babysitter to a warden."

Frank remained quiet the rest of the way to the game. I couldn't tell if he was trying to figure out if I was kidding about the warden or if he was going through his endless list of potential presents coming his way Sunday.

The Masons drew first blood in the top of the first on an error by Andre. He dropped an easy fly ball and with two out the runner on first was running all the way. But Derrick fanned the next batter and we picked up a run of our own in the bottom half on Alejandro's triple and a ground-out. Derrick's homer in the third with Denny and me aboard gave us a 4-1 lead. We tacked on two more in the fifth on Knuckles' two-run shot and coasted to a 6-3 victory.

Mom got to the game around the third inning and brought Digger with her. That seemed a little unusual, but I didn't think much of it at the time. After the game, she seemed unusually chipper.

"How many games in a row have you won, Benny?" she asked.

"Eight straight," I proudly responded. "But we're still a game behind the Elks."

I was glad to see her include Digger in our outing. This was a good sign. All the way to Hank's she chattered up a storm and even hummed along to a tune on her "oldies" station. Frank and I hadn't seen her this happy and carefree for a long time. Too long.

Mom ordered a banana split, Frank went with the double-chocolate waffle cone, and I decided on my favorite—the turtle sundae supreme. Digger had to settle for a medium cup of vanilla. About halfway through our desserts, Mom made an announcement.

"I'm delighted to inform you three that we won't have to move after all. Mr. Benton's reason for calling me this afternoon was to relay to me some good news, for a change. An anonymous donor paid off our delinquent mortgage payments and deposited enough money in an escrow account to cover our real estate taxes for the next five years."

While I jumped up to hug Mom, Frank wanted to know who "the Donors" were and why he hadn't ever heard of them.

"Where do they live? And what do crows have to do with anything? Don't look now, Benny, but someone's finishing off your sundae."

Sure enough, Digger had taken advantage of the distraction to swipe the remainder of my turtle sundae and drag it under the picnic table with him. By the time I could reach under the table, my dessert was history. I glared at him while I delivered a harsh scolding. No matter how much time we dedicated to obedience training, when it came to ice cream, even the Great Wall of China couldn't deter him.

Meanwhile, Mom was hopelessly trying to explain to Frank that "anonymous donor" wasn't an actual name and that an escrow account didn't have anything to do with crows. Eventually she gave up and turned to me.

"I think we both know who it is. Don't we, Benny?"

The Wiswalls immediately came to mind. Nora and Vera were the only people we knew with that kind of money, and with Snuffy rescued from certain death by Digger the other night, they must have felt the need to repay us in some way. Boy, did they repay us!

"When Tara, Digger, and I were leaving the other night, Vera shouted out to Ksenia to get the phone for her. I bet she was calling

Mr. Benton. I had just mentioned to them how we were going to have to move because our house was being foreclosed on. I also said we might not be able to bring Digger along with us to our new location."

"Looks like we know who to thank for saving our house," Mom said, eying our turtle sundae thief. "We're not exactly on Easy Street, but at least now we have the benefit of a fresh start. I feel pretty foolish now thinking how we might have had to part with Digger and move in with Aunt Julie."

"We all knew that wasn't going to happen," said Frank, as he climbed on top of the picnic table to guard his waffle cone from further assault.

"I can only imagine the plans the two of you were dreaming up in order to keep me from trying to place Digger with another family," said Mom.

Frank and I both gave Mom an innocent "Who, me?" look.

"Where's the trust?" I asked with a feigned heartbroken voice.

"Trust is something earned, young man. And with all the deeds and plots you manage to pull off on a regular basis, you'll have to excuse me if I don't believe every word out of your mouth as if it was the gospel truth."

She did have a point. I needed to change the subject fast, but Mom was on a roll.

"Do you realize within the last year you've been suspended from school for skipping out to attend a Cubs game—in Chicago! Then you were almost suspended from Sunday school for beaning your teacher with a snowball on a Christmas caroling outing. You followed that up charges for theft and assault following the caper at the county animal shelter. And of course there was the call I got from Mrs. Harper describing the fisticuffs on our front lawn with that dreadful thug Nestor. Is there anything I'm leaving out?"

Frank started with, "Well, there was that time this spring…" before I could reach him with my right elbow.

"I'm sure there are numerous other misadventures that don't come to mind right now, but my point is this, Benny: You need to make better decisions. You also need to trust me and always tell the truth. And be a better role model for Frank. Don't drag him into your countless escapades like the other night when you had him call me inside with a so-called emergency while you and Tara were taking Digger to the Wiswalls. And for Heaven's sake, don't include Tara in your schemes. I could tell she was very uncomfortable with that story you came up with about her lost keys. And don't forget, in a couple of months you're going to have another set of young eyes looking up to you. It's high time to start setting a better example."

"Yeah, but if we hadn't sprung Digger from the shelter, he'd be dead and we'd be losing our home."

"The end doesn't always justify the means, Benjamin."

"It did in this case," I started, as Digger set his snout on Mom's lap.

Once Mom looked into those big brown eyes of Digger's, it became obvious that I'd been able to take some of the steam out of her lecture.

Frank finished off his cone and announced, "Let's hurry up and get home. I have to tell Nicky we're not moving before he goes out looking for a new best friend."

chapter 32

SILENCE OF THE HORNS

Thursday evening's marquee match featured the red-hot Moose riding an eight-game win streak versus the revenge-minded Fire. In our previous meeting the Fire players and their coaches became distracted when they suspected André of cursing their bats before the game. Realizing later that they had been duped into believing this trickery, the Fire's coaches were looking to even up the ledger. Tonight's rematch most likely had been circled on their calendars for weeks. There was no fooling around during their pregame warm-ups. They were all business. And they looked mad.

In contrast, the mighty Moose squad looked pretty relaxed. Jimmy Patterson was cracking some new jokes he'd just heard from his older brother. Alejandro was fielding his warm-up grounders while sporting a rather large yellow sombrero. Even Knuckles, who normally spent a few minutes during pregame scowling at the opposition, was in a festive mood. Alan Gresh had painted a green shamrock on his catcher's helmet and Knuckles was proudly showing it off to the fans.

In the top of the first inning, we loaded the bases but couldn't push any runs across the plate. In the Fire half of the first, the first two batters singled sharply to left field off of Derrick. I noticed that both hitters had jumped on Derrick's first pitch. Derrick wasn't used to getting hit hard and looked a little unnerved. After getting the throw back to the infield from Alan in left field, I called a time out and paid a visit to Derrick.

"These guys are really ticked off, which is going to make them aggressive," I started off. "They'll be up there swinging from the heels. They're not looking for walks, they're wanting to tear the cover off the ball. If you can get them to chase some pitches just out of the strike zone you'll be fine."

Derrick nodded and seemed to relax a bit. His first pitch to the number-three hitter, Caleb Haines, was high, but Caleb chased it and popped up to Knuckles right between the plate near the back stop. Haines slammed his bat on the plate and trudged back to the dugout. Derrick sighed a huge sigh of relief, but he was not out of the woods yet. Their clean-up hitter, Blake Grogan, was striding to the plate wielding a large green bat that reminded me of El Diablo. Blake was one of the most feared hitters in the league. Only the Bowers twins had more home runs than Grogan. But Blake had one weakness—zero patience. No one could remember the last time he drew a walk. Derrick glanced over to me and winked. I was certain that Mr. Grogan wasn't about to see a good pitch. On the first pitch, Derrick fired a fastball three inches inside which Black couldn't resist. The pitch jammed him good. The best he could manage was an easy roller to me. I stepped on third and fired to first for an inning-ending double play. You could almost see the steam seeping out from under Blake's helmet as he hoofed it down to first base.

In the third inning we finally broke through. I hit my third home run of the year with Denny and Jesus aboard. After Derrick ripped a double to right center, Knuckles cracked one deep over the left field fence to give us a 5-0 advantage.

The Fire scraped a couple runs off of Milosh in the third inning and by the time I took the mound in the bottom of the fifth frame we had a 7-2 lead. I felt confident I could get them to chase a few bad pitches but the Fire batters suddenly became a lot more selective with their swings. After retiring the first two batters on fly outs, I fell behind their next three batters 2-0 and had to come in with some fat pitches. All three were sent rifling off various parts of the outfield fence and the

Fire bench came to life. When the next batter sent a lazy fly to center it looked as though we would escape without further damage. But Billy Sanders somehow misjudged it and it fell harmlessly to the ground two feet behind him. Now it was 7-5 and Caleb Haines was stepping into the batter's box. I got him to chase an outside pitch and he popped it up into right field. Somehow it blooped just out of Derrick's reach and right in front of a diving Andre. The score was now 7-6, Caleb was on second base, and Blake Grogan was striding to the plate twirling his big green bat like a baton. The Fire fans were in a frenzy. Several of the lazier fans who were watching the game from the comfort of their cars began obnoxiously blaring their horns. Meanwhile, on the Moose side, things were so quiet you could hear a pin drop.

I was determined to pitch around Blake and his menacing green war club. I even though about plunking him with the first pitch just to shut up the parking lot crazies and that incessant honking. But I had faith that I could pitch around him and get him to extend the strike zone. The first pitch bounced in and Knuckles had to smother it to keep Caleb from advancing. The second pitch was a foot outside, but Blake didn't chase it. I should have thrown the next two a foot and a half outside and taken my chances with the next batter. But I just knew I could get him to sucker after a high hard one. As soon as the third pitch left my hand, I wished I could take it back. It was right down the middle about letter high. Grogan crushed it high and deep into the night. I couldn't even bear to turn around and watch it disappear as it headed for a neighboring county.

The Fire fanatics erupted. Some began shaking the fence. Others pounded their thunder sticks non-stop. And the horns seemed to get louder and louder. Some clown who must not have exhausted his Fourth of July fireworks began setting off bottle rockets and firecrackers.

Knuckles walked out to the mound and handed me a new ball.

"Don't worry, Ben, we're only down one run and we still get another crack at them. Just finish off this punk and we'll get after it."

I did retire the next hitter on a one-hopper back to the mound. As we came off the field, I apologized to Coach Sanders for blowing the lead.

"Nonsense," he said. "We win as a team and we lose as a team. Now let's go out there and win as a team."

Denny led off the top of the sixth with a ground out to second. The din on the Fire side increased. But Alejandro legged out a slow grounder to short. On a 1-0 pitch, I laced a single to right center and Alejandro raced to third easily. With Derrick strutting up to the dish there was a noticeable shift in noise level and confidence. Bennie Richardson, the Fire head coach, called time out and strode to the mound for a conference with his pitcher, Trevor Martin. After a few words of confidence and advice for Trevor and his infielders, he jogged back to the dugout.

I took off on the first pitch, a low fastball. The catcher faked a throw to second in hopes of picking off Alejandro at third, but he wasn't biting. Now with the tying run at third, the leading run at second, and first base open, Richardson ordered the intentional walk to Derrick. This strategy allowed for a force at any base and the possibility of a double play to end the game. And with Knuckles, not the most fleet of foot, due up, the odds were higher yet. Personally, I was hoping for a duplication of Knuckles' third-inning home run. A grand slam sure would have looked good right then.

On the 2-2 pitch, Knuckles grounded one right to the shortstop. It had double play written all over it. The shortstop flipped it to the second baseman who pivoted to make the throw to first to end the game. But Derrick had gotten a great jump off first and slid hard into the second baseman as he was releasing the ball. To say that it altered the throw was an understatement. The ball ended up twenty feet up the first base line. Alejandro waltzed in from third and I was digging for home all the way as I rounded third. By the time their first baseman could corral the ball, I was across the plate without a throw.

Coach Richardson came stomping out to protest the hard slide at second but his protest fell upon deaf ears.

The base umpire said, "If you're looking for a sport with no contact, why don't you just issue them tutus and enroll them in a ballet class?"

That sent Richardson ballistic. He let loose with a rash of expletives as he tossed his hat out toward right field. His animated performance earned him an immediate ejection from the game. It probably didn't help his stock in the Brophy sportsmanship standings, either. Somehow I doubted the trophy was a high priority of his right now.

While the drama played out on the field, the Moose faithful reveled in the turn of events. Chants were started up by some of the mothers. Moose calls could be heard throughout the bleachers. High-fives were being exchanged in our dugout. Following Milosh's fly out to end the inning, sanity resumed and everyone dug in for an anticipated nervous bottom of the sixth.

First up for the Fire was Trevor Martin. He lofted a foul pop-up between home and third. Both Knuckles and Alan Gresh, who was playing third, called for the pop-up. Alan, Knuckles and the ball all arrived at the same time. When the dust settled, the laws of physics had taken effect. Knuckles stood clutching the ball while Alan lay in a heap on the ground. Ice packs, bandages, and smelling salts were administered to poor Alan back in the dugout. Rakeesh Patel replaced Alan at third. And the Fire was down to its last two outs.

Next up was Tavaris Jackson. He lined a 1-1 pitch down the third base line just foul by inches. The Fire's second in command, Jeff Blomberg, came out to do a little bellyaching but was chased right back with a reminder that if one more coach got tossed it was an automatic forfeit. Blomberg spun around, muttering to himself all the way back to the coaches' box near first base. I struck Tavaris out on the next pitch and the Fire was down to the last bullet. The third batter, Juan Diaz, fouled off several of my better pitches before grounding a single to right field between Derrick and Denny. Juan had pretty decent speed, but I didn't think they'd risk the final out testing Knuckles' arm. Not many runners enjoyed success running on Knuckles.

Next up was Tony Kalodimas, a decent hitter with good power. *No mistakes here,* I told myself. *Just keep it in on his fists and don't let him extend those bulky arms.* I caught a little too much of the plate on the first pitch and Tony sent it hard past my right side. I figured it was ticketed to center field but I had underestimated our shortstop. Alejandro dove to his left and snared the ball on its second hop. While still on his belly, he flipped the ball to Denny, covering second base. The throw short-hopped Denny but he scooped it up cleanly for the force out to end the game. What a perfect ending to a great game. The Moose winning streak was now at nine and the Fire squad was left shaking their heads. And best of all, there weren't any noisy horns to be heard blaring away in the parking lot.

chapter 33

STORMY WEATHER

I rolled out of bed earlier than usual Saturday morning. Behind in my yard work duties, both at home and for two other customers, I needed to get a fresh start before the day's heat and humidity could put a damper on my efforts.

Gassing up the mower while Digger patrolled the yard, I realized that my soon-to-be-eight-year-old assistant was going to be needed if I was to finish by noon. We went back inside to the kitchen, where I poured a bowl of cereal for myself and a bowl of dog food for Digger. By the time I poured milk on the cereal and secured a spoon, Digger had already scarfed down his chow.

"Go get Frankie up," I urged him. "I'll get you a biscuit if you get Frankie."

Up the stairs he bounded. A minute later he returned with Frank's blanket. Dropping it on the linoleum floor, he stationed himself under the cabinet where his biscuits were stored.

"Nice try, but that wasn't the deal." I went back to my cereal, hoping he'd run back upstairs for another assault.

Instead, he paced over to my side. Placing a paw on my knee, he took turns staring at me and at the magic cabinet above the counter that contained his treats. Finishing my cereal, I grabbed a biscuit and marched upstairs to Frank's room. I tossed the treat onto Frank's curled-up torso. Digger pounced on top of Frank and began crunching away.

"Hey, go away you two. I'm trying to get my beauty sleep."

"Tough. There aren't enough hours in the day for you to get beautiful, chump. Now get up, lazy bones," I commanded.

Not getting a response to that, I added, "You know, it's not too late for me to return your present. I still have the receipt somewhere."

That bluff worked perfectly. Reluctantly Frank willed himself out of bed and off to the bathroom. Digger hopped off the bed and proceeded down the hall, where he barged into Mom's room to perform his version of reveille. I had to laugh to myself when I heard Mom grumble, "I swear the three of you could wake up the dead."

Back outside, I was getting set to start up the mower when I noticed Tara's dad's truck in their driveway. On the front porch, Tara and her father were engaged in a friendly conversation. Not wanting to appear nosy, I pretended to be busy attending to last-minute details before starting up the mower. They exchanged a somewhat awkward hug before he descended the steps and backed his car out the drive.

"Did I hear your father mention Denver? So you won last night, huh?" I asked.

"Yeah, we nipped Cedar Rapids in ten innings, 2-1. By the way, how long have you been snooping around there, Benny?"

"I wasn't eavesdropping," I lied. "I was just getting the lawn mower ready and heard your dad mention Denver."

"Sure, right. And I'm the tooth fairy," Tara remarked as she pranced over toward me. "We're leaving Thursday for the mile-high city. I'm so excited. Mom's going, too. We've never seen the Rockies. I can't wait. Not only do we get to play softball, but we get to hike and camp in the mountains, too."

It was refreshing to see Tara this happy and excited. And talkative. Hopefully her father's visit had something to do with it.

"Just don't get eaten by any bears while you're out hiking in the mountains," I joked. "I heard they're partial to gabby softball players."

"Actually, they prefer nerdy boys for their snack, so you'd better stay put here in 'Corn Corners.' Speaking of staying put, could you take care of Rufus while we're gone?"

"No problem, but if you get gobbled up by a bear, I get to keep him."

Frank and I finished up our landscaping duties well before noon. Since it was getting warmer by the minute, we decided an afternoon at the pool was in order. Denny and Derrick were already there by the time Frank and I arrived. Luckily they saved me a lounge chair. It seemed as though half the town had the same idea and open chairs were hard to come by. Frank met up with Nicky and they spread their towels, not coincidentally, right next to the snack bar before plunging into the water.

The three of us spent the next three hours rotating between the tornado slide, the high diving board, and the lounge chairs. And of course there was the "occasional" girl-watching going on. Derrick insisted that was the reason God invented sunglasses. About thirty feet away from our chairs were a few girls from our class: Cheryl McAdams, Ella Turner, and Lauren Gildemeister. Across the pool catching some rays were some of the girls from the next freshman class, including Tara. What a difference a year makes.

Feeling like we'd had enough fun in the sun for one day, it was time for one last splash before our exit. Climbing the high dive ladder we decided to bend the diving board rules a little bit. The rules were posted on the fence:

1. Only one person allowed on the board at a time.
2. Wait for OK from lifeguard before advancing.
3. Jump straight out.
4. Upon resurfacing, go directly to the side of the pool and exit the water.

We, however, had other plans. Derrick went first and bounced directly to the left, where his jackknife managed to soak Cheryl McAdams and her bevy. I followed immediately with a bounce and a hard right toward Tara and her sun-drenched friends. I managed to land a perfect cannonball that doused them quite respectably. Denny eluded the suddenly alarmed lifeguard but was thrown off balance. Whatever his intentions were, he ended up in a painfully landed belly flop.

By the time I came to the surface, I was eager to see the fruits of my labor. Instead, I was face-to-face with a revenge-seeking Tara, who leaned over and shoved my head back under water. Unfortunately for her, she lost her balance and toppled into the water as well. I skedaddled out of the pool before she could administer another dunking. Whistles were blaring away from everywhere. I glanced across the pool to where Derrick was being jettisoned toward the exit. Two lifeguards were assisting Denny. His painful belly flop and the resulting discomfort to his midsection certainly seemed to have taken the starch out of him.

A female lifeguard by the name of Janna stormed up to me and simply stated, "GET OUT." She didn't seem to be the kind of person to beat around the bush.

"But I have to get my little brother first," I started.

That was met with another short but sweet "GET OUT–NOW."

By now Tara had hopped out of the pool.

"I'll see that Frank gets home OK. You'd better leave before they slap you with a lifetime ban."

On my way to being escorted off the premises, I stopped to collect my sunglasses and towel. Trying to maintain as much dignity as possible under the circumstances, I popped my shades back on and began folding my towel quite deliberately. Trying to avoid the bum's rush that Derrick was given, I only managed to infuriate the pool manager, who was standing at the gate with his arms folded and a nasty scowl on his face. As I passed by, he mumbled, "And don't bother to darken our doorstep again." Unsure of whether or not that constituted a lifetime ban, I resisted the urge to ask for clarification.

Arriving home a short while later I realized that Mom was due home any minute. Not wanting to explain how it happened that I had abandoned Frank at the pool, it seemed like a good time to take Digger for a walk. Digger was more than glad to visit all the trees, bushes, and fire hydrants in the 'hood'. Fifteen minutes later along came Frank and Tara on their way home from the pool. Tara was the first to chime in.

"The lifeguards didn't seem too impressed with your little stunt, Benjamin."

"That's because they obviously lack a true sense of humor. Some of them need to get a life. Maybe if they'd lighten up and smile once in a while, they wouldn't be so uptight."

"The two girls running the snack bar got a kick out of it, Benny," added Frank. "They got to laughing so hard at Denny's belly flop that Janna finally stalked over and told them to knock it off and get back to work."

"See, not everyone's a stick-in-the-mud, Tara. You were even laughing until Janna started flipping out."

"I was just wondering why it took you so long to start trouble. Three whole hours of behaving and obeying the rules must be some kind of a record for you. It must have been killing you."

"Actually it shows how mature I'm becoming." That got a snort out of both of them. Tara shook her head and muttered, "That'll be the day."

After Mass on Sunday morning Mom began setting up for Frank's party. Nicky's dad came over with the large inflatable castle and got it set up. Frank and I got the Slip and Slide ready while Mom set out some clues for a scavenger hunt. Seeing as there would soon be a dozen seven- and eight-year-olds running rampant through the yard, I thought it best to send Digger next door to play with Rufus.

Everyone had a great time at Frank's gala affair. The noise level never slipped below ninety decibels. There was only one bloody nose from all the jumping and bumping in the castle. Stephen Borden got his foot temporarily wedged under the fence when he slid too far off the Slip and Slide. And Desmond Friested lost a baby tooth on his third helping of peanut brittle. All in all, the casualty report was deemed to be within tolerance.

Frank ripped into his presents like a house on fire. He hardly took time enough to thank the benefactor for one gift before tearing into the next one. He seemed to especially enjoy Mom's present—a thousand-piece Lego set. He loved building Lego structures although we were never quite sure what they were supposed to resemble. But it kept him quiet for hours on end, which I'm sure was on Mom's mind when she bought the set. My present to Frank was a large set of Lincoln Logs. The fact that I enjoyed playing with Lincoln Logs more that Frank did was not lost on Mom as she eyed me suspiciously. Frank would be so busy with all his other treasures that he wouldn't notice me borrowing his Lincoln Logs from time to time.

By the time the party was wrapping up, dark clouds were appearing overhead. As the last little jasper departed with his goody bag in tow, thunder could be heard in the distance. Mom turned on the radio, and the forecast called for severe thunderstorms. Knowing that Digger wasn't too fond of thunder and high winds, Mom sent me next door to fetch him. Meeting me at her fence was a worried-looking Tara.

"Digger is starting to wig out," she noted.

Sure enough, he was racing frantically back and forth along the fence line while loudly barking at the invisible thunder. When a flash of lightning appeared in the darkening sky, he hunkered down and began digging madly in the lawn. This storm had him spooked like nothing I'd seen before. Rufus seemed oblivious to the approaching weather front, but his calm demeanor didn't seem to be rubbing off on Digger.

"I'd better get him home before he makes Swiss cheese of your yard."

"Here, take Rufus's leash to lead him over to your house. In the state he's in, I'm afraid he might bolt."

We knew that storms bothered him for some reason, but he was worse than ever right then. The lightning flash seemed to send him over the edge. I clipped the leash on his collar and rushed him indoors. He seemed a little better once inside, but was still nervous. He paced about the house, pausing occasionally at the front picture window to bark at the ever-increasing thunder and wind. When another lightning bolt lit up the neighborhood with a loud crash, he freaked out. He raced down the hall and into the den. By the time I reached the den, he was madly digging away at the carpet in the far corner. In no time at all, he'd managed to shred a decent-sized patch of carpeting and even the padding underneath. Frank brought him his favorite biscuit treat and I tried to distract him by throwing a tennis ball across the room. He was having none of it as he continued to shred away.

Mom wondered if with all the experience Tara had with animals, she might have an idea. After a quick phone call, Mom rushed to the den closet to grab a quilt. She brushed past us and forced Digger on his side while she covered him with it and then wrapped him up tightly in the quilt until it was almost like he was in a sleeping bag. That did the trick. He calmed down noticeably. Frank scratched his ears for a few minutes as the storm died down and passed by. When we unraveled the quilt from around him he popped up, scarfed down his biscuit, and pranced out of the room with the tennis ball in his mouth as if nothing had happened.

Before I could ask, Mom explained her conversation with Tara. What Digger had just gone through was not uncommon, according to Tara's experience working at the shelters. Getting something tight to wrap around a dog was often the key to getting him to relax.

"I wonder if something in his past had something to do with it," I offered.

"Could be. Tara mentioned that sometimes when a dog experiences a traumatic event, the memory of that experience can stay with him for the rest of his life. We'll have to keep this quilt handy because I doubt that's the last storm to visit Glidden."

"Where did Frank sneak off to?" I asked.

"If I remember correctly, there was one piece of chocolate cake left over from the party. I'll bet you a dollar he's in the kitchen right now."

"No way. I know a sucker bet when I see it."

By the time we reached the kitchen, Frank was shoveling the last piece in his mouth.

"Told you it was a sucker bet," was all I could say.

chapter 34
UP IN FLAMES

Monday evening I received a phone call from Helton's coach, Maury Shenberger, with some good news. I was named to the all-star team! He was going to coach the squad and our first practice was Saturday morning. Joining me on the squad from the Moose were Derrick and Knuckles. I felt sorry for Denny, but it would have been next to impossible to get more than three players named from the same team. It promised to be an eventful week. Tuesday night was our rematch with Helton's and Thursday evening was the 'game of the century' with the Moose taking on the Elks in the regular season finale. If we knocked off Helton's tomorrow, Thursday's game would be for first place. And now with an All Star practice on Saturday, it was almost too good to be true.

I ran next door to give my batting coach the good news. She was already packing for her trip to Colorado. Even though she was going to be gone for less than a week, she was bringing enough clothes for a month.

"I thought you weren't leaving until Thursday morning. And what's with two suitcases and a duffel bag? Are you moving there?"

"Pipe down and mind your own business. For your information, it gets cold up in the Rockies and I plan on being prepared."

My idea of packing was tossing a few duds in a Hefty bag five minutes before departure. I just didn't understand girls.

"Don't forget to leave some room for your bear spray."

"Thanks for the tip. But tell me you didn't barge into my house just to pester me."

"No, actually I come bearing good news. Guess who made the All Star team?"

"Well, congrats, slugger. I knew you could do it."

"Of course I did have a little help along the way from a certain drill sergeant batting coach."

"Only because it's the one way to get through that thick skull of yours. And speaking of skulls, don't be getting too full of yourself about the All Star selection. You do have a tendency to let success go to your head."

I hated it when she was right.

"I'll try and squeeze that enormous skull of mine out the door now. If you're done packing by tomorrow afternoon, maybe you can pitch me some batting practice. I'll even throw in a free autograph for you."

Tuesday's batting practice was productive despite the constant nagging (coaching) from Sergeant Mangolin. "Keep your head still. Hands back, I said. The next time that left foot steps towards third base I'm sticking it in a bucket of cement." All said with love and tenderness, of course.

Tuesday evening found the Moose matched up with Helton's. Given our last encounter with Helton's, I half expected to see a yellow police tape wrapped around the field. But all was calm and normal. Coaches Sanders and Shenberger even shook hands and exchanged pleasantries before the contest.

There were several Elks players in attendance—pulling for Helton's, of course. A Moose loss would give them the league title. Eager to disappoint them, we jumped on Helton's big time in the top of the first. Alejandro and Denny both singled, I doubled them home and Derrick smacked one over the center field fence. It was 4-0 before some of the fans even got settled in. The game never did get closer than that. By the time the final out was recorded it was 12-3. The Elks players had long since departed on their bikes, and to the delight of Commissioner Deverman, no punches were thrown.

On Wednesday evening, Frank and I decided to take Digger for a walk. It was purely a coincidence that our walk took us to Hank's. On our return trip, we heard sirens in the distance. As we continued on, we could see smoke billowing up into the night sky. We picked up the pace considerably until a right turn on Brown Street revealed the source of the blaze. Flames were shooting out of every window of an older two-story house in the middle of the block. Several fire engines were parked out front and an ambulance was at the end of the drive. Police were busy trying to keep onlookers back at a safe distance. Creeping up closer, we spotted Father Bill sitting on the back of the ambulance with his arm around an elderly lady. She looked familiar but I didn't know her name. We overheard a woman who claimed to be a next-door neighbor explaining to some people who had just walked up what was going on.

"Harold must have fallen asleep in his Lazy Boy in front of the TV. It's not the first time he's done that with a cigarette going. I must have told Kathy a dozen times that it would catch up with him. Kathy was upstairs reading in bed. Luckily Riley—that's their cat— made enough of a stink to get her attention. By the time she made it downstairs there was smoke everywhere. She's not near strong enough to pull him out of his chair, and the smoke was overcoming her by then. She tried to wake him up but it was hopeless. I have little doubt he was past waking up at that stage. Between the smoke and the countless beers he downs every night someone would have had to carry him out of there. Kathy and Riley managed to crawl out of there though. She made it over to our house. Charlie and I were just getting ready to turn in for the night when we heard the doorbell. Charlie was convinced it was some neighbor kids pulling a prank, but I peeked out through the blinds and was I surprised. There on our front stoop was Kathy coughing away with nothing but her nightie on, holding Riley close to her chest. I couldn't believe my own eyes. I glanced next door and saw smoke pouring out their side windows. I yelled for Charlie to call the fire department and started down the stairs. He asked, 'What for? It's just kids having some fun is all.'"

"I stormed back into the room and told him, 'It isn't kids, you fool. The Burtons' house is on fire.' He told me I was crazy and couldn't see anything without my glasses. I told him if he didn't call right now, the only thing he'd be seeing was stars. I swear that man sometimes is dumb as a box of rocks."

Inching closer to the ambulance, I could hear Father Bill trying to get through to Kathy, who was apparently in shock. It was clear from his tone that Harold hadn't survived the blaze. A grim-looking coroner was getting into his car. As he pulled away, so did a black vehicle resembling a hearse. With that, Kathy became hysterical. It was all Father Bill could do to calm her down. With his arm draped around Mrs. Burton, he assured her that he'd accompany her to the hospital, where they needed to check her out further for smoke inhalation.

In moments like this, the importance of having someone like Father Bill is immeasurable. Being able to help parishioners get through the most tragic of events is a blessing not everyone possesses. If Father Bill were still wrestling between his commitment to the Church and his feelings for Ms. Dillon, something like this would probably tend to pull him back toward his ordination vows. He sure was good at what he did, and Mrs. Burton's need right then was critical. With the ambulance's lights disappearing around the corner, I couldn't help but think that she was in for a rough time of it. Having Father Bill in her corner was at least a silver lining to a very dark cloud.

chapter 35
THE RIGHT THING TO DO

It was still dark early Thursday morning when I woke up to a racket coming from next door. Peeking out the window, I could see Tara and a couple of her teammates trying to cram their luggage into a car-top carrier. With the amount of belongings they were bringing along it might have been better to rent a bus. I couldn't resist getting one last dig in before she left.

"You know they have weight limits on those mountain roads in Colorado," I shouted out the window.

"Go back to sleep, Dork," Tara answered back. "You're gonna need all the rest you can get for the drubbing the Elks'll put on you tonight."

"Sounds like a bet to me. I've got five bucks that says the Moose take home the hardware tonight."

"You're on. You guys got lucky last time." With that, the three of them went back to packing up and giggling away. I shut the window and went back to bed. But there was no going back to sleep. As I tossed and turned all that came into my thoughts was the big game tonight. We just had to win.

A short while later I heard moaning coming from Frank's room. Mom and I got to his door at the same time. As we entered the bedroom it was clear to see that Frank was having a nightmare. A concerned-looking Digger was on the bed nervously pawing away at his legs. Frank hadn't had a nightmare in months, but this one was a doozy. He was thrashing about the bed while he shouted, "No, no, let go of me."

Mom rushed over and gave his shoulders a light shaking. "It's all right, Frankie. Everything's going to be OK."

Frank's eyes popped open but a frightened look remained on his face. After a few seconds he offered, "I was dreaming our house was on fire and I couldn't find Digger. The firemen had a ladder up to my room but I told him I wasn't going anywhere without my dog. The fireman was mad at me and called me stupid. Then he reached out and dragged me through the window. All the way down the ladder I kept hitting and punching him, but that just made him laugh. He said I punch like a girl."

The nightmare involving a fire was obviously implanted in Frank's head from last night's horrifying blaze on Brown Street. I never should have let Frank witness that scene. I don't know what it is about fires, train wrecks, or car accidents. Even if you figure out you shouldn't look, you still can't take your eyes off it.

While Mom was hugging Frank she was giving me the evil eye. Without saying a word, it was clear what she was thinking. *We finally got through his nightmare phase and what do you do, Bozo? Drag him to a fiery blaze where someone perishes. Good one, noodle brain.*

"Don't worry, Frankie," I told him. "We've got smoke alarms in the hall, the stairway, and downstairs. We'd have plenty of warning. Plus, if we did have a fire, you wouldn't have to look for Digger. He'd be on your bed howling loud enough to drown out the smoke alarms."

"There will be no more talk of fire," Mom declared. "Now the two of you make your beds and brush your teeth, and I'll meet you downstairs for breakfast. I'm making French toast, bacon and oatmeal. I figure a big breakfast is what we all need."

With visions of a morning feast, we raced into action. When I got out of the bathroom, I noticed Mom standing on a ladder at the end of the hall testing the smoke alarm.

"Never can be too sure," is all she said as I headed down the stairs.

The weather Thursday evening was as close to perfect as it got in northern Illinois. A slight breeze from the north offered a welcome relief from the oppressive heat and humidity of the past several weeks. As game time approached, the Glidden Little League complex took on the appearance of a small city. Henri's Hot Dog Stand was a bustle of activity. I always got a kick out of his advertisements. "World famous." "Best hot dog this side of Chicago." "Known coast to coast." The popular notion in town had it Henri had an aunt in New York and a cousin in L.A. That would explain his claim of being known coast to coast.

Also in attendance—with front-row seating compliments of the handicapped section—were the Wiswalls. Ksenia figured the fresh air and excitement would do them both good. They seemed to be thoroughly enjoying themselves. Vera called me over to inquire why we weren't using wooden bats. I explained to her that aluminum bats had pretty much taken over in place of the old Louisville Slugger wooden ones. She looked at me like I was crazy. Nora had her Cubs hat on, while Vera was gracefully adorned in her St. Louis Cardinals jersey. Ksenia reported that the two would argue to no end when the Cubs played the Cardinals on TV.

"They go for days without speaking to each other following close games," I recalled Ksenia telling me recently. The only thing that brought them back to speaking terms was their mutual hatred of the New York Yankees. If one of their feuds lasted more than a few days, Ksenia would bring up the subject of a recent Yankee loss. That ploy always worked to bring them back to a common goal: bashing the Yankees and their "East Coast arrogance," as they put it.

To the left of the Wiswalls in the VIP box was Commissioner Deverman. Deverman was flanked by two impressive-looking trophies. One was for the league championship and the other was the Stan Brophy Sportsmanship Award. At least we had a shot at one of them. The other one—forget about it.

Crazy Dave had his popcorn stand set up near the entrance. 'Smolderin' Joe Watson was grilling up some mean-looking ribs and barbeque chicken behind the stands near home plate. The line for Joe's meaty cuisine stretched all the way back to the restrooms. Numerous tables were set up just the other side of the outfield fence to accommodate fundraising organizations such as the Boy Scouts, the Girl Scouts, and the HATS Humane Society. There were even a few churches representing their parishes in recruitment drives and bake sales. Further down the left field line was a farmer's market offering fresh produce and other healthy choices. It seemed as though the whole town was present. The complex was taking on a circus-like atmosphere.

The mayor, William 'Wild Bill' Johnson, was making the rounds, shaking hands, kissing babies and generally taking credit for the pleasant weather.

The municipal band struck up "The Star-Spangled Banner," "America the Beautiful," and of course, "Take Me out to the Ball Game." Once the field was cleared, the announcement was made: "*Play ball!*"

The Elks, being the visitors, got first crack at us in the top of the first, but Derrick shut them down 1-2-3. The first two were easy ground-outs. Zane Bowers, the third batter, nearly took my head off with a liner that I caught more in self-defense than anything.

In the Moose half of the first, Alejandro and Denny were both strike-out victims. Zane was really bringing the smoke that night. I fouled the first pitch off over the first-base dugout. The second pitch came zinging in right under my chin. I stepped out of the batter's box to collect my wits. Glancing back I could see Nora Wiswall poking her cane through the chain-link fence and shouting out to the mound.

"One more pitch like that, Sonny, and I'm gonna come out there and wrap this cane around your neck!"

That got a few chuckles from the fans, but I was probably the only one within earshot who knew she wasn't kidding. Fouling off a couple more of Zane's best pitches, I managed to draw a walk. On the first pitch to Derrick I took off for second. The catcher's throw was high and wide of the shortstop covering second and I scampered around to third before the center fielder could scoop it up and get it back to Zane. With a 2-2 count, Derrick drove a deep fly down the right field line but it curled foul just before reaching the outfield wall. The next pitch was in the dirt and scooted past the catcher to the backstop where it took a nasty carom away from him. By the time he could corral the ball I was crossing home plate with the first run of the game—a cheap run, but a run just the same. Drawing first blood, the Moose nation was whipped into a frenzy. Zane stomped back to the mound with a look on his face like he was suffering from extreme indigestion. He ended up walking Derrick but retired Knuckles and a grounder to second.

Derrick gave up a leadoff double to Zach to start the second inning. He managed to wiggle out of the inning without any damage. A strike-out, a ground-out and lazy fly to right did the trick and left Zach stranded on third.

The score remained 1-0 going into the top of the fourth. Milosh ran into some control problems and walked the bases full with one out. Coach Sanders called time out and strolled out to the mound to calm Milosh down.

"Just relax, young man, and concentrate on Jeremy's catcher's mitt. You'll be fine. Take a deep breath and go get 'em."

Coach Sanders's little pep talk didn't seem to provide the needed effect on Milosh. He plunked Landon Mercer on the first pitch and the game was tied.

Sanders decided it was time for a pitching change on his second trip to the mound and handed me the ball with one simple instruction: "*Throw strikes.*"

Throwing strikes was never a problem for me. Keeping the ball from flying over the outfield wall was where I had issues.

After a handful of warm-up pitches, Desmond Wallace stepped into the box. If I remembered correctly, Desmond cranked one over the left field fence last year on me. We certainly didn't need a repeat performance of that right now. With all the walks, he was taking on the first pitch, so I got ahead of him 0-1. On the second pitch, he fouled it straight back into the stands. With an 0-2 count I decided to jam him a little bit. He swung at it and dribbled it right back to me. I whipped a throw to Knuckles, who stepped on the plate and fired down to Derrick at first base for an inning-ending double play. The Elks had blown a golden opportunity to put a serious hurt on us. The Moose had dodged a bullet.

It was still tied in the bottom of the fifth. Zach Bowers walked Andre on five pitches to start the inning. Jesus bunted him over to second base. With one out we had the potential lead run in scoring position. But Alan rolled out to second with Andre taking third. Now there were two outs and Billy Sanders was up. Billy was 0 for the season and Zack Bowers was throwing aspirin tablets up to the plate. Not exactly your dream match-up. It was the baseball equivalent of David and Goliath. Trouble was, Billy was holding a bat instead of a slingshot.

The first two pitches whizzed right past Billy. The ball was safely in the catcher's mitt by the time Billy got around. I saw Knuckles grab his mask in anticipation of taking the field for the top of the sixth. Billy stepped out of the box and choked up a good three inches on the bat handle. As the third pitch came rocketing down the pipe I was mentally rehearsing my standard line, "Nice try, Billy, we'll get 'em next time." But those words ended up stuck in my throat as Billy chopped one that hit a few feet in front of the plate and bounced high into the air. Zack was off balance and couldn't reach it as it landed right behind the mound. By the time the shortstop reached it and threw to first, Billy was a step past the bag. It was his only hit of the year and only traveled about sixty feet, but it couldn't have come at a better time. The Moose led 2-1. Zack struck out Rakeesh on three pitches, but the damage was done.

Three outs was all that stood between us and the league championship trophy. But with a meager one-run lead, there wasn't much room for error. On top of that, first up in the top of the sixth was Zack Bowers. He lined my first pitch toward right field. Fortunately Derrick was playing a few feet on the grass for Zack. That and the fact he was our tallest player enabled him to leap up and snag it in the webbing of his glove. When he came down the ball was part in the glove and part sticking out the top like a snow cone. Zack flung his bat angrily toward his dugout and shouted out a few things in Derrick's direction. I don't believe any of the dialogue included the words "nice catch." Derrick just smiled back as he held the ball aloft, to the merriment of the Moose faithful.

Next up was Walter Burgess. With the count 1-1, he swung for the fences but got underneath it and popped up to short center, where Alejandro gathered it in for the second out.

With two out the Moose fans were on their feet. One more out. Just one more out. Andrew Bell was their last hope. I got ahead of him 0-2. On the third pitch I tried to jam him but the pitch hung right over the plate. He hit it high and deep to left field. Alan raced back to the fence and swiped at the ball but came up empty. It hit the top of the fence and carried over. Home run. Tie score. Disaster. As the ball landed hauntingly on the other side of the fence I heard a commotion behind me. Lying on the ground a couple of steps past first base was Andrew Bell. He was writhing in pain and holding his ankle. As the coaches huddled around him I asked Derrick what had happened.

"He was rounding first and looking up at the ball. He came down on the side of the bag and I heard a crack. I think he might have broken a bone in his ankle."

A woman came out from the stands and indentified herself as Dr. Astling. While she tended to Andrew, a discussion broke out between the umpires and coaches. Home plate umpire Wayne Burger pointed out the ruling: "The batter must touch all the bases before it's an official home run. In addition, he or she can receive no assistance from any teammate, coach, or outside person." Dr. Astling insisted that Andrew could not possibly drag himself around the bases without causing further damage. It looked as though the Moose were going to win on a technicality.

I noticed Coach Sanders huddling with Burger in the middle of the diamond and wondered what that was all about. Sanders called the infield together and announced, "There's nothing in the rule book that forbids the opposing team from carrying the player around the bases. Derrick, you get under one arm, Denny, you the other, and Ben, you're in charge of holding his legs still. Make sure he can touch the bases with his good foot."

Knuckles looked at Coach Sanders like he'd lost his mind. "What are you, nuts? Why would we do that?"

"Because it's the right thing to do, Jeremy," he answered. "Now the three of you get going so he can be taken to the medical center for proper treatment."

When we got to Andrew, he had his ankle elevated with an ice pack on it. We recruited Alejandro to hold the ice pack in place and keep the leg elevated. Andrew looked puzzled as we gathered around him. "Come on, Bell," Denny said. "We're going for a little ride."

I had the easiest job. All I had to do was get under his good leg and bend it at second, third, and home to make his foot touch the bases.

As we reached home plate, I half expected Knuckles to be standing in front of it to block us, but he just stood off to the side glowering at us.

Word spread through the crowd as to what was happening as we handed Andrew over to Dr. Astling and his parents. In unison, the crowd stood and applauded. The standing ovation lasted for several minutes. The "right thing to do" turned out to be very popular with the townspeople. Even Knuckles, who at first regarded me with a look that could have been reserved for Judas, seemed to be softening a little. He handed me a new ball, smiled, and said, "I don't like it when people take advantage of my good nature. Now let's get one more out, Davies. Then we put a run across in our half and whip these dirt bags."

Good ol' Knuckles. It was always refreshing to witness his tender side. Not wishing to upset Knuckles further, I induced the next batter to ground out to Alejandro for the third out. Now, to get that run.

I was up first to start the bottom of the sixth. Warming up in the on-deck circle, I could hear Nora shouting to me.

"Blast one over the fence, Benny, and end this thing. My bunions are killing me." Much as I'd have loved to do just that, I kept in mind the words Tara had drilled into me. "Just make contact. Don't try to kill it. Keep your head still."

On Zack's first pitch I hit a hot smash between short and third and out into left field. Rounding first base aggressively, I noticed that the Elks' left fielder misplayed the ball. It caromed off his glove and bounced a few feet away. That was all I needed and slid into second well ahead of the throw. With first base open it was a no-brainer to intentionally walk Derrick. Up to the plate stepped Knuckles. Zach's first pitch whistled past Knuckles' ear. He didn't even finch. If Bowers thought he could intimidate Knuckles, he had another thing coming. The next pitch was knee-high on the outside corner. Knuckles drove the pitch into right field. It landed a few feet in front of the Elks' right fielder, Justin French. I dug around third and glanced back at the rainbow throw from Justin. Gambling there wasn't enough mustard on the toss, I kept coming. The gamble paid off as the throw barely trickled all the way to the plate. Burgess could only watch in horror as I slid past him before the ball arrived. The Moose were the new league champions. All was good in the world. The smile plastered on Knuckles' face as he danced around first base was priceless.

chapter 36

THE GAZE

As we lined up to accept the league championship trophy, a feeling I wasn't expecting came over me. The state of euphoria I was in was suddenly replaced with a kind of sadness. Actually more like a regret. Something was missing. Or to be precise, *someone* was missing. The man who coached me from tee-ball on. The same one who never missed a game of mine until this year. He should have been here with us celebrating, with that mile-wide grin of his, giving out high-fives to everyone within reach. Right about the time tears began to well up in my eyes, I felt a nudge on the back of my thigh. Digger had broken loose from Frank and decided to join us in the middle of the diamond. Bending down to give him a hug gave me a chance to hide my tears and regroup. I stayed clutched to Digger for the better part of a minute until the worst had passed. Wiping my eyes on the sleeve of my jersey I popped back up to join the celebration. Looking around the mob scene it appeared as though no one had noticed. I plastered a smile back on my face and glanced over to the fence. There was Mom, gazing back at me through her own tears. She had noticed. She always noticed, and I realized that she was thinking the same thing I was. She smiled back to me and pointed skyward. I nodded back. *Yeah, Mom,* I thought to myself, *he never missed a pitch.*

My train of thought was interrupted by a tug on my arm. It was Frank, and he pointed toward home plate, saying, "Looks like you guys are grabbing all the hardware tonight." Sure enough, reluctantly trudging out to the mound holding the Stan Brophy Sportsmanship Trophy was Lloyd Deverman. I suppose after our gesture of fair play by toting Andrew Bell around the bases to tie the game, Lloyd felt he had little choice. The paper would surely have pictures of our goodwill tour in tomorrow's edition. As deeply as it must have pained him to turn over this award to the motley Moose squad, essentially his hands were tied. With a forced smile he offered the trophy out to a beaming Coach Sanders. Coach Sanders nearly had to pry it out of Deverman's hands, as it seemed he was beginning to have second thoughts on the matter. Once it was safely in Sanders's hands, Deverman winced a little as he muttered a terse congratulations before spinning on his heels and rushing off. More than likely, he was on his way to Kelly's for a stiff drink or two to wash the taste out of his mouth.

When Mom pulled into Hank's for our celebratory postgame ritual, the line was stretched clear around the block, so she promised to take both Frank and me to Chuck E. Cheese's tomorrow evening. "You can each bring a friend," she added.

"I'll call Nicky," Frank chimed in.

"What a surprise," Mom laughed. "How about you, Benny?"

"Yeah, big shot, who are you going to ask since your girlfriend's out of town?" Frank chided.

"She's not my girlfriend, you little dweeb," I shot back.

"Oh, really. Is that why you spend so much time gazing out your bedroom window toward her house every day?"

"For your information, nosy, I enjoy spending time appreciating the view from my window of the wooded nature trail and the brook that winds through it."

"Liar."

"Snoop."

With that Mom jerked the car off the road and onto the shoulder. Putting the station wagon in park, she spun around facing the back seat and gave us 'the gaze.'

"One more word out of either of you and Chuck E. Cheese's is out. We'll dine on beets and broccoli instead. Is that clear?"

The two of us nodded in unison. The thought of having to devour a beet was enough to make me hurl. And to Frank, broccoli was considered a vile weed. Once Mom continued driving, Frank crouched down slightly, enough to be out of sight of the rearview mirror, and commenced making faces at me in a taunting manner. I did the only thing a self-respecting older brother could do in this case. I slugged him in the arm. Wincing hard and wanting to rat me out, Frank thought better of it. Not willing to risk a pizza night out in favor of a face-to-face with a broccoli spear, he sucked it up and remained silent. It was Digger who stared back at me from his perch in the passenger side of the front seat. He was giving me his 'look.' His message, although not verbalized, was just as clear. Slugging Frank was not going to be tolerated.

Friday morning's *Glidden Gazette* was teeming with pictures and articles of Thursday night's event at the baseball complex. Plastered on the front page was a picture of the four of us toting Andrew Bell toward home plate. Mom raced out to buy a few extra copies to send to out-of-town relatives and friends. This was much better press than when I was being brought up on theft and assault charges. I couldn't recall offhand any extra newspaper purchases on her part during those dark days.

I called Denny to see if he'd seen the paper yet and to ask him to accompany us to Chuck E. Cheese that night. Since Denny didn't make the All Star team, hopefully this would help to take his mind off it for a night.

"It's not just the paper that got hold of it, Benny," he half shouted on the phone. "WGN radio in Chicago had a story about it this morning with call-ins and everything. I was checking out the pictures in the *Gazette* and of course you had the easy part. Holding and bending one leg while Derrick and I were busy breaking our backs hauling that big lug around the infield."

"Well, I heard that pizza is just the thing for an ailing back, so we'll pick you up at six," I said. As I focused on the picture of us crossing home plate, Knuckles' face could be seen in the background and the shot didn't do him justice. There was a defiant sourpuss look on his mug.

Saturday morning found me back at the Little League complex for our first all-star team practice. Looking around I was impressed with the talent on the squad. Between the twin towers of Zach and Zane and Derrick we had a dominant power-pitching staff. We also had another pitcher, Jaimie Hsu, who threw a lot of junk pitches, including a knuckle curve ball. Sprinkling Jaimie in occasionally with the heat of the other three could help to throw off the timing of our opponent's hitters. Behind the plate of course was Knuckles who was as fine (and ornery) as any catcher there was. Riley Slager would be our starting center fielder. Riley could cover a lot of ground and had a rifle for an arm. At shortstop was Benito Sanchez, who was as slick as they came with a glove. Rounding out the rest of the team was Caleb Haines, Blake Grogan, Malik Brown, and Lance Calhoun.

We had a pretty intense two-hour practice before Coach Shenberger sat us down and let us in on the upcoming schedule of events. One more practice on Tuesday evening and then our first game would be a home game against Naperville on Thursday. If we won that one, we would play in Rockford on Saturday. The first two games were single elimination, so there would be no room for error. Lose and we'd be done. After the first two games, the winner would advance from district to sectional. Our sectional was in Rock Island, where a pool play system would be used. From there was the state tournament, to be held in Springfield. The state tournament was a double-elimination system with the winner of state moving on to the Great Lakes Regional. Competing against Illinois would be the state champs from Michigan, Wisconsin, Ohio, Indiana, and Kentucky. The winner of the Great Lakes Regional would qualify for the Little League World Series, held in Williamsport, Pennsylvania. Teams from the United States and countries from around the globe would then fight it out in Williamsport for the world championship.

Riding my bike home after practice I had visions of spending the latter part of my summer vacation in Pennsylvania. Of course, it would take a miracle for little old Glidden to make it to the World Series, but without dreams, what good would life be?

chapter 37

ROCKY MOUNTAIN HIGH

E arly Sunday afternoon Tara called me from high atop a peak in Rocky Mountain National Forest.

"How is it I can travel halfway across the country and still not get away from you?" she asked. "Amber got a phone call from her aunt who lives in Chicago. She heard on the radio about some wholesome heroes in Glidden. Don't tell me that you were part of the posse of Moose misfits carting some injured kid around the bases. What's going on back there in Corn Corners?"

I explained to her the circumstances leading up to our noble deed. Naturally, she wasn't buying my version of how it was my idea to carry the injured boy around the bases in a show of true sportsmanship.

"How naive do you think I am? There's no way you'd ever risk blowing the five bucks we bet on the game. Your coach must have held a gun to your head."

"That'll teach you to wager your money against the Moose. The Moose rule. And don't get gobbled up by a bear or blow all your money in one of those tourist shops in Estes Park. I'll expect prompt payment upon your return. By the way, how did the Diamonds do on the field this weekend?"

"We took third place in nationals. We lost in the semis to a team from California that was scary good. I hit a two-run walk-off homer in the third-place game to beat a squad out of Odessa, Texas. That was pretty exciting. We're having a fantastic time out here and the mountains are gorgeous. An elk ran past our cabin this morning and a herd of bighorn sheep are parading down a path about fifty yards away as I speak. Gotta run but I'll see you in a couple of days. Give Rufus a big hug for me."

"Will do," I answered. It was really her I'd rather give a big hug to but it was probably best to keep those thoughts to myself.

Derrick and Denny joined Frank and me at the dog park Sunday evening. Digger and Rufus were creating their usual havoc by stealing tennis balls and sticks from some of the less-than-energetic canines in attendance. Denny told me that there was an article in the Sunday Chicago *Tribune* about our game Thursday night and how we were shining examples of fair play with a high moral compass. The article then compared our story with that of another Little League game played in Joliet last week. In that contest, there was an argument concerning the legality of a bat. It ended up with one coach pounding the bat over the head of the opposing coach. The injured coach ended up in the hospital while the other spent the night in the slammer.

That sounded a little like our first game this year against Helton's. Hopefully that little melee didn't get mentioned in the article. That revelation might serve to put a slight dent in our moral compass.

We had to drag Digger and Rufus away from the park about a half hour later. They were determined on staying all night, but Frank needed to hurry home to answer a nature call. And it was never good to fool with Mother Nature. As we approached the house, Mom came running out to greet us.

"You'll never guess who I just got off the phone with," Mom announced.

It could have been from Santa Claus for all Frank cared as he rushed past Mom and straight into the house to the nearest bathroom. Digger and Rufus weren't exactly on pins and needles, either. A squirrel went scurrying up a tree as they jumped and clawed after it in gleeful harmony. Unless one of them sprouted a pair of wings the squirrel was safe.

"A representative of the Cubs wants you, Derrick, Denny, and Alejandro to come to Wrigley Field next Sunday as their guests. Also the boy you carried around the bases. And get this. The five of you get to be on the field for batting practice and visit both clubhouses."

I couldn't believe my ears. What a dream come true. Maybe there was something to this sportsmanship business after all.

chapter 38

BUTTERFLIES

Following Tuesday evening's practice, we were issued our all-star uniforms: maroon jerseys with gold pants and black socks. The combination was downright hideous. Whatever genius picked out these threads either got a heck of a bargain or was color blind, I thought. During our team picture I trusted that the photographer was bright enough to go with a simple black-and-white print. The only consolation was the thought of the color scheme being such a distraction to our foes that it could work in our favor. No matter what, it wasn't likely that our opponents would soon forget such a blatant eyesore.

Rumor was circulating through the practice that Magoo would be behind the dish for Thursday night's matchup with Naperville. When asked about that possibility, Coach Shenberger chuckled for a moment before assuring us that would not be the case.

"Mr. McGruder was relieved of his duties last week. A performance-based analysis along with a finding of 'conduct unbecoming of a league official' were the reasons for dismissal," he replied.

On the way home after practice, Derrick and I came up with two schools of thought on the subject. The first was that Magoo enjoyed one too many frosty mugs at Kelly's last week and spouted off to Deverman. The second line of reasoning was the fear of the Naperville fans torching the Little League complex to the ground in response to perceived 'homering' calls in Glidden's favor from Magoo. Either way, it was too important a game to put in the hands of a loose canon like Magoo. Both teams deserved better.

When I got home, Mom made me put my uniform back on so she could take my picture. When I came downstairs to display the disastrous color combination, complete with the maroon ball cap with the gold "G" in the front, she just said, "Oh dear," and put down the camera. Frank thought the uniform was "really cool" and wanted one just like it. I told Frank we were looking for a batboy so he might just get his wish after all.

Before I could escape up the stairs to change, Tara came in the front door with the five dollars she owed me. One look at my get-up and she burst into laughter.

"Can I borrow your costume for Halloween?" she asked. "It certainly looks scary enough."

I snatched the five bucks out of her mitts and dashed back up the stairs before she could unleash any further insults in my direction. When I came back down after a quick change, Tara and Mom were still laughing while Frank wanted to know what was so funny.

On Thursday night, as game time approached, I was experiencing a major case of the butterflies—a combination of anxiety and nerves. When I spotted the lineup card that Shenberger posted, with me batting second in the lineup, the butterflies began to multiply rapidly. Frank, who was pulling batboy duties, was in hog heaven. To him, the uniform was "awesome" and he had the most important job in the world. While Frank got his last-minute instructions on the dos and don'ts of his duties, I took a minute to stroll down the fence line to where Mom and Digger were stationed. Digger raced over to the fence to issue me a few good-luck licks.

Noticing my nervousness, Mom simply smiled and said, "Take a deep breath, relax, and have fun. Let the other team do all the worrying. You just go out there and enjoy yourself."

By the time I headed back toward the team, the butterflies had disappeared and things were looking brighter. It was time to play ball. Before reaching the dugout, I passed Tara, who was accompanied by

Rufus and a couple of her friends. She motioned me over closer to her and gave me a quick scouting report on Naperville's starting pitcher, Joe Drabowski, who was warming up down the right field line. He was a big—in every way—right-hander.

"His fastball is pretty good," she started off. "He throws a curve ball but it doesn't break much. In fact, it just hangs there usually. Keep your hands back and wait for that hanger. You'll be able to do some damage to it if you're patient enough."

After thanking her, I ducked into the dugout to grab my mitt. Looking back at Tara as she walked away, I just shook my head and wondered why God would bestow such knowledge and understanding on a White Sox fan. It just didn't seem to make sense.

Zack mowed down the Naperville hitters 1-2-3 in the top of the first.

In the bottom of the first, Drabowski retired Benito on a pop-up to first. His first pitch to me was a fastball that I was late on. In fact, I think it was in the catcher's mitt before I finished my swing. I stepped out of the box and heard Frank's voice from the on-deck circle.

"Want a lighter bat, slugger?"

Not exactly the confidence boost I was hoping for at that moment. His next pitch was inside – another fastball. The third was also a fastball, and this time I was right on it and fouled it straight back. Now that I had my timing down on his hard stuff, it figured to be the perfect time for his curve. Choking up an inch on the bat and reminding myself to keep my hands back, I was ready. Sure enough, Drabowski came with his breaking ball and it hung right over the plate at the letters. I ripped a liner over the third baseman's head and down the left field line into the corner for a stand-up double. Standing on second and basking in the applause I made a mental note to treat Tara to a turtle sundae for her heads-up scouting report. Zack ripped a single to right on the first pitch and I scampered home without drawing a throw. Zane followed with a base on balls and the twins were brought home when Derrick sliced a double into the right field corner. The maroon and gold had a 3-0 lead, much to the delight of the hometown faithful.

The Naperville nine never got any closer from there on out. Zane's two-run homer in the bottom of the fifth was icing on the cake on the way to a 7-1 victory. I went two for three at the plate but booted a grounder in the third. Fortunately, Riley Slager made a circus catch in deep left center for the third out with two men on so the error didn't end up costing us any runs. Riley was probably due a frosty treat as well for bailing me out. When I got back to the dugout after that inning, Frank was hounding me.

"Keep your head down, Ben. You lifted your head up and that's why you fumbled it. How many times do I have to tell you? Watch the ball all the way into your glove, for crying out loud."

I was beginning to think that getting Frank the batboy gig wasn't such a good idea after all.

chapter 39
THE FARMER'S FIELD

At one o'clock on Saturday we squared off against a squad from Crystal Lake. The game was held in Rockford at a new facility on the banks of the Rock River. Crystal Lake's starting pitcher was a wily left-hander by the name of Ramon Gutierrez. Ramon threw most every pitch known to man or beast. He had us stymied for the better part of the first five innings. We managed to score just one run on him, but we led 1-0 going into the bottom of the fifth. With one out Zane walked their number-three hitter. The clean-up batter, a bruiser by the name of Herman Rollins, belted a moon shot over the center field fence to give Crystal Lake a 2-1 lead going into the final frame.

Coach Shenberger pulled us aside before our last at-bats and implored us to be patient and try to take Ramon deeper into the count.

"Draw a walk if you can. Make him come in with a fat one. Let's put some pressure on these guys."

Benito did just that. He worked the count full, fouled off a couple of pitches and drew a base on balls. I was up next. On a 2-2 pitch I laced a single into right field and Benito hoofed it to third. Ramon was starting to tire. Zane walked on four pitches and we had the bags full with nobody out.

The Crystal Lake manager paid a visit to the mound to check on his pitcher. With Zack due up, a left-handed batter, their skipper decided to go with the percentages and let Ramon stay in to work on Zack. Quickly falling behind 2-0, Ramon had to come in with a juicy one. Zack's eyes lit up like saucers when he saw the pitch coming in. He launched a blast way over the right field fence and out into the Rock River, where it narrowly missed an unsuspecting canoeist. The grand slam gave us a 5-2 lead.

Derrick closed them out in the bottom of the sixth with only one hit and we were on our way to the sectionals in Rock Island, which started next Tuesday.

Back in Glidden that evening, the town's annual weekend festival was going on. Rockford had an event called "On the Waterfront." Dixon had its "Petunia Festival." Geneva had "Swedish Days," while Glidden was home to "Corn Fest." Musical groups came from far and wide to perform at Glidden's Huntley Park band shelter. There were also carnival rides, food booths, beverage tents, T-shirt vendors, and dunk tanks spread throughout the downtown area, and of course, a giant corn boil.

Frank was bushed from all his batboy and waterboy chores. That and all the bragging he did on the ride home about how he out-did Crystal Lake's "slouch" of a batboy.

"Twice that slacker from Crystal Lake forgot to pick up their bats in between innings," he said. "I had to run them over to their dugout myself. One time he tried to retrieve a bat while the ball was still in play. That could have cost them an interference call and an automatic out."

About the third time he rehashed that story I leaned over and told him, "Put a sock in it, Francis."

He hated it when I called him Francis. He glared at me for a moment before continuing with the critique of his beleaguered counterpart.

"That clown even knocked their water jug over in the fourth inning and spilled half of it. Some of their catcher's gear got soaking wet."

I just hoped, for that kid's sake, the Crystal Lake catcher was more forgiving than Knuckles would have been under the same circumstances.

As I cleaned up and raided my lawn care savings fund for a night on the town, Mom and Frank decided to order a pizza and stay in and watch a movie on TV.

"Don't forget to take Digger for a walk before you leave, Ben," said Mom. "He missed you two today. The poor thing spent all afternoon lying by the front window just waiting for you guys to show up. I swear every time so much as a leaf blew by on our lawn, his ears perked up and he grabbed one of his tennis balls hoping it was the two of you returning. Then when he realized it wasn't either of you, he'd just slump back down like he'd just lost his best friend. Even a small dish of ice cream was barely enough to bring him out of the doldrums."

When I turned to look for Digger he was already standing by the front door with his leash in his mouth and his tail going a mile a minute. All it took for him was to hear the word "walk" and he got pumped up. I took him on a long tour of the 'hood as well as an excursion to the river. I let him off the leash near the river so that he could chase all the ducks and geese back into the water, thus restoring order. Digger's vision of world order called for ducks and geese to be either in the sky or on the water. Birds and squirrels belonged in trees. And any self-respecting rabbit spotted outside his warren was in violation of an understood agreement between dogs and rabbits. All dogs were ordained to immediately chase them back into the thicket and out of sight. No exceptions!

As I neared our house on the way back, I noticed Tara out in her back yard tossing a rubber ball across the lawn for Rufus to retrieve. Digger just naturally assumed he was invited to the ball-chasing game and all but dragged me across the front lawn and to their gate. Once inside, the two rascals tore after each other in an endless duel to steal the ball while periodically bushwhacking each other as well.

Tara informed me she was heading down to the Corn Fest and was looking forward to catching a blues band out of Chicago featuring Buddy Guy that was scheduled for nine o'clock at the main stage.

"Say Ben, I dug up some info at the animal shelter this morning you might be interested in. It concerns a certain stray by the name of Harvey that was brought in last year on Halloween."

That got my attention. She was referring to Digger.

"Let me see it," I anxiously requested.

"No can do. But I suppose I could read to you what the report said. The shelter got a call on Saturday afternoon on the thirty-first around four o'clock from a farmer a few miles north of town. He reported that there were two dogs in his field about 100 feet from the highway. One of the dogs was dead, he figured. Probably hit by a car. The other was nervously pacing around the body. There was a nasty-looking thunderstorm blowing in and the farmer was worried about the dog."

"By the time the shelter was able to get a couple of people out to the site, it was 4:30 and a wicked storm, complete with thunder, lightning, and heavy rain, had swept in. As the two volunteers, Maria Benson and Paul Anderson, approached the scene, they could see that indeed one of the dogs was deceased. The other canine, a rain-soaked beige short-hair shepherd mix, lay on top of his companion as if to shelter her from the storm. He appeared to be deeply agitated as well as severely undernourished."

"Once back at the shelter, Paul disposed of the deceased canine while Maria attended to the shepherd mix. After finally getting him settled down, she was able to administer some much-needed nourishment to him. Concerned for the state of his fragile health, she remained with him throughout the night. Maria was able to convince an acquaintance of hers, a veterinarian by the name of Michael Bloom, to stop by and check in on him Sunday morning."

Tara continued, "After checking the dog's vitals, Dr. Bloom was astounded the dog had survived the previous night's ordeal. Dr. Bloom spent the entire morning overseeing the necessary steps to increase the odds for survival. Maria spent another night with the dog. By

Monday morning, there was a marked improvement in the dog's vitals. The worst seemed to be over. Maria decided to name the dog after her favorite mixed drink during her college days: Harvey Wallbanger."

"I'm going to have to look up this Maria Benson," I said. "I hope she won't mind that we changed his name."

"Guess that goes a long way in explaining his fear of thunderstorms," Tara added. "No wonder he freaks out with any reminder of that horrible afternoon in the farmer's field. Too bad Digger can't talk. I'd love to know what the other dog meant to him. Possibly a sister. Maybe just a close companion."

"Whoever she was, she must have meant a lot to him," I said. "To be protecting her in those conditions, they must have been awfully tight. Looks like we'll never know."

Digger and Rufus were cooling their heels in the mini plastic pool. Exhausted and panting heavily, the two of them stared out at the rubber ball lying peacefully in the middle of the yard. Neither one had the energy to continue the game.

"Come on, you goofball," I said to Digger. "We gotta go home now. I've got a big night planned. Let's get going."

Digger's response to my request was to lie down in the pool and look disinterested. As I approached the pool trying to decide which tactic would be most effective in chasing him out of the water, the pizza delivery truck pulled up in front of our house. As the delivery man waltzed up to our front door, Digger bounded out of the pool, shook his excess water all over me and dashed to the gate. He looked back at me as if to say, "Hurry up, let's go already," and all I could offer was, "Now who's in a big hurry, your highness?"

Latching on his leash as we left the back yard I had to endure another parting shot from Tara.

"It appears as though he's got you well trained, Dork."

chapter 40

A NIGHT ON THE TOWN

It was almost eight o'clock by the time I caught up with Derrick and Denny. They were stationed next to the dunk tank on Second Street that was serving as a fundraiser for the Glidden school district. My timing couldn't have been better. Entering the cage and setting himself over the ice-cold water was none other than Principal Westmont. A near brawl ensued as the three of us stormed up to the front of the line for first crack at the suddenly nervous-looking victim. Paybacks were in order. Memories of his beaming smile as he taunted us with his knowledge of our trip to Wrigley Field last September came to mind. And there had been pure joy in his voice as he doled out the two-day suspension for our punishment. But that was then and this was now.

Derrick won honors for first shot at Westmont. His second toss hit dead center on the bull's eye and sent our esteemed tormentor tumbling into the tank. Denny was next up and nailed his first pitch. It took me three flings but I got the job done. By the time my throw sent him plunging into the frigid waters of the tank, Westmont's broad smile had been replaced with some noticeable shivers. As we gleefully departed the dunk tank area, we could hear the principal's outburst loud and clear.

"Enjoy the rest of your summer, boys. I'll be seeing the three of you in about a month."

His parting words didn't exactly come out as a warm and friendly invitation. Our best hope for a peaceful school year hinged on his possessing a short memory.

Our next stop was the carnival. I tried to lobby for a race on the go-cart track. But Derrick and Denny were psyched up for the Gravitron. I balked at the idea of getting on a ride that went round and round like the Gravitron. When I was about six, I hopped on a merry-go-round at Shipman Park and was never so sick in my life.

"Nah, you two go ahead. I'll wait for you over by the elephant ears stand."

"What's the matter, Ben, you scared?" chided Denny.

Figuring that I'd outgrown my motion sickness, and against my better judgment, I gave in and agreed to give it a try. By the second rotation it was clear I'd made a huge mistake. By the fifth twirl, I was screaming to no one in particular to stop and let me off. By the time the nightmare known as the Gravitron came to a stop, I welcomed death. Stumbling down the ramp like a pinball being bounced between bumpers, I desperately searched for an isolated area to get sick. Luckily there was a narrow, deserted alleyway located only about fifty feet from ground zero. I barely made it before the hurling began. My big night out on the town lasted all of twenty minutes. What a chump.

As I stood up and started to formulate my exit strategy I heard from behind me a familiar voice.

"You don't look so good, Davies. What happened? A bad ear of corn or something?"

Standing a few feet away with a beer in one hand and a cigarette in the other was my old pal John Nestor.

"No, just that stupid Gravitron. I should have known better."

"Well it kicked your butt, that's for sure. I appreciate you not mentioning to anyone about those two lucky punches you landed on me a couple months back. Let bygones be bygones?"

If John had had a free hand I'd have been more than glad to shake on that because the last thing I was in need of right then was a pummeling.

Nestor offered to escort me home through a series of back alleys and side yards that allowed us to avoid the majority of Corn Fest revelers. In my sickened state that was fine with me. And John wasn't too eager to draw attention to himself and his beer, either. I asked John how his summer was going.

"It sucks," he replied. "My old man ran off again in early June. Nobody's seen or heard from him since. My old lady got popped for a DUI Wednesday night and was court-ordered into rehab. DCFS stepped in and split up my brothers and me into two different foster homes. Other than that, everything's just peachy."

After hearing John's grim account of his summer vacation, my temporary predicament didn't seem nearly as dire.

"Don't you have any relatives who can help you out?"

"Yeah, I got an uncle who lives in Arizona that says I could stay with him. But he only has room for me. Steve and Freddy would still be stuck here."

As we approached my house I wished him good luck and asked him where he was going next. He took one last swig of his Old Style, tossed me the empty can, lit up another cigarette and told me he was heading over to the sound stage at Huntley Park to catch the blues bands and scout out the chicks.

My only wish was that one of the chicks wasn't Tara. On my way across the front lawn, Digger caught sight of me from his perch and announced my arrival. Before I could ditch the empty beer can in the bushes, the front door swung open and there stood Mom with her mouth agape and fire in her eyes.

"Benjamin Thomas Davies! Is that a beer can in your hand? You look like death warmed over."

Rushing out in an attempt to usher me inside before the neighbors could get a good look at my unfortunate state, she glanced back over her shoulder and pleaded, "I only pray that no one witnessed my twelve-year-old alcoholic stumbling past their house."

"I wasn't drinking, Mom," I started, but then round two of the turmoil in my stomach began to erupt.

Frank took one look at me and declared, "You are so grounded, dude." I couldn't even muster a response as I brushed past him on my way to the bathroom. The last thing I heard from him before closing the door was, "You are so dead." So much for some much-needed comfort and support from my lawn maintenance assistant. As I finished emptying the contents of my belly it came to mind that the raise I promised to Frank last week might have to be put on hold for a while.

By the time I washed my face and brushed my teeth it was back into the lion's den. Mom's mood had changed from being really mad to genuinely worried. She chased Frank from the living room with instructions to go upstairs to his room. Of course there was no doubt in my mind that he and Digger had stationed themselves at the top of the stairs just out of eyesight but not out of earshot. He wasn't about to miss out on the main event. I'm sure he was anticipating a severe tongue-lashing. For once I hadn't done anything wrong but the evidence was stacked against me. I could really use my lawyer, Richard Petrino, right about now.

Before Mom could start in on me, the phone rang. She picked it up in the next room and I heard her say, "Yes, he is, but no, you can't talk to him right now." The rest of the conversation was too muffled to catch anything after she closed the door behind her. I glanced up to the top of the stairs where Frank and Digger were huddled together in anticipation of the upcoming fireworks.

Upon returning to the 'courtroom' she announced, "That was Derrick. He was concerned that you seemingly disappeared following a ride on the Gravitron. He and Denny looked all over for you but came up empty. He implied that you had reservations about the ride beforehand and the two of them felt guilty about goading you into it. I grilled him about the alcohol but he insisted that you weren't drinking while you three were together. So please explain yourself, Benjamin."

I told her of the hasty exit from the horrors of the Gravitron and my encounter with John Nestor in the alley. I related to her John's nightmarish summer of family problems and probable separation from his two brothers. By the time I got to the empty beer can she was more concerned about John's dilemma than about my motion sickness.

"I'll get you a ginger ale, Benny, and if you can hold that down we'll see about some buttered toast. And we'll include the Nestor family in our prayers tomorrow at church."

Glancing up the stairs I could see a visibly disappointed look on Frank's face. He had psyched himself up to witness a severe beat-down only to see it fizzle out prematurely.

As Frank and Digger descended the stairs he said, "I thought you were a goner, Ben, but you somehow managed to skate again. Want some pizza?"

The last thing in the world I needed right then was pizza.

"No, Frank, go right ahead. It's all yours." By the time Mom came back with my ginger ale the pizza was history.

"I'm sorry your Corn Fest evening turned out to be such a disaster, Ben," said Mom. "But at least this way, maybe you'll get a good night's sleep for the big day tomorrow at Wrigley Field."

The thought of all the plans I had for tomorrow brightened my outlook immediately. Maybe I'd try some of that toast now.

Following eight o'clock Mass Sunday morning, Denny's dad came rolling into the driveway. Derrick's father was also joining us as an extra chaperone. Another set of eyes to keep the four of us in line was probably a good idea. Andrew Bell couldn't make the trip. His ankle wasn't healed sufficiently to handle all the walking and stair climbing that was in store for us that day. Mom gave me a hug and told me that Frank and she would be watching the game on TV. She reminded me to behave myself (for a change), and stay out of trouble (if at all possible).

Frank added, "Don't mess up, Ben, and be sure to get me plenty of autographs."

I thanked them for their encouraging remarks and dashed out to the car. There seemed to be a general lack of confidence on the home front.

Once we had parked and arrived at the Player's Gate, a young man by the name of Jerry escorted us directly onto the field, where the Cardinals were having batting practice. It was really something to witness up close some of the tape-measure home runs flying out of the park.

Part of our game-day experience also included a visit to each team's locker room prior to the game. I had my Sharpie packed among the various team photos and individual shots of the Cubs and Cards, along with strict instructions from all concerned. Frank wanted Rick Monday's and Bill Madlock's autographs. Mom wanted me to hit up Jose Cardenal and Bruce Sutter. Tara's favorite was Cardinal outfielder Lou Brock. Vera was insistent I procure, at the very least, Rick Reuschel and Ernie Banks. Nora made it clear that I needn't bother to return without Keith Hernandez's and Ted Simmons's John Hancocks in tow.

In the St. Louis dressing room we had the good fortune to run into Red Schoendienst, the Redbirds' manager. He happened to be very friendly and as it turned out, quite a dog lover. When I told him about Digger and how I came to bust him out, Red's eyes lit up. We must have talked dog stories for ten minutes before his batting coach finally dragged him away.

Over in the Cubs locker room, Denny and Derrick tracked down Mr. Cub, Ernie Banks. Jerry arranged for them to get their picture taken with him. It's not every day you can get your picture taken with a Hall of Famer. Before leaving the dressing room, Alejandro received some batting tips from his hero, Manny Trillo. Being as Alejandro idolized Manny, it must have been a special moment for the young Moose shortstop.

For the game itself, the Cubs set us up with box seats right behind the Cubs dugout. The action on the field was also quite pleasant as the Cubs took a 4-1 lead into the seventh. But with two out, Cub starter Steve Stone began to tire. A walk, a single, and a homer tied it up quickly. This didn't go over too well with Stone, who took out his frustration on the next batter, Ted Simmons, by plunking him with a fastball to the rib cage. With Simmons writhing in pain at the plate, both benches emptied out onto the field and a full-blown melee erupted. Fortunately baseball players aren't particularly adept at fighting, so most of the punches found nothing but air. Several other combatants wrestled each other harmlessly to the ground while a few simply pointed fingers and acted tough.

I had to laugh to myself at the thought of the scene unfolding right then at the Wiswalls'. Poor Ksenia was certainly up to her elbows trying to separate Vera and Nora. It wouldn't be an enviable task dodging walkers and ducking flying canes while attempting to settle the two of them down during the heat of battle. Ksenia would be safer on the field in the middle of one of the pile-ups than in the Wiswall living room trying to mediate a settlement.

Eventually the tussling on the field calmed down and order was restored. The home-plate umpire sent both managers and a player from each team to an early shower.

While the Cubs new reliever was being brought in, Jerry had a tray of hot dogs and Cokes sent down to us. There was no doubt we were getting the royal treatment at the "friendly confines." A Rick Monday

RBI triple in the eighth was just enough to lead the Cubbies to a narrow 5-4 victory.

After the game, we were allowed access to the Cubs dugout, where Jerry introduced us to longtime Cub catcher Randy Hundley. Randy congratulated us on our show of true sportsmanship in carrying an injured player around the bases and noted how that differed greatly from what we had witnessed on the diamond during the seventh inning. When he asked me about it, I pointed out that the Moose squad wasn't always so well-behaved either. I related several of our episodes, including the fracas that broke out against Helton's, and the game against the Fire when Andre pretended to jinx their bats with magic voodoo dust. Hundley was in stitches, and being a catcher himself, particularly enjoyed the stories that included Knuckles. I mentioned that Knuckles could be a little temperamental on occasion. When he asked me what Knuckles was doing as we carted Andrew around the bases, I answered, "He was standing in the batter's box trying to figure out which one of us he was going to punch out first when we reached home plate."

Hundley looked back at Jerry and asked him, "Are you sure you got the same four boys who were here for their outstanding sportsmanship qualities?"

As we were being herded out of the dugout a little later, I could hear Hundley mention to Mr. Woodson, "I've got to meet this Knuckles character. He sounds like my kind of ballplayer."

chapter 41

STATE CHAMPS

The Glidden All Stars took to the field Tuesday evening in Rock Island for our quest to advance from the sectional level to the state finals in Springfield the following week. Malik Brown's two-run homer in the second got us rolling and we finished with a 6-2 victory. Coach Shenberger did a masterful job of limiting the pitch count for Zack and Zane by utilizing all four of our main pitchers, thus allowing him to bring the Twin Towers back again for the next game, which was Thursday afternoon.

Derrick was the big star Thursday afternoon against Moline with a double and a three-run blast in leading us to a 7-4 victory. I chipped in with a single, a walk, and a stolen base. But my best move of the day was in saving Knuckles from certain expulsion following a questionable call at home plate. Knowing his explosive demeanor all too well, I recognized his intention to storm the umpire. Racing down the line, I was able to sidle in front of Knuckles just in the nick of time to defuse the probable eruption. Meanwhile, Assistant Coach Richardson was able to distract the ump with some disparaging remarks and ended up getting tossed for his efforts. We could survive without an assistant coach for the rest of the game, but catchers like Knuckles didn't just grow on trees.

Friday's game didn't turn out nearly as well. Derrick didn't have his best stuff and the Galesburg offense battered him around pretty hard. Shenberger couldn't use either of the Twin Towers because of pitch counts and he didn't want to waste an opportunity to use Jaimie Hsu if he had to in the decisive game on Saturday, so he turned to me to pitch the final two frames. I held them to four runs and the final score was 14-6. That set up a winner-take-all rematch the following night against Galesburg.

A big crowd was on hand for Saturday night's championship showdown. A lot of familiar faces from Glidden were in attendance, including Mom and Digger. Mom had even planned a picnic for the four of us earlier in the day at a park on the banks of the mighty Mississippi River. We had such a good time playing Frisbee with Digger and watching all the activity on the river that I almost forgot that we had a game to play. Looking out at the huge barges and other boats was a far cry from standing on the edge of the Blackhawk River that flowed through Glidden. The largest watercraft I had ever seen navigating 'the Hawk' was a three-man canoe. There were even two eagles soaring above the river, which added to the scenery. Digger noticed the eagles and raced along the edge of the river barking futilely at the magnificent birds of prey.

As we concluded our pregame warm-ups that evening, I had a good feeling about our chances. Many of the Galesburg players looked overconfident after the spanking they had given us the day before. They must have felt any team with such hideous uniforms could hardly be taken seriously. But we possessed two decided advantages. First, they'd never faced the Bowers Brothers before. And second, their best pitcher was used up from yesterday's game.

I started off the top of the first with a double to right center and by the time I batted again, still in the top of the first, seven runs had already crossed the plate. Mercifully for Galesburg there was a 10-run "slaughter rule" so the game went just four innings and we celebrated our 14-1 sectional championship victory with a pizza party in downtown Rock Island. Coach Shenberger later remarked that he couldn't believe that Frank had devoured more slices of pizza than Knuckles. I wasn't surprised in the least.

The team's next challenge was the state finals in Springfield. The competition had definitely moved up a notch. The coaches impressed upon us the importance of mental toughness at this level.

"There aren't many glaring weaknesses in any of these teams down here," Shenberger stated. "The team that keeps their heads in the game at all times will make less mistakes. And it's mistakes that lose games. So let's bear down and win this thing."

The state tourney was a simple double elimination set-up. Lose two games and you go home. Our first match up was against a scrappy team from Champaign. They loved to bunt and slap it around. Stealing bases was also a big part of their offense. They tended to be very aggressive on the bases. Their style was termed "small ball." Being the third baseman was a demanding position with this lineup. I wanted to creep in to make the play on bunts but if one crept too close against this team, he was likely to get the ball knocked down his throat.

For the most part we were able to keep them off the bases. The few of Champaign's finest that did reach base were promptly cut down trying to steal by Knuckles. Rafael Salazar's two-out double in the fourth brought home Lance Calhoun and Blake Grogan. Zane's towering two-run homer in the fifth gave us some insurance in a 4-0 victory.

Next on the docket was a squad from Lockport. They had a couple of bruisers in the middle of their lineup that went yard on Derrick, but both were solo shots. Derrick was able to pitch his way out of a couple of jams with the help of two defensive gems. The first was an over-the-shoulder snag by Benito Sanchez on a Texas-leaguer with two on and two out in the third. Caleb Haines cut down a Lockport runner at the plate on a perfect one-hopper from right field to end the fourth. Zane cracked a three-run shot in the third. Malik Brown followed with a two-run dinger in the same inning. Jaimie set down Lockport 1-2-3 in the bottom of the sixth to preserve a 5-3 victory.

The following afternoon our team celebrated our off day with a trip to the Abraham Lincoln Museum. I thought it was pretty cool, but Frank soon tired of all the culture that wasn't to his liking. Claiming to be feeling a little under the weather, he convinced Coach Richardson to escort him back to the hotel so that he could lie down. Not trusting Frank for a minute to go back to our room and rest up, I accompanied him. As it turned out, several other culturally challenged players decided to join us and return to the hotel.

Once back in our room, Frank miraculously recovered from his illness and within a matter of seconds had donned his swimming trunks and gone racing down the hallway in the direction of the swimming pool. I almost felt sorry for the unsuspecting sunbathers and other pool denizens who were about to have their peace and quiet shattered by the whirling dervish menace barreling toward them.

By the time I got my suit on and reached the pool, Frank was in true form. The majority of poolside patrons were amused at the 50-pound dynamo and his antics. On the other hand, several others did not appear to be thoroughly delighted. Just as I was settling into a lounge chair to catch a couple rays, Frank made his biggest gaffe. An elderly woman sporting a recent perm was innocently bobbing in the shallow end when Frank decided to execute one of his infamous cannonballs.

The unfortunate lady's perm was drenched with the aftermath of his splashdown. Cursing and glaring at Frank, she made her way toward him, determined to give him a piece of her mind. Seeing the fire in her eyes, Frank quickly submerged himself and fled to the safety of the deep end.

Cornering him near the diving board I warned him, "Cool your jets, Frank, you're going to get us kicked out if you don't settle down. I'll get you a Snickers bar from the vending machine if you promise to behave."

The candy bar bribe seemed to do the trick as Frank calmed down considerably and only posed a mild nuisance the remainder of the afternoon. The rest of the team eventually filtered down to the pool and essentially chased the remaining seniors to the safety of dry land and eventually into the hotel lounge for happy hour refreshments.

Following a relaxing afternoon around the pool, a majority of the team drifted inside to the Jungle, the hotel's awesome game room. The Jungle had numerous pinball games, a pool table, two foosball machines and an impressive-looking air hockey table. Lance Calhoun and I teamed up to form a dominating foosball tandem. We remained undefeated throughout the evening.

I'd gotten to know Lance pretty well as the team proceeded through the district and sectional tournaments. But when we arrived in Springfield, I noticed that he seemed unusually quiet.

"Cat got your tongue, Lance?" I remarked after a lengthy silent spell.

"No, it's my folks. They're splitting up. Dad moved out last week and Mom's already hired a lawyer. My home life has turned into a real bummer, Ben."

"I'm sorry to hear that," was all I could muster up. Hopefully, the baseball tournament and goofing around the motel would serve as a distraction for Lance. He seemed to have a lot on his mind concerning his parents' breakup.

The next day it was back to business. Our third game of the state tourney pitted us against Evanston. We started off sluggishly and Evanston jumped off to a 3-0 lead after two innings. But the big bats got going for Glidden in the top of the third. The big blow was a bases-clearing double, compliments of Derrick. The final score was 7-4. The best part of it was that after three rounds, we were the only team without a loss.

After another off day, we faced Decatur. One more victory and the state title was ours. Decatur's squad looked a bit worn down from surviving the qualifying games just to get a shot at us. It showed on the field as we scored in all but one inning on our way to a 9-1 rout. The governor was in attendance and presented us with the State of Illinois Little League championship trophy. The trophy itself was magnificent, but even more so was the awesome feeling that little old Glidden would be representing the Land of Lincoln in the next leg of the journey on the road to Williamsport. At first I was very impressed that the governor was going to shake hands with each of us. That was until I saw the Sox hat he was wearing. My excitement level dropped a few notches upon seeing the black ball cap with the Sox emblem. When it was my turn to shake hands with him, I mentioned to him that a blue hat would go a long way in making him appear much younger-looking to the voters. He didn't appear to appreciate my sense of humor in the least. The grip on his handshake with me was a tad stronger than necessary.

chapter 42

RETURN THE FAVOR

With a week separating us from our trip to Indianapolis for the Great Lakes Regional, it was nice for Frank and me to squeeze in some playtime with Digger between our lawn jobs. Trips to the dog park and the river were often followed by a stopover at Hank's. Digger didn't exactly have to be dragged kicking and screaming to any of those haunts. On Wednesday we kidnapped Rufus, too, and made the hike to the county animal shelter to surprise Tara for lunch. Digger was a little leery at first—maybe he was afraid we were returning him. But he settled down quickly and began frolicking with Rufus and a couple of the residents.

I knew it was Tara's birthday, her fourteenth, so when nosy Frank was busy settling a dispute between Rufus and a cocker spaniel, I slipped her a gift certificate to Glidden's local cinema, the Egyptian Theater.

"Thanks, Benny," she said and gave me a hug. "You didn't have to do this."

"Well, I'm not much for baking cakes, and figured I couldn't go wrong with a movie and a box of popcorn."

"Your birthday's coming up next month, isn't it? Just think, a teenage Benjamin. Now there's a scary thought. I hate to think of your poor mother, though. She'll have a full head of gray by the time you finish your teenage years."

On the way home Frank asked me, "How did she like her present, Romeo?"

"Shut up, Squirt. You know, if you paid half as much attention in school as you do to my personal affairs, you just might get decent grades once in a while."

220 Digging for Home

"Say, Digger, I think I touched a nerve in Benny, what do you think?"

But Digger was too occupied escorting a squirrel back to his tree to give it much thought. As far as I was concerned, it was worth catching some minor grief from Frank in exchange for a hug from Tara.

As I tried to coax Digger and Rufus away from the treed squirrel and back on the trail, Frank had managed to drift ahead of us. By the time I'd gotten their leashes back on them, I noticed Frank standing near the street, talking to someone in a white van. As I quickened our pace to catch up with him, the van pulled away.

"Who were you talking to, Frank?"

"Oh, just some guy looking for directions to Sears. He seemed real friendly. He even mentioned that my ball cap reminded him of a hat he wore when he was my age."

All right, now I was officially creeped out.

"Frank, don't ever stop to talk to a stranger in a car. Haven't you ever heard that speech before?"

"It was a van. And he wasn't offering me any candy or anything."

"It doesn't matter. Promise me right now you'll never do that again."

"Don't have a cow, Benny. OK, I promise."

Maybe I was overreacting, but the rest of the way home I kept glancing over my shoulder to see if that creepy white van was following us. By the time we reached home, I was a nervous wreck.

That evening, Mrs. Mangolin stopped over and kidnapped Mom.

"You need to get out, Suzy. I have an extra ticket to *Fiddler on the Roof* tonight at Middleton Community College and you're going. You need to get out so we've planned a ladies' nights out. We're having dinner at Rosales Mexican restaurant, complete with margaritas. Of course you'll be relegated to virgin margaritas, but your ticket is free and there will be no debate. Ksenia and Lacy Halverson will be joining us for the evening."

Mom was a little nervous about leaving Frank and me alone for an entire evening, but the thought of having a night out with the ladies to enjoy hours of adult conversation was too appealing to pass up.

"Will you boys be OK?" she inquired.

"Don't worry about us," I answered. "What possible trouble could we could get into in such a short time?"

That comment was not well received and she immediately announced that she wasn't going out. It took everything Tara's mother could muster to convince Mom that everything would be all right and that Tara would be right next door to assure safety and compliance with any ground rules Mom wished to enforce. And with Digger standing guard, we were as safe as possible. Begrudgingly, Mom agreed and off they went.

If anyone deserved a night out it was Mom. Between the tragic loss of Dad and all the financial problems she'd been facing lately, just the thought of spending an evening conversing with adults and away from the horrors of dealing with the likes of Frank and yours truly must have seemed too good to be true.

Later that night as I was nodding off, Mom dropped into my room and plopped on my bed. I pretended to be asleep as she stroked my hair. "I'm the luckiest mother in the world," she whispered to me. "Thank God for you and Frankie. After Dad was gone I was feeling sorry for myself and those worthless pills I was taking were making things worse. That night I told you we couldn't afford to bring a dog into our life, I couldn't sleep. Something, or someone, drove me down the hallway to check in on you boys. Once I saw the two of you sleeping peacefully, like a couple of angels, I rushed back to my room and flushed those dreadful pills down the toilet. And to think that I happened to be pregnant at the time and was unknowingly endangering my baby. I'm so sorry. I love you so much, Benny. Please forgive me."

There was no way I was going to acknowledge my awareness of this confession. My mother had just unloaded an enormous burden off her chest to what she assumed was a sleeping lug. I wanted to wrap my arms around her and tell her how much I loved her and the baby she was carrying, but it would have given me away and embarrassed her in the process.

However, as she waddled toward the door I rolled over and tried my best to appear as though I had just awakened. "I love you too, Mom."

The following Tuesday morning, the Glidden Little League All Stars set off for the Hoosier state. We checked into a Holiday Inn only minutes from the ball field. Living the good life wasn't such a bad thing.

Our first opponent in the double-elimination regional was a squad from Appleton, Wisconsin, representing the Badger State. They had a hard-throwing right-hander by the name of Logan Mueller. In the top of the first, I reached on a bunt, scooted to third on a single to right, and scored on a sacrifice fly to deep left off Zack's bat. They countered with single runs in the third and fourth to take a 2-1 lead.

In the fifth, a leadoff walk to Riley Slager started a big inning for us. A couple of singles tied it up and with two out the big blow was a three-run dinger to right field from Caleb Haines. In the bottom of the sixth, things got a little nervous. Back-to-back doubles made it 5-3. A single with two outs got Appleton within a run. That brought up their clean-up hitter, Dominic Boykin. He sent the first pitch from Zane high and deep to dead center field. Riley drifted all the way to the fence and with his back firmly pressed against it watched the ball land safely in his glove. It took a few seconds for all of us to get our hearts back out of our throats, but once we were able to exhale, it set off a wild celebration.

Back at the hotel, we got a little too boisterous and the management instructed us to all return to our rooms. Once back in our rooms, however, the noise level steadily began to increase, prompting a visit by hotel security. Coach Shenberger called us all together for a brief meeting.

"If I get one more complaint or hear so much as a pin drop the rest of the night, I'll order the bus driver to take us back to Glidden tomorrow morning. Any questions?"

One hand shot up.

"What is it, Frank?"

"Does that include snoring?"

"*Yes!*"

Apparently no one snored too loudly because the following day the bus took us over to the field for a light morning workout. Our opponent Wednesday evening was from Lexington, Kentucky. They had lost their opening-round game to a very impressive squad from Hamilton, Ohio. The Hamilton players arrived in a large, air-conditioned coach bus. The kind a college football team travels in. All the players had their own sleek-looking color-coordinated bat bags, complete with the player's name and uniform number stitched on the side. This was definitely not their first rodeo.

The Hamilton followers were in the parking lot the previous night when we pulled in, because their game against Lexington preceded ours. I was sure that one look at our traveling accommodations (a yellow school bus), our hideous gold-and-maroon uniforms, and our ragtag equipment bags gave them a wonderful impression of us. As we headed up the ramp to the complex they must have half expected that our coaches would be wearing bib overalls with the Salvation Army band following up close behind.

Nevertheless, baseball games aren't won on style points but on great pitching, solid defense, and timely hitting. That we had plenty of.

After a little batting practice and some fielding drills, it was back to the hotel with strict orders from Shenberger: No swimming or running around.

Our game against Lexington that evening started out well. Scoring three runs in the bottom of the first and two more in the second we held a 5-0 lead after two innings. But the lads from the Blue Grass State weren't about to go home quietly. They struck for four runs off Derrick in the third and managed two unearned runs in the fourth following a rare throwing error from Benito Sanchez with two outs. Knuckles cranked a solo homer to left in the bottom of the fifth to tie it up. Jaime Hsu was brought in to pitch the top of the sixth and wriggled out of a tight jam to keep it knotted up entering the bottom of the sixth.

I led off the bottom of the sixth. After fouling off several tough pitches from a lanky left-hander by the name of Herman Clay, I coaxed a walk. His first pitch to Derrick was in the dirt, and the catcher couldn't find the handle on it so I raced into second without a throw. On Derrick's ground-out to second I easily took third. With the Twin Towers due up, the Lexington coach decided to walk them both and hope for a force out at home or a double play. That brought Riley up to bat. With the Lexington coach going over his defensive alignment, Coach Richardson huddled up with Riley and me. When he told us to execute the squeeze play, we thought he was nuts. But he explained that the lefty, Clay, fell off the mound to the third base on his follow-through and it left a hole between the mound and first base. On top of that, Riley was the team's best bunter and was sure to get a strike on the first pitch with the bases being full. Clay couldn't afford a walk and certainly didn't want to fall behind on the count. The strategy made Coach Richardson look like a genius. Riley placed Clay's get-ahead fast ball just about twenty feet in front of the plate halfway between the mound and the foul line. The only person who had a chance at it was their first-sacker, whose desperation shovel toss bounced in late and wide. As I slid safely past the frustrated catcher, the Glidden team stormed the field. We were a step closer to our dream, while the disgruntled Lexington squad was heading back to their "old Kentucky home."

Thursday's contest was against the home state Hoosiers from Ft. Wayne. Ft. Wayne was 1-1 thus far, so they also were facing elimination with a loss. But the Ft. Wayne nine had their hitting shoes on and jumped on Jaime for seven runs after three innings. With us trailing 7-2, Coach Shenberger, after reviewing the modified pitch counts for the regional series, decided it might be best to sacrifice this game in order to save more innings for our big three pitchers. He sent me to the mound for the fourth and fifth innings. Some outstanding defensive plays kept the game respectable but even after a top-of-the-sixth rally that netted us three runs, the final score was 12-6. The Hoosiers remained alive and now our backs were against the wall too.

Friday's game against Lansing, Michigan, was a barnburner. The wind was howling out to left field and the Lansing boys had some boys in their lineup that could poke it. Fortunately, so did we. When my high fly in the top of the sixth carried over the fence it was Glidden's sixth home run of the night. Lansing had four blasts of their own, but when the dust had finally settled, we'd captured the slugfest 14-11. Lansing, who had defeated powerful Hamilton the night before, was going home. That left us to face Hamilton Saturday night with a trip to Williamsport on the line.

The first thing I noticed when we reached the complex Saturday was the TV truck. Several vans with TV emblems were also present throughout the parking lot. By game time, the stands were packed and a sizeable group was stationed on the berm surrounding the outfield fence. A large contingent of Hamilton folks could be spotted in the crowd. It was comforting to see that plenty of familiar faces from Glidden had also made the jaunt to Indianapolis.

In the top of the first, I led off by bouncing back to the mound. Derrick was retired on a routine fly to right. With two dead, Zack ripped a single to center and Zane brought the Glidden fans to their feet with a towering homer to left center. Hamilton threatened in almost every inning but some highlight-reel defensive gems from Benito at shortstop squelched the Buckeyes' chances for some big innings. At the end of five innings, Hamilton led 5-3.

Benito started us off with a bunt single in the top of the sixth. Knuckles rapped a single to left and we had the tying runs on base. Caleb's sacrifice bunt moved them both into scoring position. Malik Brown was up next and his high fly to right center brought Benito home to make it 5-4, but it also was our second out. With Knuckles on second, two out and the season on the line, it was my turn to step to the plate. To say that I was nervous would be a gross understatement. The Hamilton coach came out to make a pitching change. Just what I needed—more time to worry. While the new pitcher threw his warm-ups, I strolled over to the dugout. Frank was there with a huge grin on his mug.

"Tell you what, Ben. Get a hit here and I'll forgive you for scarfing down the last fudge bar out of our mini fridge last night."

I was about to argue that he'd already gobbled up four bars out of the six-pack, but then realized he was only trying to distract me from the pressure I was feeling.

With a 1-1 count I took a cut at the pitch on the outside corner. It was nearly off the end of the bat but it floated out to right center and fell safely to the grass. The right fielder tried to nail Knuckles at the plate but his throw tailed up the third baseline. Knuckles slid into home with the tying run as I took second on the play at the plate. I tried to act calm taking in the scene in the dugout and the stands, but my heart felt like it was going to jump out of my chest. Derrick followed with a line drive single to center, which brought me home with the leading run.

Zack grounded out to end the inning. We needed three more outs to earn a trip to Pennsylvania.

No one expected Hamilton to go quietly into the night. They were too good a team for that. The first batter Derrick faced singled sharply in the hole between Benito and me. The second hitter rocketed a one-hopper off Derrick's glove and into foul territory for another single. Their next batter tried to advance both runners into scoring position with a bunt but Derrick hopped on it and fired to me at third for the force out. The next kid rifled a blue dart to right field. Luckily, it was right at Rafael Salazar, and we had two outs. The next batter, a stout left-hander, pulled two pitches deep down the right field line but foul. On a 3-2 pitch, Derrick lost him with an outside pitch that almost evaded Knuckles. Bases loaded, two outs and Hamilton's first baseman, Nate Bolton, was digging in at the plate.

Shenberger called time and called us in to the mound. Derrick and Knuckles were pretty cool customers, but all four of us infielders had lumps in our throats the size of apples.

"Just relax, everyone. We've got a force at every base so don't panic. If you can't field the ball cleanly, at least knock it down and keep it in the infield." Turning to Derrick, he added, "Three strikes and we're going to Williamsport. Go get 'em."

With the count 2-2 after throwing four straight fastballs, Derrick threw Bolton an off-speed pitch. Fooled by the pitch, Bolton swung awkwardly and the ball went off the tip of the bat. It snaked along the ground toward second baseman Lance Calhoun with an incredible amount of topspin on it. As Lance went to field it, the ball, which clearly had a mind of its own, managed to evade his glove and scoot right through his legs and onto the outfield grass. With one run in, the boy coming from second never slowed down as he rounded third and headed for home. Lance dashed out into short right, grabbed the evil orb, spun around and fired a perfect one-hopper to Knuckles. The runner beat the throw to the plate but Knuckles had it blocked. At least that's the way I saw it. And so did most everybody else. The only person that really mattered, however, to the dismay and chagrin of the Glidden faithful, flattened out his palms, ruling the runner safe.

Just like that, the dream was over. The Hamilton players and coaches swarmed onto the field. Knuckles went toe-to-toe with the ump, pointing to where the runner was stopped short of the plate. Shenberger and Richardson charged out of the dugout to vent their anger at the man in blue. Derrick, usually not one to blow his top, was screaming at the top of his lungs at the beleaguered ump. Even Frank got into the act by questioning the umpire on the results of his most recent eye exam.

Not knowing if I wanted to cry or cuss, I looked out into short right field where the loneliest boy in the world knelt down crying his eyes out. Feeling like we were well-represented in the admonishing of the umpire, I jogged out to where Lance was.

I'd gotten to know Lance pretty well over the last few weeks. With his parents' recent split-up, the last thing he needed right then was a guilt trip over missing a grounder that cost us a trip to Williamsport. Remembering how horrible I felt curled up in my room last winter, and how good it felt to have someone to put their arm around me and offer some kind words, I figured it was time for me to return the favor.

Grabbing his hand, I helped him to his feet. Putting an arm around his shoulder I told him, "That ball would have squirmed through any of our legs. You made a great recovery and that throw to the plate was perfect. I'm proud of you, buddy. Now let's shake their hands, go back to the pool, and find some trouble to get into."

While it wasn't exactly a Knute Rockne pep talk, it was the best I could come up with on short notice.

chapter 43
SLOAN PARK

A rriving back in Glidden early Sunday afternoon, our bus was greeted at the Little League complex with a surprise welcoming committee. The municipal band was belting out a familiar tune that I couldn't put my finger on as we piled out one by one. The mayor was on hand as well as a healthy number of townspeople and parents. Mayor Johnson had officially declared the day Glidden All-Star Day. Coach Shenberger was forced to say a few words to the crowd. In the middle of his speech, I caught sight of Mom and Digger. Digger had spotted Frank and me and was tugging on his leash with all his might. Mom finally gave up and let go. He rushed up the makeshift podium nearly sending the mayor head over heels in the process. Nearly squealing with delight, he bounced back and forth from Frank to me for head scratches and hugs.

That afternoon, while Frank was swimming in Nicky's backyard pool, I decided to take a little bike ride. I needed to pay someone a long overdue visit. At least a dozen times over the past few months I had pulled up to the gate at the entrance of Perpetual Gardens only to chicken out and return home. Several times Mom had asked me to accompany her on a visit there, but I always managed to come up with some lame excuse to weasel out of it.

This time I was determined to go through with it. As I approached the gravesite, which was located to the rear of the cemetery under a tall maple tree, my eyes became fixated on the gray headstone.

PAUL WARREN DAVIES

BELOVED HUSBAND

LOVING FATHER

WE MISS YOU

I stood motionless for a full minute before the words and tears began flowing out of me non-stop. Having dreaded this moment for months, I was amazed at how naturally the emotions and thoughts came forth. The weight of fear and guilt was lifted off my shoulders immediately. I felt totally at peace with myself for the first time all year. It was a feeling I'll never forget. All this time, I'd been living in the fear that Dad was gone forever, and that he was no longer a part of my life. That paralyzing fear no longer existed. By the time my visit was over, and as I walked my bike past the cemetery gate, there was a peacefulness and comforting condition in me that had been missing for some time. I couldn't explain how I knew it, but there was no doubt in my mind that he'd been with me every step of the way.

Early Monday afternoon, Denny called. He was excited about the birthday present his folks had given him, a remote-controlled model airplane that he was dying to try out. I told him that Frank and I were taking Digger out for a walk and we'd meet him at Sloan Park in a half hour for his inaugural flight.

I called Tara and invited her and Rufus to join us for Denny's big air show. She told me she could use a good laugh, so off the five of us went to Sloan Park.

"Sorry to hear about your tough loss Saturday night," Tara offered on the way to the park. "It's gotta be rough to be that close to Williamsport only to have it slip away."

"Yeah, I think the home-plate umpire ended up needing a police escort to his car," I said. "It's not likely he'll be showing his face around Glidden in the near future."

"He was Indianapolis's version of Magoo," Frank added.

About a half hour into Denny's air display, it was evident he was going to need a little fine-tuning before he was ready for the big time. The plane did more crashing than flying. When his pride and joy finally smashed into a large oak tree at the edge of the woods, the show was over. Denny retrieved the crumpled mass and declared, "My dad's going to kill me."

"It's not your fault, Denny," I told him. "Whoever planted that blasted oak tree a hundred years ago is the one to blame."

We wished Denny good luck in explaining his damaged aircraft to his parents and told him it was time for us to depart. We were having some good laughs at Denny's expense as we walked toward home. No one noticed the white van that had been circling the park for the past twenty minutes. As we approached the corner near the boulevard, Digger decided it was time to do his business. He was a little shy about his pooping duties, so he marched into the thicket a few yards for some privacy.

Tara, Frank, and Rufus proceeded around the corner and I told them we'd catch up to them in a minute. When he finally sauntered out of the brush, I said to Digger, "About time, fussy."

But he wasn't listening to me. He came to full attention with his ears perked up and shot off, like the time with the coyote and Snuffy. He was around the corner before I could blink. "What now?" I said to myself.

I gathered up his leash and treat bag and hustled to get around the corner to see what the big emergency was. Rounding the corner, I still couldn't see anything because there was a big lilac bush blocking my view. Once I stepped clear of the lilac bush, there was a scene unfolding before my eyes that was both baffling and terrifying at the same time. The first thing that caught my eye was a large, disheveled-looking man in a dark blue sweat suit, slamming the sliding side door of a white van and limping around to the driver's side. Rufus was gnawing away on his leg every step of the way. The man looked as though he were in a world of hurt. The sight of Tara limping toward the van was the second shocker. She had her back to me and was shouting frantically, I could only assume, at the strange man who appeared to be leaving in a hurry. As I approached the developing nightmare at a full-out dash, the van screeched out of the secluded gravel maintenance drive and onto the boulevard with Rufus in hot pursuit. There was a heap in the shade next to where the van had taken off. As I passed Tara, I freaked out at the sight as terror struck my very soul. The crumpled heap consisted of Digger lying on top of Frank.

There was blood. Digger was panting heavily, and Frank wasn't moving at all. Tara turned to me and pointed to a phone booth on the corner, about fifty yards away. It was evident she'd been injured. Her face was scraped up and she held her right arm close to her body as she raced toward the pay phone. A college-aged woman rushed up from behind me. Carefully sliding Digger off Frank, she immediately checked Frank's pulse. There was a damp rag of some sort on the ground next to Frank. A few feet from the rag was a blood-stained knife. I didn't realize until then that a person could literally be frozen with fear. But that's exactly what was happening to me.

The woman picked up the rag and smelled it before quickly pitching it aside as she started coughing. As her coughing subsided, the jogger introduced herself as Clare. Pointing to the rag, Clare spat out one word: "chloroform." She continued to examine Frank as she gave me her version of events.

"I was jogging along the bike path and noticed a van parked over in the corner of the lot behind these shrubs. I didn't think much of it at first, but about a hundred yards further down the path, something made me look back. That girl, she said, motioning toward Tara, who was on her way back now, "was face-down on the gravel and some man was carrying this boy to the van. He put the boy down to open the door."

By then, Clare had turned her attention to Digger. She poured out the contents of her water bottle on Digger's two horrific-looking wounds, one on the side of his neck, the other a lengthy gash along his side. Clare had also shed her sweatshirt and was applying pressure to the gash on Digger's side as she continued.

"The man bent down and was lifting the boy into the van when this dog showed up. The dog lunged at the guy and almost tore his shoulder off. The guy reached inside the van, pulled out a knife and slashed the dog with it. He made one more attempt to lift the boy up with one arm but the dog was having none of it. This time the dog went for his face. The man slashed the poor dog again and the dog landed on top of the boy. He raised the knife to stab him when the beagle launched himself at the guy's midsection. That sent him slamming back against the side of the van and knocked the knife clear out of his hand. By this time, the girl was yelling at the man to stop. You saw the rest. We both got here about the same time."

"What's wrong with my brother?" I screamed, pointing to Frank.

"From the odor, my guess is chloroform."

"Is he going to be all right?"

"Your brother should be OK. His pulse is healthy. He doesn't seem to have any injuries. This dog, on the other hand, might not be so lucky. This gash is pretty deep. He's going to need immediate attention. If any of his major organs were nicked, he'll bleed out."

I was too terrified to cry. I just knelt there, still frozen. Glancing over at Tara, I could see the terror in her eyes.

"Are you all right?" I asked. She had grass-stained knees with gravel embedded in both. Her nose was bleeding and she was gripping her right shoulder.

"I hurt all over, but I'll live. Something smashed into the back of my shoulder. The next thing I knew, I was face-down in some gravel with Rufus licking my ear. The first thing I saw when I got up was this horrible man getting ready to load Frank into a van. The cavalry arrived just in the nick of time. I got the license plate number and so do the cops by now."

Sirens could be heard in the distance. In what must have been a matter of minutes, but what seemed like an eternity, the first squad car came barreling up to the maintenance drive. Following close behind was an ambulance. Everyone was glad to see them except Rufus, who was very reluctant to let any more strangers approach Tara. While the paramedics tended to Frank and Tara, Clare slipped into the back of the ambulance and lifted some tubes of antiseptics and a roll of bandages as she continued her work on Digger.

"Are you a doctor or something?" I asked her.

"Something," was all she answered. "We need to get this dog to a vet right now or we're going to lose him."

The third police car to arrive on the scene was driven by Officer Woodson. Clare had stolen into the back of the ambulance again and this time came out with a board.

"Son, slide this board under the dog while I lift him up a few inches." With Digger on the board our dilemma now was hitching a ride across town to the vet.

"Mr. Woodson, we need a ride to the vet right away or Digger's not going to make it. Please."

Derrick's father surveyed the scene. "Well, I suppose these other officers and paramedics can handle things for a few minutes." Clare and I were loading Digger into the back of the squad car before he could change his mind.

I ran over to check on Frank and Tara. Tara assured me that they were both doing fine. Frank was coming to, but he seemed groggy. A paramedic was checking out Tara's right shoulder. Every movement of the shoulder was met with a painful wince but she stared at me through her tears and said, "Go, Benny, I'll keep an eye on Frank and get a hold of your mom." I hopped into the front seat of the squad car and off we went. Clare stayed behind. In all the rush, I didn't even get a chance to thank her.

As we pulled out into traffic, I asked Mr. Woodson anxiously, "Could you turn on the siren?"

"Don't push your luck, Benny."

Officer Woodson did however call dispatch and told them to notify Franzine's Animal Hospital that we had an emergency case on the way and that it pertained to police business. Five minutes later we pulled up to the front door and rushed Digger through the lobby and into the surgery room. Digger's breathing was getting shallower by the minute.

Mr. Woodson wished me good luck and excused himself with, "Duty calls."

A woman in a white coat introduced herself as Deirdre Luney and started to examine Digger.

After several minutes she announced, "We'll do what we can, but I don't want to get your hopes up. He's lost a substantial amount of blood and with this deep of a gash, there's almost certainly internal bleeding to deal with."

Tears came springing forth from my eyes. I walked around the table, kissed him on the head and whispered, "Hang in there, little buddy, and don't you dare give up. We're going to make it, just like I told you when we busted you out of the shelter. Just keep digging and you'll make it."

His eyes, open just a slit, were glazed over, but I knew he heard me. As I was being led out of the room I gave the same message to Deirdre, "Don't give up on him. He's going to make it."

Sitting in the lobby, it was like I was marooned on an island. The enormity of the situation suddenly came crashing down on me. My brother was nearly snatched away from us by some lunatic, maybe never to be seen again. Tara was battered and my dog lay near death, just twenty feet away. How could this be happening? Was Frank going to be OK? Was Tara injured badly? Was Digger going to live? Did anyone contact my mom? Surely somebody got a hold of her. Where was she? Probably on her way to the hospital. My head was spinning with questions and turmoil. Less than two days ago all I cared about was going to Williamsport. It seemed like a lifetime ago. Right now I couldn't care less if I ever stepped foot in Pennsylvania.

A short while later the lobby door swung open and Father Bill entered. Boy, was he a welcome sight.

"Your mother just called me in a panic. She was so hysterical I had a difficult time understanding what she was trying to tell me. I was finally able to figure out she needed me to get my hind end over to the animal hospital and not let you out of my sight under any circumstances. Benny, what's going on?"

I tried to calm down and catch him up with the nightmarish events of the afternoon, but I did more stammering and blubbering than anything else. He looked more confused than ever by the time I finished.

Getting up and grabbing a cup of water from the dispenser, he returned to his spot next to me.

"Benny, I need you to take a slow drink of water, relax, and tell me again about what happened—in English this time."

So I went over the entire scenario step by step with what I had seen and what Clare had witnessed.

"No wonder your mother's fit to be tied. She must be a nervous wreck. I'll make some calls and get us an update."

The update proved encouraging. Mom and Sara Mangolin were at the ER. Frank was all right. The only thing he was complaining about was that he was starving. That was a good sign. He had no idea what had happened to him. He said he was walking home one minute and the next thing he knew, he was sitting in the back of an ambulance watching some man putting Tara's arm in a sling. He asked her if she fell. Not knowing what to tell him, she'd just replied, "Yeah, something like that."

Tara had sustained a dislocated collarbone along with an assortment of minor cuts and bruises. None of the cuts required stitches, so they were in the process of being released and would soon be joining us at Franzine's.

Father Bill suggested I pray to St. Francis of Assisi, the patron saint of animals.

"It sounds like Digger could really use some divine intervention right now, Benny."

Picturing Digger lying on top of Frank reminded me of the story about the time the animal shelter volunteers rescued him from the farmer's field in a driving thunderstorm. He was lying on top of his companion in an attempt to shelter her from the weather even though she was already gone. He was lying on top of Frank today for the same reason – to protect him. Now it was Digger who needed an advocate–St. Francis, perhaps.

Twenty minutes later, the refugees from the hospital joined the vigil. Mom wasn't ready to reveal the true horrors of the afternoon to Frank quite yet, and explained to him that Digger had been entangled in some barbed wire while pursuing a rabbit. Frank wasn't buying it.

"Why don't I remember any of this?" he asked her. "And don't tell me that Tara just fell down on her own. What's going on?"

While Frank was giving Mom the third degree, Tara and her mother pulled me aside to get an update on Digger's condition. I was giving them an account of the grim outlook when a squad car pulled into the lot and Officer Woodson stepped out. As he approached the door, Mom asked Father Bill if he would take Frank across the lobby to the vending machine to get him a candy bar. Frank was reluctant to miss out on what Officer Woodson had to report, but his craving for a chocolate bar trumped his curiosity.

With Frank safely out of earshot, Officer Woodson gave us the scoop.

"It's all over, I'm happy to report. Morgan David Whitmore was the perp. When we ran the license plate number Tara read off to the dispatcher, it lit up the system big time. Whitmore was sentenced to twenty-eight years in prison eleven years ago. He was granted an early release two months ago by a parole board in Michigan who declared him rehabilitated and no longer a danger to society. He skipped out on his parole officer two weeks ago and disappeared."

I had a feeling that a certain parole board in Michigan was about to receive an unannounced visit from my mother—and her purse.

"The county police got a read on him a couple miles south of town. Within ten minutes, squad cars from the city, county, and state boxed him in out on McGirr Road. They tried to talk him into giving up, but he was adamant that he wasn't going back to prison. Eventually he came charging out of his van firing away at the officers. It didn't end well for him."

"Good," was all Mom had to say.

"I wish they'd saved me a shot at that cretin," added Sara Mangolin. "I'd have blown his…"

"Hello, Father," Tara cut in as he and Frank returned to the group.

"Mr. Woodson," I said. "We never got a chance to thank Clare for her help. She was fantastic. Did you get a phone number or anything so we could let her know what's going on?"

"You mean that woman who was working on Digger? She was long gone by the time I got back to the scene. I'll ask around, someone must have gotten her statement."

"Who's this Clare and what scene are you talking about?" asked Frank in between bites of his Snickers bar.

We were all spared from further interrogation when a door opened and Deirdre came out.

"How's he doing?" I asked, all the time trying to read her face.

Mom rushed up and pulled Deirdre aside before anything about slashes or stab wounds could be blurted out in Frank's presence.

Between the body language and Mom's facial expressions, the news seemed to be mostly bad. I edged close enough to hear Deirdre's final foreboding forecast: "It's probably just a matter of time, Mrs. Davies. I'm sorry."

The room that Digger was in was too small for everyone to be in at once, so we split up into twos to visit him. First Mom and Frank went in. Then Tara and her mother took a turn. Finally Father Bill and I entered. Digger's breathing seemed labored. He looked so vulnerable lying there on the table. Father said a prayer over him while I talked non-stop in a low voice about all the adventures we'd been through and all the mischief we were going to get into in the coming years.

Mom peeked in a half hour later and told us she was taking Frank home and that Tara and her mom had already left. I could see the rosary in her hand and knew full well she'd be working the beads all night.

Shortly after Mom and Frank left, an attendant came into the room and announced it was closing time and that we'd have to leave. I'm not sure if it was the look on my face (the look that said wild horses couldn't drag me out of there) or the possibility that she just didn't feel right about kicking a priest out. Father asked her to call the police station to check with Officer Woodson and assured her he would vouch for us. That seemed to satisfy her and she wished us good luck.

Father Bill secured additional sodas and chocolate bars as we dug in for a vigil. Digger most likely wouldn't survive the night, but even more certainly, he wouldn't be alone when his time came.

chapter 44

LABOR DAY

Labor Day weekend. And more importantly, my thirteenth birthday. On our way to the picnic at Pioneer Park, I announced to Mom that now that I was a teenager, she could expect to see a calmer, more levelheaded, mature young man. An hour into the picnic she still hadn't stopped laughing. Not only did she think it was funny, but everyone she mentioned it to also found it to be amusing. It appeared that no one shared my vision of a sedate teenage existence.

We had a three-team bocce ball tournament going while Father Bill manned the barbeque grill. Frank and I were drubbed first by Derrick and Denny and then again by Tara and Stephanie. With the other two teams fighting it out for bragging rights, Frank and I reclined in the shade and enjoyed some homemade lemonade that Nora and Vera brought. Ksenia was trying to distract the two of them because they had Father cornered.

"Why did the church do away with the Latin mass?" pestered Nora.

Vera was bemoaning the phasing out of "Holy Ghost" in favor of "Holy Spirit."

"It's as if the Church just swept the Holy Ghost right out the door without so much as a thank-you. That's a fine how-do-you-do if you ask me."

I mentioned to Frank, "It looks like the hot dogs and veggie burgers aren't the only things being grilled."

"Who's the Holy Ghost?" asked Frank.

"See," cackled Vera, "just like I told you, Father, the younger folks don't even recognize the term."

I offered Padre some of my ice-cold lemonade (he looked like he could really use some) when a sudden movement caught my eye. A rabbit had bounded around the corner and into the woods. Rufus came screeching around the corner seconds later and after a few sniffs at the edge of the forest decided the bunny wasn't worth any further effort. After all, he'd done his job by chasing it back into the underbrush.

A moment later, another familiar mug came gimping around the corner and into view. Nose to the wind, Digger could detect the odor from the barbeque wafting through the air. The bunny was soon forgotten as the two made their way toward the grill. As people started calling their names, Digger's limp became noticeably more pronounced. He had quickly picked up on how sympathy for his injuries translated into more attention and added treats.

Deirdre Luney had been delightfully shocked the morning following Digger's surgery when she arrived at her office. She actually burst into tears when he opened his eyes for the first time.

"This is the highlight of my career," she proudly announced. "There is no way I thought…" and her voice trailed off.

"You obviously did a fantastic job," Father commented.

"A lot of the credit should go to the ambulance paramedics. The work they did to get to the wounds cleaned up went a long way in preventing infection. Plus the job they did in bandaging that nasty gash along his side to stop the bleeding was instrumental in buying us time that at least gave Digger a fighting chance. Still, I can't figure out, with those internal injuries, how he managed to survive the night."

"The Lord often works in mysterious ways," Father Bill added.

When I informed her that the ambulance personnel weren't responsible for Digger's pre-op, but instead a passerby named Clare, Deirdre eyed me skeptically. She immediately dismissed my version of events to sleep deprivation delusions. I did notice, however, on Digger's follow-up visit the following week that there was an addition to the décor in Deirdre's office—a St. Francis statue.

And now, three weeks after the fact, still no sign of Clare. The police canvassed the neighborhood but nobody could ever recall seeing anyone matching her description. The city council even drew up and official proclamation with a certificate honoring her with a Good Samaritan award. But no one's seen hide nor hair of her so it's still unclaimed. When I asked Father Bill what he made of the mystery surrounding Clare, he just smiled and said, "Usually there's a logical explanation for what happens in life, and then again, sometimes one's faith is allowed to step in when logic fails."

I wasn't exactly sure what that meant, but I did know we sure were grateful that Clare, or whoever she was, showed up when she did. Hopefully, some day we'll meet again, preferably under less stressful conditions.

Two days after the incident at Sloan Park, Mom mailed off a scathing letter to the parole board in Michigan that had been responsible for the decision to release Morgan Whitmore. Father didn't believe that the letter accurately depicted her true Christian values, but I happened to notice him chuckling several times as he read it.

Megan Dillon accepted a teaching position in Milwaukee and moved up there a week ago, leaving Father Bill to shepherd his flock in Glidden. With some of the wayward sheep in our parish, he certainly has his hands full.

I called Maria Benson yesterday. Maria was the volunteer who rescued Digger from the farmer's field during the horrible storm last October and watched over him until he returned to health. She's currently living in Minnesota. She'd caught the story of the aborted abduction on the news, but had no idea that her Harvey, now Digger, was one of the hero canines involved.

"I knew there was something special about that dog when I first laid eyes on him in that cornfield," she mentioned. "There was certainly no quit in him, I'll tell you that." I thanked her and promised to keep her updated on his progress.

Tara and Stephanie came laughing and high-fiving over to the picnic table to grab some lemonade. Having dispatched Derrick and Denny in a hotly contested match, they were eager to rub it in. Tara had been cleared Friday by her doctor to practice with the high school volleyball team. She received a sizeable check last week from a Michigan children's rights organization that had posted a reward for information leading to Whitmore's capture. It was her phone call that led to his capture. Of course, after treating the volleyball team to a pizza night, she donated the bulk of the funds to area animal shelters. One of those shelters, Oaken Acres, informed her the other day that the fox we rescued from the trap a couple of months ago was scheduled to be released back into the wild within the week. While Tara's happy for his sake, she'll still miss ol' Freddy. Tara's father, Earl, seemed to be improving for a brief period, but a couple of recent relapses have clouded his future in regard to a possible reconciliation with her mom. Tara didn't seem to be particularly eager to roll out the red carpet for a second chance either.

The coroner's inquest into Whitmore's death was a story unto itself. The coroner started out with the nonlethal injuries Whitmore sustained, including several deep lacerations that were presumably canine-inflicted wounds. Then he got around to the cause of death: thirty-seven gunshot wounds. When the coroner questioned Sheriff John Low on why there were thirty-seven gunshot wounds in the deceased, Low simply replied, "Because we ran out of bullets." Sheriff Low's approval ratings jumped sky-high following that comment, and he is a virtual shoe-in for re-election in November. A far cry from the paltry support he endured in the wake of the Griswold debacle.

Speaking of Marvin, rumor has it that he caught on with the carnival that passed through Glidden during Corn Fest. In all likelihood, he's in charge of the dreaded Gravitron.

John Nestor is currently incarcerated in the juvenile detention center, in Kane County, following his arrest on breaking and entering charges. Mom's been driving me there once a week for supervised visits. We play some cards and I pass along some news from his brothers. John seems to understand the seriousness of his predicament and appears to be making strides in getting his attitude straightened out. He's going to need it, because he's got a long road ahead of him.

I followed Hamilton's progress in the Little League World Series in the papers. The pride of Ohio made it to the semifinals before being edged out by a team from South Korea. I suppose we'll always be left to wonder what would have happened if little ol' Glidden had advanced to Williamsport. But that's life. And as I looked over toward where Frank and Digger were playing tug of war with a battered Frisbee, I couldn't help but to recall the words Father Bill spoke to me last winter: "You'll be better served appreciating the things you do have rather than resenting the things you don't."

The Cubs, meanwhile, managed once again to drop out of sight in the pennant race. The Cubbies' search for the holy grail, [World Series], was going to have to be put on hold once again. Wait till next year.

With Tara entering high school Tuesday, I'm still stuck with a one-year sentence in that purgatory known as junior high. Our eighth-grade team did start football practice this past week. The coach has me playing cornerback. With Knuckles at middle linebacker, teams won't be prone to pound away at us on the ground too often. Hopefully, that will add up to more passes coming my way to be picked off.

This morning, the Davies family traveled out to Perpetual Gardens for a birthday celebration. It was a tradition in our house for Dad to cook a big breakfast on my birthday. His specialty was chocolate-chip waffles and bacon. So we brought out our propane Coleman grill and did it up right. Mom even purposely burned one of the waffles because that's the way Dad liked his. The only snafu in the outing occurred when Mom went to straighten out the flowers around the headstone and unwisely left her half-eaten waffle unguarded. The unattended waffle did not go unnoticed by Digger, and he made quick work of it.

And here it was, almost time to eat again, and as usual, Frank had managed to edge his way to the front of the line for first dibs at the chow. By the time he makes it through the food line, the rest of us will be lucky if there's a few scraps remaining.

With all the publicity surrounding the attempted kidnapping, it was impossible to shield Frank from the truth. Once Digger was released from the animal hospital, Mom and I sat Frank down to explain to him what went down that day at Sloan Park. Occasionally, in the past, Frank would complain that Digger was a little too needy, or always seemed to be underfoot when he got up to go someplace. Once Frank learned the truth about what Digger went through to protect him, he hasn't once mentioned any concerns regarding Digger's hovering tendencies. In fact, the first week Digger was home following his release and was unable to climb the stairs, it was Frank who grabbed his sleeping bag and pillow to camp out in the living room with him every night. Evidence I discovered the following mornings led me to believe that numerous midnight raids had been conducted on the refrigerator during their campouts.

In fact with his new around the clock security detail shadowing him constantly, I think Frank's better protected than the president. The other night I ducked my head into Frank's room to rag about him leaving the cap off the toothpaste again. He was sound asleep, or at least pretending to be just to deny me my rant. There at the foot of his bed was his security detail curled up and keeping an eye on him. I believe that most children have a guardian angel, complete with wings and a halo. Frank's, on the other hand, has four legs, an aversion to thunderstorms, and a fondness for ice cream. But I wouldn't sell Digger short. He seems to be every bit as effective as any of the celestial beings.

I jumped into line behind Tara—just a coincidence, mind you—and when we got to the grill I politely asked, "Padre, could I please have one of those delicious-looking veggie burgers? I'm thinking of taking a break from meat for a while."

Tara beamed and snatched one off the grill for me before Father could determine if I was kidding or not. Mom glanced suspiciously in my direction. Vera nudged Nora, who was taking a little nap. Father Bill winked at me in approval. Digger cocked his head sideways at me as if looking for an explanation. Frank shook his head and commented, "Benny, you're a real piece of work sometimes."

Tara was proud of her newest convert to vegetarianism and rushed over to sit next to me at the picnic table.

"What should we wear Saturday, Benny? Something nice or just casual?" Saturday morning, Digger and Rufus were being honored at a ceremony at Sloan Park. They were scheduled to receive honorary lifetime memberships in the Glidden Police Canine Unit. Of course if the award turned out to be something they couldn't devour, it was unlikely either one of them would be visibly impressed.

Seeing as I didn't really own anything nice that fit me anymore, I replied, "Let's just go casual."

"Well, so how's your burger?" she asked.

"Delicious," I fibbed. "Are there any more?"

As Tara went to check on the status of the veggie burgers, I tried to convince myself that life as a vegetarian wouldn't be so bad. I could survive on peanut butter and jelly sandwiches, green pepper with onion pizza, and an occasional fish sandwich at McDonalds. And any failures

I encountered at home, say at Thanksgiving, could be discreetly covered up with a small bribe to Frank in order to keep his big clam shut. Yeah, I had faith I could pull it off.

Mom had baked a cake for my birthday—my favorite, German chocolate. As she was lighting the thirteen candles, Frank asked me if the candles represented my I.Q. I was able to land one quick punch to the arm before his security detail stepped in. As friends and family sang "Happy Birthday," I whispered to Digger, "See, this teenager gig isn't so tough after all." I'm not certain if I was imagining things or not, but I swear he winked at me. I winked back and said, "Come up here and give me a hand. It's time to blow out the candles. Frank's already got his fork and plate ready to go, and we both know it's never a good idea to keep him waiting when there's dessert involved."

Before Frank was halfway through his dessert, I noticed Mom sitting on her folding chair with a pained look on her face. She motioned to Mrs. Mangolin and the two of them huddled together for a moment before Sara bolted toward the parking lot.

Waddling over to the dessert line Mom announced, "I'm sorry, Benny, but it appears as though your sibling is bound and determined to start out life off as a party crasher. Sara is going to run me to the hospital now." Turning to Frank she added, "Save me a piece of cake if at all possible."

Fat chance, I thought to myself.

Between swallows, Frank could only muster one question. "If the baby and Benny end up sharing the same birthday, does that mean we get two cakes next year?"

As Mom shook her head in bewilderment over Frank's response, I walked over and gave her a sideways hug (a frontal hug was out of the question at this point) and offered, "I'll bet you're hoping this one's a girl."

She smiled back and cracked, "You think?"

EPILOGUE

Isabelle Marie Davies did indeed join the residents of Glidden later that evening. She was so darling that I didn't mind sharing my birthday with her one bit. She had Dad's brown eyes and, according to Mom, his chin too. Not being much of an expert on chins, I guess I'll have to take her word for it. Arriving home after a brief two-day stay in the hospital, it was hard to believe that a person weighing only seven pounds and ten ounces could have such an impact on a household.

Her first couple of days at home had Digger thinking she was part of an alien invasion. But the light bulb eventually went on in his head and he realized she was simply a new member of the pack. During late-night nursing sessions, Digger patrolled the upstairs hallway between Mom's and Frank's rooms much like a sentry. Frank, meanwhile, continually bragged to anyone within earshot what a great big brother he was, although he managed to be conspicuously absent whenever diaper duty presented itself.

Tara, not having any siblings, unofficially adopted Izzy as her little sister. This was fine with me because Tara stopped over almost every night under the premise of giving my mom a break. Mom did seem tired quite a bit but I can never remember seeing her so happy. And why wouldn't she be? After enduring a couple of bulldozers like Frank and me, she was due peaceful thoughts of shopping for little dresses and making May baskets in the spring. When Isabelle got old enough to be out playing in the neighborhood, Mom most likely wouldn't have to flinch every time the phone rang in anticipation of complaints concerning trampled flower gardens, broken windows from errant throws or loud and inappropriate behavior by her ill mannered children.

The other day I decided that Digger and I were overdue for a little excursion to the north forty. Just the two of us. It had been a while since I had him all to myself and missed the one on one play time and just hanging out. After a half hour or so of fetching and rough housing Digger trotted up to me as I rested on the ground. He sat right in front of me and stuck out his paw for a shake. It reminded me of the first time at the shelter when he did the same thing.

"We've been through quite a bit together big fella. Haven't we?"

There was that wink of his again and I wasn't imagining it this time. The way I figure it, the first shake at the shelter was his way of claiming me. Probably the look we shared in each other's eyes that day screamed to both of us–SAVE ME. This shake was to remind me not to worry. Even though he had numerous chores such as protecting Frank and Isabelle, along with half the neighborhood, we were still best buddies. I hugged him and gave his ears a good scratching. Nothing needed to be said. It was all understood. A couple of minutes later we were homeward bound because it was time for Digger to get back to work.

One night I accompanied Tara back to her house following an evening of watching over Izzy and playing poker with Frank and Nicky. I had something on my mind, but felt a little nervous about how to bring it into the conversation.

Finally I just blurted it out. "Have you ever kissed a boy before?"

"None of your business," was her reply.

I took that as a no but left it at that.

"Well, I was just wondering if, you know, maybe you could do me a favor and, well, you know…" Nothing was coming out right and I was out of "you knows."

Tara looked at me skeptically while I stood there on her porch. Things weren't progressing as smoothly as I had envisioned. It was like dying a slow and painful death. Finally, her eyes softened a bit. "Just this once, Benny. And don't get any ideas in that big head of yours. One time only."

As I floated across the front lawn following the greatest three seconds of my young life, something drew my attention to the upstairs window of Frank's room. Frank, Nicky, and Digger were all cramming their noggins out the window and looking in my direction. Nicky had a disgusted look on his face. Digger released a couple of good-natured woofs. Frank simply smiled down at me and gave me a big thumbs-up.

As I took in the view of the three stooges with their heads hanging out the window, I had to laugh to myself with Tara's words echoing in my head.

Just this once, Benny.

Just this once, huh? We'll see about that.

ACKNOWLEDGMENTS

I would like to thank the professional staff at Windy City Publishers for their assistance in navigating this rookie author through the minefield of modern-day book publishing.

I also deeply appreciate the dedicated volunteers at TAILS humane society in DeKalb, IL, who rescued many pets following the devastation caused by Hurricane Katrina in 2005, including my dog, Digger. Digger would like to send along his appreciation as well.

ABOUT THE AUTHOR

JIMMY BALL grew up in DeKalb, Illinois, home to Northern Illinois University and endless corn fields. He enjoyed a 36-year career with the United States Postal Service before retiring in 2007. Married for 35 years, he and his wife, Barb, are empty nesters with two daughters off and married on their own. In addition to writing, retirement includes part-time work at the University bookstore, reffing high school football and basketball, walking his dog, Digger (a rescued dog following Hurricane Katrina), and spoiling his grandson. A long-suffering Chicago Cubs fan, he optimistically awaits "next year."

CPSIA information can be obtained at www.ICGtesting.com
Printed in the USA
LVOW100719021212

309631LV00001B/47/P

9 781935 766643